ALSO BY JORDY ROSENBERG

Confessions of the Fox

Night Night Fawn

NIGHT NIGHT FAWN

A NOVEL

JORDY ROSENBERG

One World
New York

One World
An imprint of Random House
A division of Penguin Random House LLC
1745 Broadway, New York, NY 10019
oneworldlit.com
penguinrandomhouse.com

Copyright © 2026 by Jordy Rosenberg

Penguin Random House values and supports copyright. Copyright fuels creativity, encourages diverse voices, promotes free speech, and creates a vibrant culture. Thank you for buying an authorized edition of this book and for complying with copyright laws by not reproducing, scanning, or distributing any part of it in any form without permission. You are supporting writers and allowing Penguin Random House to continue to publish books for every reader. Please note that no part of this book may be used or reproduced in any manner for the purpose of training artificial intelligence technologies or systems.

ONE WORLD and colophon are registered trademarks
of Penguin Random House LLC.

Hardcover ISBN 978-0-593-44800-7
Ebook ISBN 978-0-593-44801-4

Printed in the United States of America on acid-free paper

1st Printing

First Edition

BOOK TEAM: Production editor: Andy Lefkowitz • Managing editor: Rebecca Berlant • Production manager: Sarah Feightner • Copy editor: Shannon Barr • Proofreaders: Kevin Clift, Alicia Hyman, and Brianna Lopez

Book design by Fritz Metsch

The authorized representative in the EU for product safety and compliance is Penguin Random House Ireland, Morrison Chambers, 32 Nassau Street, Dublin D02 YH68, Ireland. https://eu-contact.penguin.ie

For my sister, who escaped these pages

Let us make a film in which the representation of Fascism would engage with the fascism of representation. A film, shall we say, which follows the life story of a member of the SS in all its pathos—

(. . .)

[W]hy should it not be possible to produce a dialectical lyric about such a character?

—GILLIAN ROSE, *Mourning Becomes the Law*

Contents

PART I:
Overture: Static in the Air
1

PART II:
My Life, by Barbara Rosenberg
11

PART III:
Vogelfrei
193

PART IV:
*Papers and Communications:
J. Rosenberg, Abe Rosenberg, Sar-El,
San Francisco County Records*
249

PART V:
Fawn
271

Part I:

Overture:

Static

in the Air

A WOMAN

MARKED FOR DEATH

Roused from a damp OxyContin slumber into the dirty orange Manhattan night, I lay there, trying to pick the nocturnal sounds apart. The ocean squall of traffic, constant. The intermittent beep of a forklift at the post office loading dock. The wind pouring down the canyon of East Sixty-ninth Street.

And something else. An ambient noise, like static in the air. From inside the apartment.

I pushed myself to sit and swung my legs out of bed, sliding them to the floor. There was the terrible ache I've come to expect, but they didn't fold, so I pumped myself into a stagger, one hand on the bottom of the bed, the other on the dresser, and made my way toward the door.

I did not have a weapon, I realized, as I reached the mirrored dressing table at the threshold of my bedroom. In addition to that, I am a Woman. A woman marked for death and caught in the jaws of a notoriously lethal illness. An arrhythmic banging came from somewhere and then a terrible, vague sloshing. On my dressing table I spotted my pink and black Tweezermans, sharp as little baby teeth. I grabbed them and, holding them out in front of me, advanced farther into the apartment like Rita Hayworth sneaking around the Mundson mansion in *Gilda*, the hem of my robe flittering along the carpet.

In my daughter's bedroom the traffic along Second Avenue cast stripes of light through the blinds; they floated across the ceiling like empty frames of film reel ticking off after a show. My eyes traced the perimeter. Small writing desk, wheeled office chair, slim bookshelf. And then, along the far wall—my god!—a coffin, quiet as a turd, lewd and horrible. Heat flew up my neck. How did someone get a coffin in here? And who was inside it? Or—I trembled—was it for me?

Cars whirred past down below, indifferent. Then the bedroom glowed red. The light had changed and the traffic paused. The shadows fleeing across the ceiling paused. Shapes sharpened in the dark. The coffin resolved into its ordinary form, just an empty twin bed sagging against the floral wallpaper, pink blossoms pale with time.

The noise, meanwhile, had become a low rumble punctuated by thuds.

I backed out of the bedroom and crossed the living room. I began to make out choking, gurgling sounds. Locking my elbows, I pushed the Tweezermans farther out in front of me and turned the corner like a cowboy sliding into a saloon, flicking on the light with the back of my shoulder. The fluorescent ceiling ring sizzled to life, and the thin needle of the galley kitchen flashed bright as a surgical theater. A shiny cockroach toddled across the Formica and slipped into a crack between the sink and countertop.

My eyes searched every surface until they reached the small dishwasher, chugging its load. Of course! I'd turned it on before I went to bed. Exhaling with relief, I sank against the doorframe, bubbly with decades of thick acrylic paint.

Making my way back across the living room, crisis averted, my legs began to shake. I had exerted myself too much.

Silly Barbara, I muttered.

I felt a bolt of fury at Stephen for being dead and unable to do his husbandly duty of investigating weird noises. And maybe a little teasing appreciation of my hysterics. Say what you will—and seventy years of life have clarified to me that people always do, though rarely to your face—I loved it when he treated me like a dumb shiksa bimbo.

Then, underneath the dishwasher's slurp and rattle, there was a whisper. I froze.

Someone was standing between the plastic fern and the credenza, facing the wall and sighing, like a teacher getting composed before addressing an unruly class. I begged the vision to become something benign. Furniture, a shadow, a mirage. But the image held. The figure began to turn. The room radiated with the inevitability of our encounter.

I had seen glimpses before. Always out of the corner of my eye, always in the middle of the night. Once, getting up to pee, I caught a flash of something darting around a corner. Another time, teetering to the kitchen for water, I swore I heard a peculiar scratching behind me, like claws moving across the carpet. What was I to do! It's a dream, I convinced myself, scuttling back to bed.

But, after each of these episodes, I'd wake with the feeling that someone had been in my room. Accompanied by the strange, deflated sensation of having been scolded for hours on end, and the overpowering sense that I needed to apologize for my life.

The face was familiar—that was the most unnerving part.

Because my terror did not vanish when I realized that it was familiar. Actually, my terror increased. Something was very wrong with the face.

Its nose was not a nose.

Or, maybe it was a nose. But it was not made of nose flesh. Where a nose should have been, something hard and black curled down into a shiny tip.

The figure just stood there, blinking at me. And as I was staring back, the inscrutable hard black thing on its face began to take shape.

It was a beak.

A big, hawk-like beak.

And then the figure opened its beak.

And said, *Mom*.

THIS OTHER YOU

The next morning when you came to check on me, I shuddered and pulled the pilly yellow blanket all the way up to my face, the worn satin edge soft against my lips. My eyes peeked out like a child at a scary movie. I couldn't get this image of you—this other you—out of my head.

You, meanwhile, were acting like everything was normal. Your nose looked nose-like again. Maybe it had retracted like a flaccid penis back into your regular nose. This is one theory I am developing. You were acting like I wouldn't remember, probably telling yourself that I had been so out of it that I couldn't put two and two together.

You leaned across the bed and placed one of those green shakes you're always forcing on me onto the dresser. I followed you with my eyes as you started back out the doorway. Eager to go make one of your endless phone calls.

Am I awake? I heard myself slur against the blanket's wet rim.

You turned back, exasperated, which wasn't fair. It's not like I'd been haranguing you all morning. I'd been lying there for hours, frankly parched.

What do you mean?

Is this real?

Is what real.

I tunneled one hand out and waved it around at the gargoyling mahogany bedroom set, the constantly playing television, the pawn shop paintings of Parisian dancing ladies. *This*, I said. *All of it.* You squinched your face, assessed the row of pills along the edge of the dresser. *Your doctor said the OxyContin could have a "derealizing effect," remember?* You had that cloyingly calm, ultra reasonable tone you always have now. I know exactly where you get it from. I found it infuriating when your father used to do it, so you can just imagine how I feel about it coming from you.

But you were enjoying this. You have all the power now and you know it. I'm wearing a diaper, after all.

The thing is, though, I saw something sticking out from between your shirt and the waist of your jeans when you bent over to put down the shake. A feather? And at that moment I realized several things:

- I wasn't dreaming last night.
- (But you'd like me to think I was.)
- You are changing.
- (And I can't tell you that I know.)

This is my punishment for having been cruel to you. Isn't it enough that I should die with only you as my caretaker? That I should end up needing the specific individual I had successfully purged from the family decades ago?

Back then, in the 1990s, I had been at the height of my powers and I was just not having it. I was not having my daughter running around in combat boots and no lipstick. Frankly, I am proud to say I didn't budge one goddamned inch. It wasn't so hard. In fact, things were easier without you around. For two decades I simply told everyone you were still dating that one boy from high school and no one asked another thing about it. (There is a yenta code of ethics, believe it or not, which is to leave people alone in their misery.)

So isn't it humiliation enough that after all these years I should have to admit I needed help? From you, no less. Isn't it enough that I should have to die overhearing you conduct your sordid business, wishing (multiple?) women good night on the phone. Talking filthy, using syrupy words. That I should die completely at your mercy.

But now this.

My daughter, what have you become?

AN ANTIC GOD

Believe me, I've tried to pray. But to whom!

The Jewish God doesn't do miracles. Though apparently Karl Marx does. Take, for example, the commodity—balm to my soul, enchantress, enigma. You say that for Marx a commodity is an abomination. A thing that lives while people die. But also that for Marx, this commodity, this abomination, is a kind of miracle. An antic god, a clown, a bag blown with unnatural life, cavorting among us, livelier than us, impossibly alive, and yet alive still.

The doctors are telling me there's no hope. But you say there is hope in Marxism. So I, Barbara Rosenberg of Second Avenue and East Sixty-ninth Street—an address in which, as everybody knows, there is no honor—call on Karl Marx, god of impossible things. I am at the mercy of a monster. I must give it what it wants. My confession, my apology, my prayer.

Part II:

My Life,

by Barbara

Rosenberg

LIKE A FLOWER WITH THE MAJORITY OF ITS PETALS PLUCKED

IF SOMEONE PUT A gun to my head and said *When was the beginning of the end*, I would have to say: Which end? Lives have multiple endings. Sometimes those multiple endings happen all at once, although you couldn't really have known it then. Looking back, my mother-in-law's funeral in 1983—that moment, just before Sugar Becker entered, fresh from the West Coast—was one of those times. That moment when, standing over the coffin, looking down at Blanchie (200 pounds in the flush of life, now a prune reposing on satin), I realized suddenly and without a shadow of a doubt that I could not allow my daughter to win our weeklong argument regarding the movie *Flashdance*.

Not technically a lesbian film, but who are we kidding.

And boy, did I try to kid myself. Why on earth would an eleven-year-old girl beg with such abject passion to see *Flashdance*, I had been asking no one, or God. The question had been keeping me up at night. As if I didn't know. I *did* know. I knew enough to say, on instinct, no *Flashdance*. Over my dead body would I be taking her to this film. I told her it was age inappropriate. To which she pointed out that I had dragged her to see *Saturday Night Fever*, a surprisingly violent movie about disco dancers, at age six. My daughter had watched wide-eyed, immobilized with terror in that chilly budget theater on Eighty-fifth and Second. Well. We ate cheeseburgers afterward, on English muffins at an Irish pub. My way of apologizing. It's all gone now, that theater, that bar. But the point is, I had a ball that day. The *dancing*, the *Bee Gees*. A *ball*. As long as I didn't have to look over at my child trembling in her seat. For this I'm sure I could be forgiven. My other sins not so much. But I needed to see John Travolta, and if I had to schlep my daughter to this movie, so help me god I would.

About *Flashdance*, however, I was not to be moved. The more my daughter pleaded and howled to see *Flashdance*, the more firm was I in my resolution. Thou shalt not see *Flashdance*, not on my watch.

There was something very wrong in her level of desperation. In the history of knowing my daughter, no movie had evoked such histrionics. And the strangest thing was, this was a girl who didn't give a shit about dance. In fact, she had at one point been suspended from school for refusing to participate in ballet, and now the sudden interest? The pouting, the pleading, all to watch a movie about—well, when I thought about it, when I really faced the truth—this was a movie about women in Pittsburgh who took off their clothes.

For whatever reason, looking at Blanchie in her burial outfit was when it all hit me. The specter that had haunted me throughout my married life—distant, for-no-good-reason-haughty Blanchie—now a shrivel in a blue dress. Seeing the violable, pitiable thing that she now was (and that, on some level perhaps, she, and thus I, and thus all women, had always been), I finally did the math. Blanchie's enshrivelment cleared something in my brain that I would have preferred not cleared. And I realized then and there that all of my dreams had died.

In case it seems like I am the kind of person who likes to get a good gander at dead people, I would rather not have had anything at all to do with Blanchie's body, but I was in the process of being silently, unjustly accused of having tampered with the contents of the casket. Specifically, a photograph had gone missing, one that was meant to be buried with Blanchie. And I knew, from the way Stephen's brother Saul was glaring, that suspicion had fallen on me.

Meanwhile, Saul—this glarer, this accuser, this absolute *zhlob*—had the brilliant idea of bringing a cheese and cold cut platter to a casket viewing. For Saul, a mother's funeral was no reason to stop being a digestive tract in motion, a shark on legs. Nothing was sacred. Even the reverence of death had to be pickled in mundanity and the stench of deli meat. I marched to the window and cracked it open, trying to make a point.

Saul, however, was plowing through a plate of chopped liver and deep in an inquisition of the funeral home director, who insisted that the casket had remained untouched since it arrived by freight on its flight from Florida two days prior. In fact, no one noticed me airing out the room except for a pair of dogs taking syncopated dumps on Coney Island Avenue. A thread of sooty air leaked in, casting a chill across the shins of my pantyhose. There was something about the combination of this shin-chill with the odors of the cold cut platter that made me nauseous, and my stomach twisted with that high note that lets you know that queasiness is a prelude to actual vomiting.

* * *

I would have liked to blame Stephen for everything, but I couldn't. The truth was that I had bound myself to this man and his cold cut–bringing family decades prior, and from thence came all the rest of it.

Including giving birth to a daughter who, it turned out, not only wanted to see women take off their clothes but wanted also to be a man. Hadn't I done my best, trying to keep her away from the corduroy blazer she was forever digging out from the depths of Stephen's closet?

In fact, just that day I had conducted one such enterprise—not so easy, by the way, in a shoebox apartment. Three rooms that opened onto each other like a flower with the majority of its petals plucked. One might think it would be impossible to conduct clandestine operations in such a small space, but I had a way of imagining myself as double agent Karin Geza from *Top Secret*, alert in a silk slip dress, forever waiting to poison a Nazi with a doctored glass of bourbon.

Sitting in the living-room-cum-den-cum-dining-area, I could perceive each individual noise of our abode without turning my head. If I sat there long enough, still enough, I would sort of *expand* and become the apartment. I was a map made solely of family sounds—the rustle of Stephen turning newspaper pages in the bathroom, the irregular blasts of sitcom laughter from behind my daughter's bedroom door.

When I was assured that everyone was otherwise occupied, I slipped over to the shallow little nook next to the entryway, aka "the hall closet," a ridiculously tiny cost-shaving compromise common to that whole swath of apartments that had sprouted from Fifty-ninth to Eighty-ninth streets, east of Third Avenue, after the war. At night when he returned from work, every moment of Stephen's routine would be audible from any other room. Unpacking his briefcase in the living room. Snapping open the buckles, placing the neat piles of papers, pipe tobacco, his Day Runner onto the coffee table. Sitting down on the couch to untie his shoes, and the couch's exhalation. The whir of laces pulled through eyelets. The shoes falling to the floor with a humph like sad dogs.

Each week it seemed another friend from the old neighborhood was installing themselves within one of these apartments. You'd go across the street for a game of poker and—boop!—find yourself cramming your overcoat into the same little void you crammed it into at home. At the time it felt kind of comforting, like a Catskills bungalow colony or a college dormitory. Not that I had ever lived in a dormitory.

As time passed, though, I started to dwell. Who were these presumably WASP engineers who had deemed such minuscule containers suitable for us? From whence came their sadistic agreement that the Jews of Yorkville should have only tiny cubbies in which to hang an entire family's coats? Jews should be happy to even *have* an apartment in Manhattan and not be dead in a ditch in Europe, I guess.

However, just that day as I heaved open the humidity-soaked door from its suture to the jamb, I indulged a hope based precisely in the losing proposition of this closet and what it represented about the slummyness of our lives.

In the smallness of this nook lay its promise: the genuine sequestration of the corduroy blazer.

And Stephen's sport coats did constitute a kind of fortress, packed to the point of being practically grouted into that miniature span of wall-void. They made a forbidding barrier, which I shouldered aside, not without a touch of erotic pleasure, as I frothed up the scent of my husband into the microenvironment of the closet. A trench coat exuded Stephen's musk: peppermint Life Savers, pipe tobacco, old rain. I sucked it all in like the dregs of a Camel Light.

With barely an inch to move in the hothouse of the closet, I hunted and shoved and shouldered until I came to the corduroy blazer, light of my daughter's sartorial life. Wrenching its hanger neck from the millipede of other necks, I removed the jacket from its position and then launched myself through the small opening I had momentarily managed to pierce in the citadel of blazers, javelining the corduroy one behind the row and catching it on the belt hook along the back wall. I pushed the closet door closed, raking up dust from the wall-to-wall pink pile carpet, then secured it against the paint-shedding jamb with a bump of my hip and retreated to our bedroom, where I sat down at my dressing table to prepare my makeup for the day.

Who would believe that this offspring, this golem of upside-down gender, persisted? Not five minutes before we were to leave the apartment for Sherman's Flatbush Memorial Chapel did I stumble upon my daughter modeling the sport coat in the full-length mirror on the interior of this very closet door. An elf twisting and turning in a sail of corduroy, pinching the blazer at the small of her back to affect the mirage of tailoring. I cannot communicate the level of despair this scene inspired in me.

"This is why," I said, under my breath, emerging from behind so that we were both briefly reflected in the mirror—me in my black Anne Klein belted blazer dress with my hair out to here, and her in, well, also sort of a blazer dress if you think about it.

I folded my arms as she turned to face me. I was not technically blocking the way, but once you are a mother you become differently sized, and certain things can't be helped. I felt my own power radiating off me, something in which you might think I would have reveled but which I never entirely liked, because while on the one hand as a mother you do become larger, you also become smaller. I will come back to this point later.

"Why what?" my daughter had the audacity to ask. Methought the blazer was giving her unusual boldness.

"You know what," I said, arching an eyebrow.

"Everyone else in my class has seen it!" she bleated. But she turned bright red and un-blazered herself, throwing the sport coat onto the carpet and darting around me into her room to fetch her sanctioned outfit, a pleated black wool skirt and black V-neck topped with a burgundy velvet knee-length duffel coat from Gimbels.

Look, we didn't know any better then. Certainly I didn't. Where exactly was I supposed to have learned "better," Ocean Avenue? Don't make me laugh. But listen, I have had a lot of time to reflect lately. Not to mention I am nothing if not always up on the latest trends such as, at one point, Jazzercise, and I have had to reckon with some developments. Modern developments. Developments that have caused me to ask a question I never wanted to ask. Namely: What is a man? The truth is, it doesn't have to do with corduroy jackets. And in fact it doesn't have a thing to do with genitalia, either. Neither clothes nor sex makes you a man. What makes you a man is how you die.

Stephen's father, now *that* was a man. Teddy had two years of college and had majored in pre-law, but "due to the

Depression"—which was everyone's excuse for everything including why you had to save even a single curl of used aluminum foil, musical chairs'ing it from tuna tin to tuna tin—what Stephen's father had been was a gangster, managing Rosemere Trucking out of an office on Thirty-eighth and Tenth from before the war until the day after his retirement when he succumbed, while mowing the lawn, to an embolism brought on by undiagnosed bladder cancer. Outside the bitter gruel of his routine, Teddy's body just ceased functioning. His body was an instrument tuned to a rhythm of breaking legs, playing blackjack, and enjoying a diet of Pecan Sandie cookies, Carlsberg beer, and Flor del Fumar Perfecto cigars. On the weekdays.

On the weekends, he was a domestic taskmaster, a conduit of assimilation and success for his family. He kept his hair neat, his cologne fuming off his skin in successive waves like a military regiment in attack formation, and his pants pressed. A garmento, a mid-level Jewish mafia grunt was what he was. And what he couldn't have for himself, he would have for his son. He laid himself, his law ambitions, and all his hopes down. He made his body a bridge between the clamor of the city and the hushed, aspirational lawns of Nyack, so his family could walk across—grind the heels of their polished Florsheims into his crisp Catskill-strutted guayabera, deep into his broad, mole-pocked, sallow Semitic back. At the end of it all, he would be crushed into the suburban lawn like the butt end of a Flor del Fumar, dying the way all men should, like beaten animals, piles of bones and meat in the grass. But his family? They would make it to the other side.

Every dead man is a felled tree. But women die ignominiously, like dried raisins stuck to the bottom of a Sun-Maid box. Life has an order, a gendered order, no matter what shenanigans certain people may think possible. And what I was realizing that day was that a woman's body was, essentially, a desecratable thing.

Case in point: Blanchie in her blue dress.

It's strange the way connections get made. I was standing there looking at Blanchie, and I flashed on a vision of my daughter in the corduroy blazer from earlier that day. I grasped then very clearly the enterprise on which she was set—a lifelong enterprise, if she had her way, and one against which I realized I would have to stake my own life. All this business with men's clothes that had begun in tears over patent leather shoes at the age of three was evidence of a major misunderstanding on her part: She actually believed she could *accoutre* herself out of the misery of femaleness. My feeling was: It's not so easy to give degradation the slip. Even the makers of *Flashdance* knew it.

And yet my daughter in her fascination with this blazer was trying to tunnel her way out.

Something about the hubris of this insane proposition infuriated me.

I'm trying to explain something, and it's hard to know where to start. Karl Marx, or so I hear, said that beginnings are difficult in all scientific endeavors. Especially, I would like to add, yenta science. Look, I'm talking about how people (for example, women) become things, and how things (for example, corduroy blazers) become quasi-people, or take on a vitality of their own. This very shitty situation has actually defined both my and my daughter's lives, as much as we might hate to admit it.

To make matters worse I had to bear the force of realizing this thing about women's thingliness while having to watch Stephen's timidity about *what had to be done*. Someone was going to have to hunt in the folds of the casket for the photograph. We had conducted all the peering we could conduct. The physical scouring of Blanchie's body needed to commence. If Stephen wanted to protect my reputation, he would do it. He knew it and I knew it. Yet here he was, bouncing from foot to foot in front of the coffin, hesitating. It seemed like part of a grander refusal on his part to acknowledge facts about the world—his waffling, his hemming, his hawing, his willingness to see both sides about everything. Even things about which there were very clear sides to take.

I mean, this was a person who had touched dead bodies before, and yet such dillydallying I never saw.

To be fair, it was probably not so many dead bodies. A deputy health director (aka a glorified numbers cruncher in the employ of the city) neither touches dead bodies as a matter of course like a real doctor would, nor touches a paycheck of any significance. Still, Stephen had indeed touched one or two dead bodies, at some point in medical school back before he had abandoned his goal of becoming a practicing doctor. Certainly that should have been enough to acclimate a person to the feel of it, or at least more so than was, say, Saul, hulking by the cold cut plate in a sharkskin suit with shoulder pads so large and, really, ridiculously buoyant that the word "pluming" would not be inappropriate to describe the overall effect of this jacket. Though, who knew what Saul did on his excursions to Scranton or Hartford. For Saul, it must be said, lived on the edge of propriety, not only in the flamboyance of his pluming suits, but in his omnipresent cigars and his brand-fucking-new Chrysler LeBaron with the leather seats and wood detail.

So it was not out of the question that somewhere on his travels, he might have encountered a dead body. But Saul and his unknowable familiarity with dead bodies aside, the point is that my husband, Stephen Rosenberg, in all his experience or lack thereof with dead bodies, was not prepared to be, on that day, plunging his hands wrist-deep under the buttocks of his dead mother.

The man needed a nudge. I crossed the room to Stephen's side at the coffin's edge.

Why do I want to say "shore"? "The coffin's shore"?

I suppose I have not so nicely always associated Blanchie with whales, and now she was beached, so to speak; but I think it also has to do with my current condition, which some would call high as a kite on OxyContin, and others might more generously describe as extremely free-associative. For example, just now as I was narrating this particular memory, my mind sort of skipped out and suddenly I was remembering this dream I had the other night:

Stephen was alive, and we were on another planet. I guess I was channeling him. Stephen loved the stars, as most men do.

Whereas I have never cared much for outer space. To begin with, I have always hated to fly. Also, there is no shopping in space. Before you decide this is a superficial comment, consider a thing of which I have been apprised by the left-wing guerilla that is my erstwhile daughter, called "Communist Luxury." This is an actual perspective of some Marxists who believe that after the revolution we will all have Chanel bags!

Someone should inform science fiction writers about this, because a novel about *that* I would read.

* * *

In my dream I'm standing with Stephen on a cliff above a violet ocean. The shoreline is glittery dark sand, and when the sea washes over it, the beach turns the color of Elizabeth Taylor's eyes.

I want to say something to Stephen, but when I turn and look for him, he's gone. Only his briefcase, which he brought from Earth, is there, sitting next to me on the cliff. And then I remember. He's *dead*. When I start wondering if I'm dead too, I wake up.

So I guess that's where "shore" came from. It's hard to hold on to time. Now I'm realizing that I wasn't nauseated that day at Blanchie's funeral. I must be remembering it that way because I'm very nauseated right now, in the year 2011 if you can believe. But at Blanchie's funeral, in 1983, honestly I think I would have liked to eat from the cold cut platter. Specifically, a spoonful of chopped liver. I need to add that to my running list for when I start to feel better.

1. Salted matzoh with mustard and a slice of Swiss cheese
2. A slice of coconut cream pie
3. Ba-Tampte pickled green tomatoes, sliced on a plate
4. Chopped liver

So while it is probably true that I really wanted the cold cuts, no way was I going to gratify Saul, the platter-bringing *zhlob*, by affirming the usefulness of having these pungent meats close to hand. Especially not while the Mystery of the Missing Photo still needed to be resolved.

I made my way back to the coffin, snack-free, with my stomach a sourball of hunger, and stood next to Stephen, issuing very specific instructions *sotto voce*. *Sotto voce* and yet still somehow enunciating each word with all the precision of a trained actress—a trained actress, let me add, who was supposed to have gone on to grace the marquees of countless New York City *thee-ah-tahs* instead of starring in nothing but the reception desk of Eli Zilch, the (nominally) Upper East Side plastic surgeon (his office was east of Third Avenue, which everyone knows doesn't count) whose business consisted largely of all-cash payments from the bosses of the Brighton Beach Bratva for the gigantifying of their goomars' breasts.

Or worse—which I would have preferred no one to know, but it's the truth and what does it matter now—cleaning up the exam rooms after Zilch rammed his lipo spear repeatedly into the flanks of said goomars. Yes, I was the official baller-upper of the grease-stained blue paper upon which the mistresses of the Bratva had sat their asses while being speared. This was my lot in life. Fucking *this*. Understand that I balled up other people's ass-grease paper for a living while my so-called daughter was learning to play Debussy uptown among the children of every single major royal family in exile. It seemed that anytime a country's people rose up against their monarchs, there was a private jet waiting to squire the ousted royals to a triplex on Park Avenue, and next thing you knew, these children were enrolled at the Spence School with my financially aided own. This is how I came to learn such things as that the royal family of Denmark are not allotted an actual last name beyond "of Denmark" (my daughter's roll call was like being in a film: the latest Vanderbilt child, so-and-so del Drago, *Eloise of Denmark*...), whereas the Swedish nobility had long names that did not correspond to the word "Sweden," and in fact they never spoke of their iced homeland in mixed company, probably out of guilt for their complicity in the Holocaust. Which was ironic, because the Austrian and German Nazi heirs wore their own last names so entirely without disguise or shame that those few Jewish mothers whose children had gained entrance to this storied institution and its equally tony brother school became so accustomed to it we forgot to watch in amazement as such things as—*So, nu, what's going on with your daughter and that nice Globočnik boy?*—escaped our mouths like cartoon thought bubbles as we stood around waiting to pick up our children from, if you can believe it, *squash practice.*

Dear Jordana? J-something? What am I supposed to call you (if you are even you now)? I am asking genuinely.

This letter will be written over many weeks (if I have that much time). I must begin by acknowledging that you have been here for me above & beyond what I deserved. Mistakes were made by me, but only because I wanted the three of us to become four, then six, then maybe more & to have a lifestyle & holidays and summers in a way I dreamed about. I don't know if you can understand this. I realize those were my dreams & mine alone. So all I can do is apologize for my dreams & probably cruelty. I can't fix the past, I can only try to find ways to make the future more tolerable. The fact that you & I have a relationship again says more about you as a kind, loving human being (??) than it says about me, but I am learning & trying. You can see I am trying, telling it to you in your language. Your Marxish. How am I doing?
   I am sorry about earlier. And by "earlier" I mean this morning when I spilled my green shake (yes, on purpose) & "earlier" as in all of it. Your whole life. My whole life.
   I spoke with the doctor on the phone today. He said I would experience a period of plateau after the treatments & then I would "go downhill." But Judge Judy had this & beat it. And Ruth Bader Ginsburg. So I have to hope for the best.

HEAR YE HEAR YE

HONESTLY, I WOULDN'T HAVE cared about the ass-grease paper so much if it weren't clear that my daughter was not only not going to fulfill her god-given duty of multiplying our family, but was well on her way to becoming a permanent embarrassment, a *shanda* to the max. I would have been happy to give my life and every single workday to balling up ass-grease paper if the fruits of my mothering were going to pay off.

But they were not. I saw that now. I guess what I want to say is that it's a question of a return on an investment. I don't mean to be crude, but some things are just true.

There is no royal road to science and only those who do not dread the fatiguing climb of its steep paths have a chance of gaining its luminous summits, my "daughter" likes to lord over me, quoting Karl Marx in his French Preface. She loves to say "French Preface." She loves to extemporize on how difficult it is to analyze the world. Hear ye hear ye, I don't need a French Preface to explain that sometimes you need to slog your way through something in order to really understand it. I have slogged through so much, hello, and yet not a single piece of advice that I have ever given my daughter has she taken.

Editorially speaking, moreover, I would have preferred a descent-into-hell metaphor myself. As someone who has practiced the science of balling grease-stained ass paper for a living, I can tell you that the summits are anything but luminous.

The point, suffice to say, is that I had long ago dispensed with squeamishness.

So yes, I did egg Stephen on in the pursuit of a missing photograph, which I myself had placed in the casket in Boca Raton before Blanchie's body was flown for burial at New Montefiore. This was a missing photograph for which I would surely be blamed; and it was toward the locating of said photograph that I enunciated with well-trained high dudgeon and yet somehow also *sotto voce*, as Stephen gingerly tiptoed his fingers around his mother's body, palping the pillow, the crevice between the soft little bed and the satiny walls, the inch or so just shy of the feet—the safer extremities, let's say—for any absconded photographs—"Stephen," I hissed with frankly exemplary enunciation and perfect diaphragmatic control just like they'd taught me at the High School of Performing Arts—not easy to get into, by the way—waving my hand toward the body of my dead mother-in-law and my gentle anxious husband, the non-practicing-physician-cum-municipal-servant—"Stephen," I was saying, and here I held my hands out, curling my red-taloned fingers into two upwardly turned cups, indicating the approach he ought to be taking toward his mother's dead body—"Stephen," I sibilated, "you've got to *dig*."

Meanwhile, Saul. Looming and shiny in his sharkskin suit, nobody's idea of svelte, a disco ball with a beard occupying an entire corner of Sherman's cheapest reception room. Saul who had left the top down on his LeBaron when he valeted it at the door; Saul who clearly had no intention of putting the top back up and was preparing to participate in the funeral procession along Belt Parkway with the top down and the wind shooting daggers of November cold through his bizarrely still-full head of black-brown hair. Saul with his usual blank gaze. Emotionless Saul. Giant, bushy-headed and bushy-faced, glittering-suited Saul, a man about whom it was genuinely impossible to believe he had ever been a hairless infant squeezed through a vaginal canal; or if he had been, surely it was only to have pounced upon the waiting nipple with the greedy vigor and porcine lack of embarrassment with which he enjoyed his cigars.

And if Saul had done *that*, then why couldn't it be *Saul* attempting to unearth photographs from beneath his dead mother's ass?

Somebody in this room was going to have to step up and be a man and it sure as shit wasn't going to be me, and please god it was also not going to be my daughter, who was marching across the room while uttering that phrase that let me know beyond a shadow of a doubt that this daughter of mine was indeed a bulldagger. Yes, I watched with unblinking eyes as my husband cringed his way around his mother's body, and Saul glared from the cold-cut-plate corner, and here came my daughter, speaking that universal lexicon of bulldaggery, that language of hyper-helpfulness—oh yes here she was, approaching the casket, rolling up the sleeves on her scrawny eleven-year-old arms like a foreman at a construction site, saying oh so tellingly: "I got this."

* * *

I shook my head at my daughter and flashed the eyebrow again. No she did not *got this*. *Getting this* was for men. Not a person in the room understood what I was managing; no one comprehended the sheer effort that needed to be marshaled at all times to try to steer her back into the fold of femininity. Stephen, in particular, refused to grasp the tragic path upon which she was set. My daughter needed to be righted, like a ship slurping seawater. I understand that to people of today I sound like a monster, but this was a motherly concern I had, and between *mother* and *monster* no one in the history of philosophy has yet been able to distinguish, so why I'm even trying to explain this I don't know. I felt a fear for her, an unspeakable terror for her life. Because I've been to those clubs—don't ask me when or where, but I've known those people—and gay people are very lonely people.

But my daughter had no fear of the consequences of her actions. Why? Because she had inherited the Rosenberg belief that it made you a good person to suffer. And for what? This urge toward suffering didn't come from me, and yet I had married into it and given birth to more of it and now look.

I'll give you an example. Shortly after Blanchie died, we moved for a time to Israel, where Stephen had taken a visiting post with the Health Ministry that had us living on literal pennies (shekels, actually, which were worth even less) in a bare-bones stucco cottage in someplace I had never heard of called Ramat Gan. I'll come back to all of this later. But for now I want to convey one small riddle: What's the difference between toughing it out under a thin blanket on a cot in some *frontierische* little hut versus being toasty warm at the King David Hotel watching the planes shriek by over cocktails and borscht? *Nothing*. This is what I mean about the Rosenbergs and suffering. Stephen wasn't any better than any other man who thought he'd find his dick in Israel. At least the fundamentalists and power brokers admitted it. At least they didn't accept a pittance so they could flatter themselves that they were going there to "help." Help schmelp. Help who? These men had exotic fantasies. All of them.

Including, undoubtedly, Saul. Although it may have seemed that Saul was too stupid to know the Middle East existed at all, bar mitzvahing your children at the Wailing Wall was all the rage for the parents of Rockland County. And so even Saul had made the trek, which galled me no end, as he now considered himself "worldly," which was a hoot. Listen, you can be inhaling a boatload of I Can't Believe It's Yogurt! at the Nanuet Mall one night and shitting it out in the bathroom of the Tel Aviv Hilton the next day. *Lawrence of Arabia* this is not.

In any case, it was the photo of Saul's children—Leon and Ari—that had gone missing. Thus Saul was the aggrieved one, and he was going to lurk in the corner, letting his brother fix this fuckup. Yes, he was going to lurk, staring me down for as long as it took me either to miraculously produce the item in question from his mother's ass crack, or to admit that I had never placed the photograph in the casket to begin with.

12:30 a.m.

I'm rethinking this apologizing for my dreams thing. Sometimes you're here, sometimes you aren't. You're up to something. Out at all hours. With a woman in Chelsea. A colleague. I told you, don't mix business with pleasure, but no one listens to me.

Such a saint this one. So persecuted. So wounded. And yet I hear you shoveling horseshit to multiple women multiple times a day on the phone. Is this the behavior of a traumatized little mouse? Sometimes you come in at three in the morning when you think I'm asleep. Sometimes you have someone with you. In your childhood bedroom, yet. This apartment isn't a crash pad from which to conduct sexcapades. This apartment is my prison. This apartment is my tomb.

And what do I have left but my dreams. So I should apologize? How about this bulldagger, gallivanting all over the city.

Meanwhile I think I'm overdosing on oxycodone. Not that anyone cares. I run out before the due date & Dr. Norman just prescribes more. Tonight, I don't even remember how many I took.

SUGAR BECKER

SO THERE WAS MY daughter approaching the casket with the idea of saving my reputation—which was an upside-down gallantry performed by the very person from whom I did *not* want such things—when, like a guardian angel, entered Sugar Becker.

She took one look at the situation and swept through the scrum of Rosenbergs, seized my daughter by the shoulders, and with all the drama of Indiana Jones crashing through the doors of a lonely Himalayan watering hole and straight into the arms of proprietress Karen Allen, instructed my daughter to go fetch her a seltzer water; Sugar was *absolutely parched.*

Off my daughter hastened to the little table of drinks, and the problem of who was going to take care of this photo situation reverted back to its correct location: my husband.

Sugar was clad in a glorious mink. It is possible to love a person and be consumed with envy at the same time, I had long had to conclude vis-à-vis Sugar. This mink, however, threatened that delicate equilibrium. Light reflected off a billion glossy needles of fur as Sugar minked her way through the constellation of relatives toward me. She was halted en route by Stephen's uncle Abe, who fancied himself a czar of all things, including, for whatever reason, culture, despite knowing no more than the average television watcher. Probably less. Still, Uncle Abe considered any piece of information that he had gleaned from the world to be privileged knowledge, the property of a select few *noticers* such as himself.

"Sugar," I called, removing myself like a wild electron from Stephen's side and triangling between her and Uncle Abe. I slid my arm between them. Mink met parody of mink as I twirled my arm up Sugar's like a barber's pole and pried her off at an oblique angle.

"Oh Barbara, what a loss!" she said, projecting her voice loud enough for Stephen and Saul to think I gave a shit.

I was accustomed to Sugar looking slightly different each time I saw her. The result of some new aesthetic treatment or L.A. fashion. She had known about frosted lipstick a full year before the East Coast did, for example. Same with peasant blouses. This time, though, she had an entirely new affectation. She spoke with her three middle fingers hovering over her nose and her head ducked, as if trying to cover a laugh with her mouth full, but constantly. She had mentioned a recent "botched" nose job over the phone. With this new face-covering move she was doing, though, who could tell.

"I like your mink," she said, reaching out with her free hand and stroking my arm. She didn't mean this, but Sugar had a tendency to attempt to level the financial playing field with tender but bald-faced lies. It was one of the things she did that made me ongoingly uncomfortable, having to pretend I was the fool who didn't know the difference. But I knew. To put it in my daughter's Marxish, *First mink as tragedy, second mink as farce.*

"The studio car brought you all the way out here?" I

changed the topic, hoping for a neutral tone but even I could hear how overly interested I sounded (*I always sounded*) in the details of Sugar's fancy Hollywood life.

"Actually, I'm not here for work." She still had her hand partially in front of her nose. Her cheeks and the area around her eyes were unnaturally placid, like a fish gazing unblinkingly from a bowl. This was presumably an effect of a combination of Botox and Sculptra, which had produced skin so taut that her cheekbones gleamed, frozen across the humps of an artificially boosted facial structure. We had only recently gotten Sculptra in the office, but by the evidence of Sugar's face I deduced that it must have already been in wide circulation in Los Angeles.

"When we spoke, you said you were coming here for work." I couldn't help but nudge.

Sugar had very distinctly said she was coming for work, not one week earlier on the phone. My catching her in this fabrication caused Sugar to remove her hands from in front of her face and perform ignorance.

She raised her hands, palms up. "I mean, technically I can write from anywhere."

Now I caught a glimpse of the nose. It was in fact pretty botched. The bridge and nostrils were too thin—pencil-thin—which accentuated its length and consequently highlighted the length of her face overall. She had a kind of stretched appearance, like a stuck film negative warping under a projector's heat.

Sugar saw me seeing her and caught my eye with a kind of pleading squint. "Is it bad?"

I smiled. A very genuine smile, because actually it was pretty bad, and so I was filled with magnanimity because this nose was in fact leveling the playing field a little bit between us. Zilch sometimes did nose reconstructions where he added volume back in, though the profession liked to keep these quiet, as a rule, because no one liked to think that nose jobs could go wrong when in fact they routinely did.

"Neil's doing some casting."

My magnanimity faded. Yet another project for which I wouldn't be considered even as an extra. A project of which I hadn't been apprised in advance lest I actually prepare a plea. The rise of Sugar and Neil had been so unstoppable, so meteoric, and they'd laid down the rules for me right away. They hadn't made any mistakes, had probably consulted with other Hollywood friends about what to do when you hit it big. *Don't raise expectations in your old friends. Don't give anyone anything to hope for, not even a crumb, not a bit part, not even a nothing throwaway role. Not Amy Irving's brassiere-fitter in a risqué comedy, not the counter girl in a deli, flirting with Elliott Gould.*

Saul, extravagantly working his post-charcuterie gum in his thick jaws, began paddling his way over to us.

"Find anything." Saul delivered this not as a question, but as an expression of triumph, the detective's *aha* revelation of a bloody footprint. "Find anything," inspector Saul repeated.

He gave me that look. Regarding my coat like it was a gun pointed at Stephen's head.

What was Saul, the mink police? I knew what he was thinking: *Don't you see how hard he works; you're killing my brother for an imitation mink.* Always me killing him. What about the way *he* was killing *me* with his ambitionless dreams to be a servant of the public's health. That's a thing—ambitionless dreams—if you didn't know. For example, a medical doctor who instead practices public health and is paid peanuts by the city is, despite all odds, a thing. Stephen dreamed of saving the world, and this dream kept him from worldly ambitions. As long as he didn't make money he was good. This *fakokta* equation had ruined my life.

"Look, Saul, if you really wanted to make sure the photo got in there," I said, "you should have been at your mother's bedside instead of tra-la-la'ing around at some *yenemsvelt shtarker* convention."

"National Association of Garmentory Executives." Saul balled his hands in his pockets, extending his hips to the width of his shoulder pads.

"*Executives?*" I coughed.

Stephen, listening in, emitted a quiet *humph* of either protest or agreement. These expressions of his were never clear. His humphs were a simultaneous recognition of the world and total refusal to intervene in its outcomes; that's how Stephen humphed.

Stephen humphed again and began to rummage.

If only, I thought, as I watched Stephen rifle with increasing confidence, if only Saul knew that the man I supposedly held hostage, regularly vacuuming his wallet for imitation-mink money—if only Saul knew how his faultless older brother gorged on my body, no matter what this high-minded philosopher thought of my base materialism and other vices.

And now Stephen—his right hand nuzzled deep under his mother's dead body, with his eyes turned toward the ceiling—blinked and humphed again. He drew his hand out slowly, his mother's navy dress settling back against the satin bedding. In his hand, a crumpled photo of Leon and Ari in yarmulkes and giant, ill-fitting blazers that were a mini version of Saul's own steroidal travesty, squinting impatiently at the camera with the sun slashed across their faces. The Wailing Wall loomed across the background, caper plants bursting from the stones like the pubic tufts of bar-mitzvees.

I grabbed Stephen's wrist and waggled the photo in Saul's direction. "What did I tell you? What did I fucking tell you, Saul?"

I was expecting some *farbisine* retort and began readying myself for one of our skirmishes, but instead a silence that was more than silence fell over him. It was one of those silences in a movie before a bomb goes off, a fraction of time when sound deadens at some deeper level. In one of those ominous vacuums of sound, Saul's face crumpled and the spongy balls of his cheeks scorched.

Then his eyes scorched too, and a tapestry of capillaries blossomed across their dingy whites. It appeared that Saul was starting to cry. This was an alarming sight I was pretty sure few had ever seen. Worse, he was crying *at* me. Loud, burping sobs. Staring and shaking, and then he was opening his mouth.

I bugged my eyes at Sugar. *Do something,* I mouthed.

Like what, she mouthed back, shrugging her shoulders.

Like a paramedic assigned to an emotion-prevention unit, Saul's uncle Abe materialized and rushed over, throwing a thick arm around Saul's shoulders. He yanked him into his chest sideways at a stilted right angle, a pile of damp dark suits.

"You're alright, Saul," Abe insisted. He pumped Saul's shoulder a couple times, repeating *You're alright,* as if Saul were a tire that needed to be inflated back to its proper level of masculinity.

"I"—Saul gasped—"I can't . . ." He was still staring at me. Other relatives were emerging, clustering around Saul.

"What *can't* you?" Abe prodded, more concerned than Saul was by the deepening crack in the carapace of Saulness. "You need money?" He started reaching for his wallet. Saul shook his head.

Dear God, I prayed, *I will never smoke a single cigarette again if Saul just shuts the hell up and we move on.* There was a thing I was concerned Saul was about to bring up.

"*Leon . . .*" Saul garbled. His cheeks kept reddening. He was becoming incandescently overwrought.

Saul's son Leon was a solid C student permanently marinating in Saul's rec room with his gang of monosyllabic friends who since puberty had all begun to take on the aura of underbaked loaves of bread, mounds of dough puffing inside soft, crustless rinds. It was hard to imagine anything dramatic happening to Leon, but whatever it was did not appear to have to do with me. I was relieved. God, or whoever, had heard my prayers, and this meant I would have to make good on my promise never to touch another cigarette. I felt a new wave of panic wash over me as I imagined the sheer poundage that I would put on. This—it was clear to me from my numerous friends who had quit smoking only to subsequently assume the jiggly physique of a waterbed—was inevitable. But it hit me then that, on the upside, if I saved my unused cigarette money for six months, I would be able to afford the pair of gold teardrop hoops I had been ogling in the window of Fortunoff's, as well as a suite of step aerobics classes at the newly opened Jack LaLanne on Second Avenue. And if you want to know the truth, I did stop smoking shortly thereafter, and I did get those earrings, and I really threw myself into step aerobics, and I *lost* weight, much to the amazement of everyone I knew.

". . . decided on a pre-med program. *Leon.* Leon's going to be a doctor. And I can't"—Saul dipped his head—"I won't ever be able to tell Mom."

Abe threw his hands in the air. "But this is *a miracle,* Saul!" His expression—like a dog trying to puzzle out the workings of a doorknob—suggested that Abe was as bewildered at the rise of Leon as I was.

"*Mom,*" Saul mewled into his own chest, and I did see him then as an infant, beefy in his crib. All his needs, his hunger, his unabashedness.

2:20 a.m.

Woke up with terrible cramps.

Called for you & you weren't home. See what I'm saying?

Ran a bath for myself. Could barely do it. Laid in it for a long time. I fell asleep. I could have drowned! You're playing a game with me, aren't you.

FROM THIS DIRTY LINEAGE, A MIRACLE

I HAD LET NOT a flicker of emotion cross my face during Saul's outburst. I saved it for after the funeral, at which point I immediately took to Stephen's and my bedroom, crying, with the rest of the family clustering in the doorway like a pack of squirrels.

"Barbara?" Stephen sounded—as he always did—utterly mystified by the expression of any emotion whatsoever. It wasn't that he was cold; he was unfailingly room temperature, like a scrap of chicken cutlet you scrape off your plate after dinner. Stephen unobtrusively mirrored the average aggregate heat of any room he was in. He was a rhythm guitar of a person.

There were times—many, actually—when I found this quality of Stephen's comforting. But at that moment I was wild with grief and tears. Not over Blanchie, who frankly, especially after she had seen fit to skip off to Boca as a widow, shirking her grandmotherly duties at the age of sixty-five to start a second life putting on budget musicals at the Century Village Hadassah, I did not care for. And not over Saul and that thing I was concerned he would bring up, although I would have been pretty mortified if he had. No, I was wild with grief over my daughter. Because I had realized something about gender that day, and I couldn't unsee it. My daughter was rubbing the bottom of her socked left foot absently over the top of her right one the way she used to comfort herself as a baby, staring at me sobbing, curled on the bed like a snail.

"She puts me back in the bad place." I pointed.

"The bad place?" Stephen came to stand by the bed, squeezing my shoulder in a half-assed effort to reassure me. He said *the bad place* the way someone speaks to a child about an imaginary friend. This was because Stephen actually did not believe bad places were real. Bad places, for Stephen, were just misunderstandings that could and should be sorted out by considered, reasonable discussion. His indulgent but patronizing concern plus his pitiful shoulder squeeze drove me further into despair. Stephen was trying to smooth things over as quickly as possible, probably because he—like I—had just noticed the competitive sobbing start, with tears squeegeeing out the corners of my daughter's eyes.

There is something about my daughter's sadness that has always completely enraged me. I know it's not right, and no one will admit this, but it's entirely too easy to feel enraged by your child's unhappiness. I'm not talking about the wailing of a baby, which is frustrating but not enraging. I'm talking about something that comes on later, glimmering into view around age six, and taking on its own animal shape until it becomes unavoidably apparent somewhere around twelve, thirteen. A *bugbear* begins to appear over your child's shoulder. *No, Barbara*, someone out there probably wants to object— *it's not that. It's that you felt competitive for Stephen's sympathy in this moment when he was torn between wife's and daughter's tears. It's Oedipal. Or Electral. Or whatever.*

It's true that Stephen's boundless yet sort of removed sympathy for his child—he "objectively" had sympathy for all humans, that was Stephen's gambit—was its own species of galling. But, to be clear, this *bugbear* thing was the epicenter of my anger. Actually, I would argue that this *bugbear* thing is the epicenter of most parents' anger. But in my especially miserable case, my daughter's *bugbear* was not some normal obsession or fixation; her *bugbear*, tragically, was a corduroy blazer. And about this blazer I shared the universal parental woe of witnessing your child wrestling with the existential void and coming up as empty-handed as you are, or worse. A combination of despair at being unable to make it better and outright inflamed disbelief that no matter what you had done to stave it off, your child was going to tangle themselves in their own lifelong knot anyway. And not only are you ultimately helpless to prevent it, but despite your best efforts, *you* would be unfairly named the antagonist, the cause of this knot, until the day that child themself dies.

And somewhere in there my own sadness had decreased in value in the emotional economy of the family, dwindling in importance in the face of my daughter's approaching tragic personhood. Because I was "the mother," my disappointment could only be monstrous, and the fact was that even if I tried to explain what was upsetting to me, no one in this family would ever understand. My daughter was headed for a gender disaster. I could see it and Stephen couldn't, and so I was alone in facing down the urgency of this whole situation, which was going nowhere good and which Stephen kept calmly diagnosing as just one dot on the grand spectrum of human variation. Meanwhile, not so incidentally, this girl had been our ticket out of everything, and here we were still mired in the cold cut platters of this world.

* * *

By the way, this thing about my impossible sadness is what I was getting at earlier about the larger-ness and smaller-ness of motherhood. How somehow you become two totally different things at once. This irresolvable conflict-and-yet-entanglement of two mutually exclusive qualities (larger-ness and smaller-ness) constitutes motherhood as a state of being. It is also, I am compelled to mention, the definition of the dialectic, a concept which is dramatized perfectly by the tiny hall closet, which embodies the punishment of the Jews of Yorkville for their efforts at assimilation, and, simultaneously, a promise: that of hiding a corduroy blazer from one's daughter. I'm talking about snatching victory from the jaws of defeat. That's dialectics.

When my daughter was young, maybe six or seven, I began to institute evening "enunciation practice." I would lead her to my dressing table chair, an armless, slip-covered, rose-and-white-striped chair that I inherited from my mother. When this chair is sat upon, the hot dust of old upholstery married with the baked-in pungency of generations of ass and genitals puffs out. It recalls my mother—her permanent hunch, and the sour scent that her thin old skirts gave off—so long gone now in the cold city night, soot blowing in the windows as her soul blew out. But I digress.

Wearing my favored style of nightgown—a long silky slip in bronze or peach or pink—I would sit my daughter in my lap, and with the gore-red talons I retouched at night while watching *60 Minutes*, would lay index cards on a cleared spot on the makeup table, which also held a glass of Tab diet soda with crackling ice cubes and a bendy straw.

"*T-youna, T-yousdiy.*" With one hand, I would pick up and read off the cards in the faux-British inflection I'd learned and practiced from 1940s and '50s American films; with the other I smoked a Camel Light.

The goal of the game was to stave off the inheritance of a Brooklyn accent, and the game made my daughter shy. If she didn't repeat after me right away, I would twist one Oil-of-Olayed knuckle into her ribs, spilling ashes into the crevice of the seat. She would squirm and laugh nervously and repeat the words back to me. But there was one particular word she could never consent to saying in the way I wanted.

"Nood," she would say, defying the dictates of the lesson. Nood. Like an Ocean Avenue hoodlum.

I could feel my thighs getting stony underneath my child's ass. "N-yuuuud," I would emphasize, twisting my knuckle.

"Nood," for some disaster-courting reason, my daughter would repeat. Again with the Brooklyn accent.

I am supposed to feel sorry for a lot of things, but these enunciation lessons are not one of them. I began conducting them, for one thing, just as my daughter enrolled at the Spence School, a six-story limestone mansion on Ninety-first Street between Fifth and Madison avenues, inside of which, as I said, studied and frolicked and progressed toward graduation hundreds of the wealthiest daughters of the borough—nay, *the world*—along with my daughter and a few sundry other infiltrators.

This was the late '70s and early '80s, and the city was deserted, selling entire apartment buildings on the Lower East Side for a dollar. So my child was able to slip into the Spence School through a unique historical crack of peculiarly low enrollments combined with tuition remission paid for by Stephen's evening job, adjunct lecturing at Columbia University.

Stephen, by the way, had no idea what the Spence School was. I was the one who learned of it, and who had gotten my daughter into this fortress of power for screaming little girls in patent leather shoes and sparkly bangle bracelets from Le Monde des Enfants on Madison Avenue. Not that I grew up knowing of the Spence School, either, but I had been made aware of it in 1976 via my friend Phyllis at our Jazzercise class at the Yorkville Community Center. Phyllis had just secured a place at Ramaz for her own daughter. One of our Jazzercise enemies, Jackie—an unappealing woman who looked like a tree stump in a mauve bodysuit—said something nasty about how it was easy to get your kid into the Jewish schools—Ramaz, Dalton—but the *goyishe* schools were another thing entirely. "Spence," for example, she said, or "Nightingale." I fixated on the former, though I had no idea of the difference between the two, simply because "Nightingale" sounded like a poem, or a joke.

"Spence" on the other hand, sounded like a tower of clout. And while Phyllis was content to send her children to Ramaz where they would marinate in a stew of mediocrity, I would have none of that, even though I was from exactly that.

In his old age, my father liked to visit the stores along Third Avenue in Bay Ridge requesting change for a nickel. It's pretty bleak when your desire is not to trade up, but simply to barter what you've got for something even more irrelevant. Well, it's pretty something. And this pretty something of a man was my father. Someone who tried to turn nickels—the already thankless backbone of transaction—into pennies, transaction's shit.

In his pockets, my father used to carry around these pennies, along with a supply of nougats and the steel insignias of automobiles (Dusters, Pacers, Pintos), which he would pry off parked cars as he walked from the 68th Street–Hunter College subway station to our apartment. When he visited my daughter he would gift her the nougats, and the insignias too. But the pennies he kept for himself.

From this dirty lineage, a miracle. My daughter was born—I cannot emphasize this enough—*blond*.

I really thought I'd made it. Me, Barbara Rosenberg—née Horowitz; not the Horowitz-Margareten matzoh fortune Horowitzes, just the regular Horowitzes who you never heard of. The doors to Spence had opened and my blond daughter was taken to the dusty, florid heart of the ruling class. A fine gentile hand to lead her away from the crowded beaches of Brooklyn, the clamor of Junior's Deli, the stolen car insignias, the pennies, the nougats, and the Coney Island batting cages, polar lit into the night. My daughter, educated amid a freshly washed and fragrant mob of six-year-olds in plaid tunics who were always coming from or going to Gstaad, and whose homes were humorless, huge mini-statelets. My daughter! Classmates with so-and-so of Denmark, and all the rest of them.

Stephen and I had won. My daughter joined Spence's elite; she waved at us and we joined it too.

Brooklyn receded behind me like a dirty sock. My daughter learned to say croissant the right way (*cwahsahn*), the way Nazi scions and princesses in exile did, and slept at those heirs' and exiles' apartments with floor-to-ceiling drapes shut against the Park Avenue morning light, and ate *cwahsahn* for breakfast, and sat in their box seats at the MTV Video Music Awards and the New York City Ballet, and attended private disco parties at Studio 54 and Limelight where the DJ played the first Madonna album for the very first time for a bunch of eleven-year-olds on roller skates.

* * *

So what's wrong with cold cuts?

Nothing. There's nothing objectively wrong with cold cuts. But we didn't scrimp and save to supplement the financial aid of an neoclassical palace of education where "Etiquette" and "Typing" were actual courses my daughter took for credit so she could shuck off the gifts with which she had been bestowed and become a mannish woman with a thing for books. We didn't purchase Victorian bloomers for her to perform gymnastics in front of absconded Nazis and disgraced royals for this to be the outcome. Try to imagine the feeling of taking everything we sacrificed for her education and setting it on fire, because that's what it felt like.

But it turns out you can't be to the manor born if you're not born to the manor, and it was at Blanchie's funeral that I realized I had to face facts. The putrid claw of vulgarity had come to claim my family. My bulldagger daughter, headed straight into the maw of penniless spinsterhood.

And irony of ironies, it was *Saul*—the world's biggest schmuck, with his satin tracksuits and beer belly—who was going to make it after all. My daughter was bound for a life of clunky shoes and corduroy blazers and single-ply toilet paper, and Saul's son—a son whose idea of culture had been foosball tournaments in a Nyack basement—was going to confidently tap through the halls of Mount Sinai in Gucci wing tips, conducting rounds. On patients! Actual patients! It was too much to bear. Had it all been a dream? Had I ever really watched my daughter play piano high in Spence's limestone eaves with the sunset congealing into a red paste through the iron-wrought panes, a slim gentile teacher standing over her, slipping her fingers under the hinges of my daughter's own, nudging them into the proper piano-playing shape? Or worse, was my daughter meanwhile having some kind of finger orgasm from the contact with this, now that I thought about it, suspicious-looking piano woman in the middle of a recital? I thought of all the bake sales in whatever the hell a "Drawing Room" is, the way the dust motes played over mahogany tables piled high with Rice Krispie treats in the powdery light, and how I'd truly believed that we alone among the schmucks of our extended family—my blond girl playing Debussy with arched fingers—were the lucky ones. But I saw then that Saul, who had raised his children like animals, was going to win.

This brings me to my point, which I know is going to piss some people (aka Marxists) off. There's dialectics—the sublation of tiny hall closets, a punishment that is also an opportunity, etc. And then there are some things that are just *true*. One person wins, one loses. Saul wins, I lose. Sugar's mink and her movies win; me and my imitation mink lose. Some things may be an endless play of dialectics, but some things are just a battle to the death.

6:27 a.m.

I was high on Oxy when I found myself calling you in & asking for help last night. The MTA had begun its damn excavations for the Second Avenue Subway Line. To top it off, they're putting the transfer station on the corner, right below where my bedroom looks out on Second Avenue. Earlier we had been warned that the MTA would be "blasting the schist" in the evening, whatever that is supposed to mean. You read me the building communiqué that had been emailed to all residents. No, actually, you deigned to shout this information from the living room as you tra-la-la'ed out the door for the day.

By the evening, the drilling & explosions were constant, punctuated by frequent blasts of the warning horn & then building-shaking booms as explosives detonated deeper & deeper into East Sixty-ninth Street, drowning out my food program on the television, a tiny David in the face of the MTA's Goliath. I'd been watching without hearing a single ingredient or instruction for hours. I couldn't find the clicker to turn up the volume & truth be told I didn't have the energy to shake out the blankets or even sit up & hunt farther than the radius of what my arms could reach. I'd just been lying there making snow angels in the bed, hoping for contact. By the time I heard your key in the door, I had been snow angeling & popping Oxys for quite some time, & before I knew what I was doing, I heard my voice, in sort of a put-on babyish whine, calling for help.

*   *   *

When you came to the door you looked out of sorts, actually. Your skin was leathery & your face was sharp & tired. You peered at me for a second, sliding your backpack off your shoulder & dropping it to the floor in an annoyed way. When you came closer I had a moment of vertigo, because how you were moving was not normal. You hopped into the room is the only way I can describe it—a light bobbing, or floating—& yet when you got to the edge of the bed I had the strong feeling that you were bigger, actually, occupying more space than usual. I felt very loomed over. Were you getting fatter? Or taller? Maybe I was just shrinking. I knew I made a pathetic sight, swaddled & diminished while the room shuddered with sound.

The clicker? you said, unnecessarily loudly—*a ham actor broadcasting to an audience what you were doing onstage instead of just doing it. You peacocked around the bed in the pink of health, rifling through the blankets officiously until you seized on the clicker, which somehow had made its way down toward my feet.*

You were in one of your self-congratulatory moods where you clearly felt very good about how helpful you were being—your service to me a reflection of your irreproachable ethics. I did not at that moment choose to point out that how you really could have been of service to me would have been by getting married TO A MAN years ago & contributing to this family in the ways a normal person should, instead of absurdly flaunting your clicker-finding now as some proof of the goodness of your existence.

Volume? you shouted, brandishing the clicker.

Oh how you clicked this clicker. You clicked the clicker with a sense of your own profound importance, waving it in the air while pecking at the volume button. You clicked this clicker like you were giving me a blood transfusion, or CPR, or a grandchild.

Sometimes I worry this was all my fault.

A JEWEL-ROOFED CITY IN A CLOUD OF SMOKE

IF YOU MUST KNOW, the truth was I *had* thought about not putting the photograph of Leon and Ari in the casket. Although this was only because I had thought about not putting any of the photographs in the casket.

There I was at Blanchie's apartment in Boca organizing her stuff, including the photo of Leon and Ari, and wondering *What if I just threw all these damn photographs in the garbage.* The air was that aquarium-heavy Floridian stew, and even the wicker furniture was radiating heat off its spines. My patience was thin. Blanchie's heart had finally gone to sea in its own fluid, Stephen was in the living room speaking with the Florida shipping associates of Sherman's—large goys who affected morose silence as a passable substitute for gravitas—and I was on the verge of something petty and irreversible. I studied the photos Blanchie had selected to accompany her into eternity. Leon and Ari, egomaniacally radiating the supposed weight of history in front of the Wailing Wall. And my daughter at the Parrot Jungle in Miami. Other girls her age are visible in the background, in frosted lip gloss and dangly earrings. And my daughter, standing there, in shorts and a polo shirt, arms crossed, feet planted like a coach at a losing soccer game, scowling at the ground with jowls full of chewing gum and a parrot looming on her spiny shoulder like a ventriloquist's puppet. A goddamned diesel dyke. A diesel dyke at the Parrot Jungle. This is the photo Blanchie wanted to share with all the congregants at the funeral and all the eternal dirt.

It's a phase, I tried to calm myself. *It must be a phase.* Or, okay, I would make it a phase by refusing to inter—and thus monumentalize—this photograph at New Montefiore in the family plot. I was hit then with the utter freedom of that moment, the ethical crossroads at which I sat poised. I felt overcome with the conviction that my daughter would never come around, never blossom into femininity, indeed would forever remain a sulking Mack truck if I sanctioned the reality of this photo by including it in the casket. In which case I would be doing my daughter a favor in the long run by getting rid of the photos. I would, in flinging the photos away, fling myself and all of us forward in time to a moment at which this *mishegas* would be but a hazy memory. I could anticipatorily erase this blight. I could do this by throwing out the photos without a further thought, like a dermatologist tossing a skin tag into a wastebasket. I could do this for my daughter. To give her a chance at a life—at children, a family. I could do this, simply, because I had to do it. Daily, my efforts to shoehorn this girl into femininity crumbled off her like a soft, dry snowball chucked against a window. Who would know if I just forgot to put the entire set of photos in there. Yes, the *entire* packet. Because god knows I wasn't going to eliminate my daughter's photo from its pride of place in the casket while showcasing the photo of Leon and Ari.

I'm talking about narratives, and shaping them. Does it matter what "really" happened?

Consciousness—Dr. Freud said (or so my daughter once lectured, her nose poking over a book)—begins at the point of our forgetting. An excitation occurs, an insupportable one, and consciousness is the print it leaves. A jewel-roofed city in a cloud of smoke.

I didn't do it, but I would have.

That's what it means to be a mother. I don't care how nice you are, becoming a mother grants a certain capacity to take action, like a hot holiday chestnut cracks open inside you. The absolute misery of having a child who themself remains childless is that they will never have any inkling of how many times you've had to take action on their behalf. I'm not saying the photo of Leon and Ari was one of those times, because I *did* put the photos in the casket, but I'm making a point about the fact that before you're a mother you can weigh situations, you can waffle. Afterward, forget it.

There are some people who would contend that I'm not a very good mother. To those people I say,

Fuck you.

NO CLASS? KISS MY ASS!

WHEN I PICKED UP the phone at Zilch's the day after Blanchie's funeral and heard Sugar's nasal drawl—*Baahhhbruh?*—I suggested we meet at the Soup Burg diner near the American Express office on Fifty-fifth Street and Lexington Avenue so I could get traveler's checks.

"I'm awfully busy with last-minute preparations for our posting to Stephen's engagement with the Health Ministry," I explained.

I was being absurdly *hoity-toity*.

Sugar knew we were going to Israel. She had known for months—as long as I had, practically. So I didn't need to put on a show of purchasing traveler's checks. But seeing Sugar at the funeral—*seeing Sugar, shimmering in her mink, seeing* us *at Blanchie's shabby sendoff*—required a correction, and if I had to deliver this small skit of jetting off last minute to the King David Hotel with a pocketbook full of last-minute traveler's checks and a handful of mints like the Queen of Sheba, then so be it.

In actual fact, thanks to my passion for organization, our five suitcases had been fully packed for at least a week and a half. I had no idea what the accommodations and amenities would be like, and I did not want to forget anything. Ninety-nine percent of what I knew about Israel, I knew from *Exodus*, a movie in which no one ever shaved, or bought a tube of mascara or a Band-Aid. Beyond the scenes of diplomats in suits at the King David Hotel, things looked pretty rustic. In *Exodus* someone was always either dying on a cot, or hoeing a field. The closer we got to the trip, the more questions were being raised for me. Such as: *Were there hair dryers there.*

Meanwhile, Sugar said only, as she always did when we discussed it, "*Ach, Israel!*" as if Stephen had been demoted to the Staten Island Bureau of Sanitation.

That was how Sugar was about Israel. She supported the fact of it, but she would never get her hands dirty actually going there. Going there was for commoners and fanatics. I guessed she thought I was the former.

There was silence, and the far-off sound of long nails clicking absently against a receiver. Then Sugar suggested we go to a matinee of the Holocaust thriller *Judith*, starring Sophia Loren, at the Metro instead. I could see she was offering a compromise.

My weakness had always been film, and Sugar's superior understanding of it. I did a quick mental calculation about whether I could get to the American Express office on a different day and consented to meet her at her hotel.

"Come by after my one P.M.—say one-thirty?"

Sugar and I had worked out an informal truce over many years around the difference in our stations. Some periods were more precarious than others, but all in all we had come a long way from the first time I laid eyes on her, at which moment I correctly appraised this jumble of limbs and curly dark ginger hair worn parted down the middle and always in danger of closing to a near-slit the view of her freckled face and long nose, as a daughter of the Five Towns, heiress to an in-ground pool and a dowry. A girl, I determined, whose understanding of drama generally and tragedy more specifically was drawn solely from the wellspring of feeling she had about the fact that her looks did not match her caliber.

She could have made an effort to address this disjunction. There are ways. But at fifteen, Sugar seemed to have just decided to go the wall-of-hair route, as if she would forever look out on, and judge, the world through a one-way mirror. This, I thought at the time, was a route one could only take if one had the money to afford not to be looked at. On our first meeting, I did not care for her.

"Williams or Miller?" I asked that first day. This was the regular way of doing introductions at Performing Arts. By this means one could ascertain which of the two most likely dramatists a schoolmate had chosen as their audition monologue to gain entrance to the school.

Infrequently, someone would say "Beckett." Generally it was Williams or Miller.

I had assumed Sugar would say Miller, which was the choice of elitists, but instead she said "Belle Barth," which threw me for a loop. Belle Barth was a filthy Borscht Belt comedienne whose act I had never actually heard, but had caught plenty of whisperings about among adults. The idea that Sugar had auditioned for Performing Arts—*and been accepted?*—on the basis of gutter schlock, the very thing from which I was fleeing into the world of actual theater, erected a wall between us immediately. This person was not a serious actress.

"That's a pity," I said, putting on my best cultured accent. Sugar looked bemused, which further annoyed me. After this encounter, she and I did not speak another word to each other by tacit agreement for the remainder of the school year.

The summer after ninth grade, however, my older cousin Ellen stole a copy of Belle Barth's *The Customer Comes First* from her summer job as a stockgirl at Colony Records in Times Square. We listened to it in snippets on her parents' record player when my aunt Lil would go downstairs to sit on the stoop and smoke, and I realized that Sugar was on to something about Belle Barth. My mother used to tell Ellen and me a story about a boy she didn't marry—someone she'd dallied with just before she'd met my father. One night, she had gone on a double date at the soda shop with my aunt Lil, and at some point over sodas, my mother's date told Aunt Lil that she had "no class." To which Lil shot back, "No class? Kiss my ass!" This line really stuck with us kids. In fact, the only time I was allowed to curse was when Aunt Lil would come over. Right when she opened the door, I would sing "No class? Kiss my ass!" gleefully to Aunt Lil's half-hearted reprimands.

There was something about Belle Barth that reminded me of Aunt Lil and all those neighborhood ladies. That secret voice they used among themselves—that's the voice Belle Barth used to the world. I didn't know if Sugar was on to this fact or not (I doubted anyone spoke this way in Hewlett Harbor), but I knew that, because of her intuition about Belle Barth, I now not only wanted to spend time with Sugar, I wanted to draw close to her. Sugar had realized a very specific truth about performance and the direction it was heading in this country: Soon we would all be using our secret voices openly.

* * *

When I saw Sugar after that summer, it was as if the wall between us had dissolved and somehow we both knew it. Some things don't need to be talked through. We practically ran right up to each other. I couldn't wait to tell her that I'd listened to Belle Barth, and that Sugar had been a genius to do her audition with a Barth bit. *Well,* Sugar said, *the future of theater is airing dirty laundry. That's all it is.* By the way, I don't think Sugar thought her own laundry was dirty, and maybe that's why she wanted to be friends with me as much as I wanted to be friends with her, because my family was dirty laundry. It didn't matter, though, because I'd noticed something in making my excited confession to Sugar. It didn't lessen me to admit I'd been wrong, because realizing I'd been wrong was part of making a private world with Sugar of things we loved.

We began having movie dates every weekend. Memorably, we watched *Stalag 17* at the repertory theater on Fifty-seventh and Seventh, and—I think because it combined the stiffness of noir with the texture of *secret voice*—it became our favorite movie. When *Stalag* finished its run, we lobbied the librarian at Performing Arts to buy a copy, and we screened it often after school, just us, studying every moment. We always went out for root beers and coconut cream pie slices afterward, and we would practice lines together and make plans for our big Broadway breakthroughs.

Sugar was an unstoppable prodigy. She became the star of our class, and somewhere along the way everyone fell in love with her—in part because she combined a sharp analytical mind with an uncensored embrace of vernaculars; and in part, I thought, because falling in love with her proved to us that we could love not-terribly-beautiful people, and this made us fall in love with ourselves as well—even our blowhard classmate Neil, whom we'd mocked for years because of his pomposity, and whom Sugar nevertheless married right out of high school. Next thing you knew they were headed to Los Angeles. And soon thereafter, Sugar was working as the first female head writer at *The Tonight Show* with Johnny Carson, and I began my clerical career and we moved into a phone relationship, talking every week and seeing each other once a year at most.

We never talked about how we could have loved theater together as much as we did, and planned together the way that we did, and still ended up living completely different lives. The answer, really, had been obvious from the first day.

For all these reasons, I would have loved to sweep into the Sherry-Netherland wearing a real, thick sable, dense with the morbid odor of the human domination of nature. But my imitation mink would have to do.

Underneath, at least, my outfit was unassailable—wide-legged tweed jodhpur pants, a bright green silk blazer with a purple silk blouse, and ankle boots. My hair was massive and frosted. Clacking through the rosy tomb of the lobby to the elevator, I rifled around my pocketbook until I found my twin pack of Doublemint gum. I selected two slices and waited for the elevator. There was a blond family waiting as well, each with a pristine green Orvis bag in adult or kid sizes. When the car came, I let them press their lower-floor number first, and then I pressed the Penthouse button with a dramatic excess of nonchalance, my index finger floating toward the button, arcing into a press, followed by a snappy recoil before sailing back toward the pocket of my coat.

* * *

Sugar's one P.M. meeting turned out to be an interview with *The New York Times*. An assistant let me into the suite and shushed me all the way across the foyer to a formal, armless accent chair positioned in a corner. From there, I had an oblique angle on a parlor where Sugar was sitting across from the interviewer. The room was darkened, the floor-to-ceiling white satin drapes drawn against the daylight.

Sugar turned to look at me, and as her hair parted and resettled, her face was lit by a shaft of sun that shouldered its way through the drawn curtains. The contrast erased some of the sharp angles of Sugar's new nose, and she looked, suddenly, as she had in high school. She hadn't been as plain as I had thought then, I realized. Rather, the woman I was looking at had had a sex appeal that I did not understand at the time—a coiled, coltish power boiling inside pale freckled limbs. She held my gaze and sort of waved, curling her long, thin fingers at me one by one as if playing the piano in midair.

The reporter was assiduously not looking up from his pad. He sat, elbows on his knees, studying his notes like Torah passages.

"One last question—maybe a bit more personal?" he said, massaging the eraser-end of his pencil absently against his bottom lip. "About your job. Do you find the atmosphere in the writers' room uncomfortable?" Pink rubber crumbs snowed from his lip onto the coffee table.

Sugar tightened her crossed legs and began pulsing the heel of her pump against her ankle. It meant she was angry. I recognized the move from table-reads, specifically when Sugar was frustrated with our classmates for botching their lines. "You know . . ." she said, banging her pump more powerfully now—and then she paused.

I knew how hooks worked. It would be so easy to sell a story about the secretly appalled interior life of Sugar Becker, the bitter kernel of how it felt to be daily, dramatically wronged in the writers' room, that dungeon of filth. Everyone who was anyone in the industry knew that any script that made it to air was so bowdlerized as to be an unrecognizable, chaste ghost of its former self—a demure baby spewed from a womb of cigarette smoke and midday scotches-on-the-rocks.

From everything I had heard, the writers' room *was* a hotbed of misogyny. But from what I recalled of Performing Arts, Sugar probably thrived on it.

Alone among the female cohort of Performing Arts, Sugar had liked writing with the squadron of boozy instructors the school would bring in to deliver seminars. Divorced, pale men. Shufflers, mumblers. Men whose threads attaching them to the industry were even more attenuated than those hanging from their pilly cardigans. None of the other female students had had much interest in doing extra credit with this group. But Sugar liked the scandal of being the only woman; she took pride in parrying their infantile sexual jests at some moment of collective writers' block. She had a thing for being one of the guys. She was competitive. But more than that. Sugar had this real, insatiable, and unanxious *curiosity:* She was confident in her ability to traverse the levels of social depravity, let's say, and come out the other side. As was evident from her Belle Barthian audition monologue, she had a thirst for descending to whatever depths men permitted themselves. This, however, seemed a thing impossible for the interviewer to imagine. Not because he couldn't picture women handily navigating their own objectification, but because he was having a hard time seeing Sugar as this kind of woman.

What this nebbishy interviewer—in his argyle sweater vest and bulky corduroys with wales as thick as nightcrawlers, who frankly was in no position to judge anybody's looks—was really asking was: *Are men attracted enough to you to harass you?*

I silently cheered as Sugar made not a single expression throughout her entire extra-long pause, and then answered, completely stone-faced.

". . . honestly," Sugar continued, finally, delivering what I was sure was a bald-faced lie, "everyone in the writers' room is a perfect gentleman."

The interview was over then, you could just feel it without Sugar saying anything to that effect. She had this ability to close off a scene with an intonation so final that to return the volley would be impossible. This guy knew it and I knew it, and so I stood, then, and walked into the room as if entering from the wings on cue. Sugar smiled and stood, shook the guy's hand, and we were off.

10:30 a.m.

Like I was saying, sometimes I worry this was all my fault, this detour you took in life. Stephen & I were never physically affectionate in front of you. Who knows why, because Stephen was always very physically affectionate with me in bed, as I may have mentioned. But around you I don't think we ever kissed for more than a swift peck. Sometimes we held hands. So maybe you got the wrong idea about heterosexual love? A sterile example. But it was a different time.

 Sex was not a regular topic in our household, or any household, I would like to point out, although we tried to be modern. We bought a book titled Where Did I Come From?. It was full of bright cartoon drawings of chubby pink people with copious amounts of dark pubic hair engaged in intercourse. I put it on the bookshelf in the living room, like leaving cheese out for a mouse. By the next morning the pages were rumpled & it had been returned upside down on the shelf. Certainly it had been pawed through. The pages looked as if they had gotten wet? Perhaps from fingers perspiring with excitement. Coming face-to-face with this evidence of your interest, I reeled with disgust. Before I knew it, I was ripping out all of the relevant pages in some kind of a mania & slipping it back on the shelf. Why didn't I just throw the book away? But I had been possessed in my destruction of this document & bizarrely felt the need to cover up my crime by acting like everything was normal. The book now skipped from first-date spaghetti to a happy hospital room, complete with washed baby & pink, smiling parents. The spine of the book was raw with fronds of thread, waving into the empty space where pages had been. I didn't think then about the consequences of my actions, or the strange missives we were sending each other across these pages. Maybe that was another mistake.

Eventually, in part due to my own destruction of the sex-ed book, it became necessary to explain the birds & the bees ourselves, & somehow the task fell to Stephen. I guess because he was the husband & supposedly the proprietor of knowledge about sex.

Oddly, he went the literal route, using actual birds as protagonists.

The female bird lies on her back, *Stephen began haltingly, holding one hand out, palm up, to symbolize this female bird sex posture, as you watched, cross-legged, on the matted living room carpet in front of us.* And then the male bird flies above the female & hovers. *He held his other hand way up in the air above the submissive female-bird hand splayed open underneath; these birds were as far as they could possibly be from each other.* Then he aims & releases his—cough cough—semen, which just—cough—kind of *falls into* the female bird. Later she has a baby.

What this lady chicken lying on her back & a rooster flapping wildly to stay aloft while taking complicated aim at a cloaca could possibly have to do with human intimacy, I did not know. But I had chosen this man. I had chosen him because the boys of Flatbush had hooded eyes & didn't leave the borough & became *garmentos* or went into butchering, accounting, or diamond sales. Thick, brutal apes who marched straight to work with their heads bent toward the ground & did not look up once until the day they died when, for a flicker, they permitted themselves to remember the last time they had laughed, sitting on the stone hedges of Prospect Park with all the neighborhood boys, the park a cool green at their backs; watching us girls of Ocean Avenue pass by, cracking gum, drenched in the bitter breath of Aqua Net.

I had had all these boys already, had given them countless gropes against the rough park-side stone of the wall, holding my violet gum between sticky fingers until I could chew it again on the way home. For marriage, I wanted a boy with a coarse semitic beard but soft deer eyes, who giggled after a single Carlsberg beer, whose thick hands touched me tentatively, apologetically. And now look.

So our mistakes kept adding up & clearly you never got the right message about how to be, because now here you were, childless & partnerless, or else multiply partnered, who the hell knew, waving a clicker around, like with this you had fulfilled your daughterly duty.

But there was no volume that would cancel out the MTA explosions. The louder the television got, the tinnier it sounded, until it was a high-pitched wail that seemed to only exacerbate the cacophony from the subway project. Mute it, I said in defeat, & you clicked the clicker one more time, a depressing punctuation to your heroic click *battle with the subway noise, & laid it down on the bed next to my hand.*

Just talk to me? *I heard my inebriated self asking. I had hit a new low. What were we even going to talk about? The subjects that would have soothed me were, in this particular order: grandchildren, husbands, things purchased on sale, & mah-jongg gossip.*

What do you want to talk about? *You turned the dressing table chair away from the vanity so it faced the bed, & sat down.*

Anything, *I said, meaning one of those four things I just mentioned.*

You paused, as bewildered by this request as I had been to issue it.

Make something up, *I snapped, then overcorrected to childish again.* A bedtime story, *I weirdly kittened. I needed to take my mind off the subway noise & also my tailbone, which was aching in a particular way tonight. Bedsores, I tried to tell myself, but really I knew it was something else, pressing on my organs from the inside, & I would prefer not to think about that.*

You looked startled but leaned over, unzipped your backpack & pulled out one of those books you're always reading. It had some kind of outer space scene on the front, bright planets against a soup-dark night sky. There were two individuals embracing among the stars. One wore pants & suspenders but had a head like a seahorse, with a long snout & pricked-up ears. The other had a human face & body but was purple & had breasts & a shaved head. This book did not look like my kind of book.

What is this, *I shouldn't have said.*

Gay Marxist sci-fi erotica. *You had an expression of actual sadistic pleasure. One corner of your mouth was turned up & you kept trying to force it back down.*

Forget it, I'm getting tired, *I said, & I meant this in a very existential sense.*

Shush, *you said.* It's sublime, in a dystopian way.

To be shushed by one's own daughter! It was actually terrible & wonderful at once. As appalling as it felt, strangely it settled me like a baby. Let the chips fall where they may with this fakokta *story, I thought as you opened the book:*

THE SENSUAL FEAST

The ship was already pushing against its own entropy, spooling and shuddering, wanting to release itself upward. It seemed they'd actually get this hunker off the ground, Chiasma thought from her post at the rear systems station. The Thanato *was one of the oldest vessels in the fleet, but Litotes was one of the better pilots employed by this piece-of-shit company.*

Which one is the seahorse centaur and which is the purple lesbian? *I broke in. I couldn't believe I wanted to know this, but it was more annoying not understanding who was who.*

They're both lesbians, *you said humorlessly.*

The ship jolted and Litotes pulled the Torpor handle, throwing the ship into an intentional stall on the pad so it could blow off clogged fuel. A gust of tritium exhaust puffed from the rear thrusters and fogged the windows of the rear bunk bright lime. Chiasma coughed back against the sour-water taste—the tritium coming in the vents, which of course Litotes had also forgotten to shut. Chiasma would have to write Litotes up, unfortunately.

I woke up when I heard you closing the book.
What happened, I asked. I didn't remember drifting off.
We'll keep reading another day, you said.
It was only later that I started to wonder whether this "offer" to keep reading was more of a threat.

AT LEAST THE MARXIST BUYS YOU MINK

IT WASN'T THAT SUGAR was *un*attractive with the nose job. She was uncanny, I reflected, as Sugar checked her face in her compact, snapped it closed into her Chanel bag, then walked toward me holding her arms out.

I leaned in, pressing my powdered cheek against Sugar's powdered cheek. A puff of mingled powder spiced the air between us.

Standing at the elevator, Sugar squinted at me. "See. What were you worried about. *You've* aged into your nose."

Regret was not a Sugar emotion, and yet she continued bitterly, "Who knew *Yentl* would renew the world's Ashkenazi fetish."

No matter what kind of a strange affair Sugar's nose was, it did broadcast one thing: MONEY.

"I don't know," I shrugged, as the elevator pinged its arrival.

"Well, you look beautiful." Sugar reached across her body into the large purse, soft with leather pleats, and pulled out a nip of Absolut vodka. She unscrewed the cap, tipped her head back, and drained it while looking at me through the bottom third of her eyes as she stepped into the elevator.

I arranged myself in a variety of postures as I tried to brush off my awareness of Sugar's 25 percent new face. I belted and unbelted my imitation mink, smoothed my hair, inspected my nail polish for chips.

"So do you," I said, returning the compliment after we had arrived at lobby level and too many beats had passed.

We stepped into the lobby and clacked across it in unison. "Not in L.A. I don't," returned Sugar, in yet another effort at leveling the playing field that her mink's darkly shimmering bristles kept vastly unleveling. "Frankly I'm a nobody," she said, stretching the truth. "The closest I've come to a fan base is that one time some schmuck at The Palm asked if I was Betsy Rawls, the golf player."

I heard laughter crackling out of me like a piece of paper being crunched in a fist. Sugar had an ability to get me to laugh before I even realized I was about to do so. "What did you say?"

Sugar shrugged. "I said yes."

Then there were Neil's affairs.

It took only the fifteen-minute walk to the theater on Sixty-eighth and Broadway for Sugar to get to the meat of the matter. There was a line caterpilling down the street, made up exclusively of ladies like ourselves. "It galls me that he manages to convince anyone to sleep with him," she sighed. "He doesn't have a hair left on his head."

"Bald isn't so bad," I offered. "What about Yul Brynner."

"Yul Brynner he's not. And who are you to talk. Stephen still has his full head."

"Stephen's locks for Neil's bank account," I said, omitting *and your trust fund.*

"Money shmoney," said Sugar, *noblesse obliging* her ass

off. "What I wouldn't do to run my hands through a man's full head of hair again. Anyway, we haven't said anything to anyone yet, but"—she tossed her head back and sighed as the line began moving forward, pulling her mink tight around her thin torso—"we're getting a divorce."

"Over a little baldness!" Sugar's throwing her life open to chance had made me either anxious or jealous.

"It's more than baldness," said Sugar, rifling in her purse for ticket money, "now Neil says he's a Marxist. He's *found Marx*, like half of California. Apparently this means he gets to fuck whoever he wants. He 'relinquishes ownership' of me. He was lucky enough to fuck me in the first place—a woman, let's be honest, with very few sexual hang-ups; no one with a good face gives good pussy, it's a documented fact—and now he's willing to share? It's an outrage."

Sugar always had a saying on hand. This one made me wonder what Sugar thought about my face/pussy situation.

We had arrived at the front of the line. Sugar slid a ten-dollar bill under the Plexiglas to the ticket-taker in her booth. "The two of us," she said, drawing a line in the air between us.

"At least the Marxist buys you mink." I pushed the lobby door open. "You want a bushy-headed public servant who shares a coffee-stained desk with other do-gooders in their father's hand-me-down sport coats? If I didn't know that there was an actual, quantifiable difference between a doctor and a physician, god help me I do now."

My ability to maintain the sham seamlessness of my life always frayed once Sugar let down her own guard.

We faced the glowing hedge of popcorn that ran the length of the far wall. Sugar had stopped walking and was jotting notes on a pad she'd produced from her purse.

"What." I used that Flatbush way of omitting an inflection at the end of a question. I waved my hand in the direction of Sugar's pad.

"What," returned Sugar, glancing up and shrugging. She had learned—and mastered—this delivery from me long ago. "I remembered something I need to write down for the show." She frowned at her pad, crossed something out.

"Two popcorns, and I'd also like a Tab," I diaphragmatically projected to the teenager behind the counter, throwing my voice as if I were auditioning for the role of "Woman at the Bar," ordering a Peach Bellini over the background din of the "21" Club. Incidentally, I would have nailed it.

It didn't take me long to recognize that, despite the bottomless appetite I had for the genre, *Judith* was not, in fact, the crème de la crème of Holocaust thrillers.

We were partway through the movie, when Judith, as played by Sophia Loren—having survived both Dachau and then a lengthy Mediterranean journey stowed away in a tiny steamer trunk meant for canned goods and other provisions—emerged from her sweltering casket with eyeliner fully intact and was quickly strong-armed by the Haganah into serving as a spy tracking down her Nazi ex-husband. She was heading back into the arms of the Reich, and so soon after being liberated, too. Mournful music played as Judith submitted to her Freudian destiny to repeat the traumas of her life on endless loop.

Sugar leaned over and whispered, "This movie is not nearly as funny as everyone says."

Our ensuing giggles, and the glares from surrounding patrons, drove us out of the theater before the movie finished and into the darkening streets. We walked south, arm in arm along the inside edge of the park to meet Neil and Stephen for dinner. Wide boulevards intercut the lawns, spotlit gold by the lampposts.

I knew what she was doing, taking me to the movies. Sugar was reinforcing, prior to seeing Neil, my place as a consumer, not producer, of filmic material. It was a warning not to cross the line: *Don't ask for a part; and don't pretend not to be asking while backhandedly asking, either.* Sugar's message, in going with me, was that watching things together was our special thing and also our limit. This gift, in the way of many gifts, was intended to prevent my asking for the thing I really wanted. But something about the beauty of the night—one of those Manhattan evenings, cold currents threading through the warmer air coming off the pavement—and the sound of our walking, the syncopated clonking of our heels on the sidewalk, allowed me to at least temporarily accept Sugar's offering, which was an acceptance of my place in her (and the) world. It was enough, in that moment, just to be mothers streaming through the Manhattan winter night. I leaned my head against her shoulder and breathed in the scent of my own hairspray and Doublemint gum mixed with the gamy odor of Sugar's mink. Dry leaves cycloned in the December wind.

WHEN A WINTER SUNSET FLARES OVER A FIELD OF SNOW

SUGAR DIDN'T REALLY UNDERSTAND the extent to which acting permeated a lot of other jobs that were not, officially speaking, acting. Whereas I understood this all too well, for I had learned the hard way how to handle with great aplomb the daily demands of theater in my unglamorous life.

For instance, I answered the phone the exact same way—*Gooood morning. Office of Doctor Eli Zilch*—from the first time I picked it up to the last day I worked for the schmuck.

One of the things I initially appreciated about Zilch—who was by the way a closeted *faygeleh*, and very rich—was that we both felt that the phone should be answered with a degree of gravitas. I think that was why I got the job in the first place. Before my tenure there, the receptionists had compressed their opening salvos into toothless soundbites.

"Doctor Zilch's office."

Or "Zilch Medical Aesthetics."

Or worst of all, as if he were the local grocer, "Zilch's."

When I came for my initial interview in the fall of 1981, Zilch sat me down at the front desk and walked back to his office. Then he phoned me at the front to run through a mock conversation. At that point I delivered the line—which I had been practicing on the two blocks from our apartment to Zilch's—that would become not only my trademark opening, but the mandatory greeting for all the front office workers thenceforth.

Gooood morning. Office of Doctor Eli Zilch.

You don't end with a questioning tone. This is important. You have to end with an ambiguous lilt, the tone of which is impossible to indicate through punctuation on a page. The lilt substitutes for a question, a can-I-help-you, which, in my opinion, would be too subservient. No, you must *lilt.* We weren't taking lunch orders. We were discerning the right kind of client. That was the impression, anyway. Most people able to pay the amount of cash we were asking needed to feel like not just anyone with that amount of cash could get into Zilch's practice. Needless to say, anyone with that amount of cash *could* get in, but by the time I was done onboarding them, they would enter the waiting room as if they'd had to slay a dragon.

Zilch loved the drama that I brought to the position. But he also liked making sure we in the front office knew we were his inferiors, and part of that involved mandating things like a standard opening greeting, in addition to the fact that none of us were allowed to read the magazines in the waiting area even if the place was completely empty, or that the Perrier delivery was only for him and we needed to drink from the communal watercooler like cows at a trough. Honestly, I think Zilch enjoyed degrading women a little bit. But about the need for hierarchy and order, he and I were in perfect agreement. And so I brought in my own Perrier and my own soggy copies of *People* and *Redbook* from the magazine stand by the side of the toilet at home, even if they were exact doubles of the crisper editions not ten feet from the front desk.

* * *

I answered the phone like a pro, communicating with seven short words that I was the gatekeeper to the caller's new set of life opportunities. I happen to know for a fact that Zilch was able to bump up his estimates at least 10 percent on my trademarked greeting alone. Also, I knew that if I drew out the greeting, I'd have the upper hand with patients. I set the tone for how they were to speak to me. Formal, respectful, protocolled. You needed to do this, because with the Bratvas and their mistresses it was a contest of wills before you even spoke a word.

You had to let the phone ring exactly thrice before you picked up. Anything less and the caller would feel you were desperate. Anything more, unprofessional. On the third ring, you *slowly* raised the phone from the cradle to your ear and inhaled with an audible mixture of impatience and authoritative leisure. Then you sort of *drawled* out an exhalation; you had to imagine you were exhaling a wordless but nonetheless extremely textural sound, sort of the way Paul Newman as Brick Pollitt in *Cat on a Hot Tin Roof* drawls the breath around his *i*'s in "We're done with *lies* and *liars* in this house." It's hard to explain how to inflect a breath. In the acting world, they know what I'm talking about. But in short, you have to believe that you, like Newman, are a Jew playing an exasperated WASP.

Once you've inhaled and exhaled, only then do you say, *Gooooood morning. Office of Doctor Eli Zilch.*

And by then the caller is sufficiently on the defensive. But you can't let up. Next you need to be unable to find an appointment for six weeks. You can't get them in sooner even if the caller offers to pay up front. You can't squeeze anybody in for any reason at all. Dr. Zilch is exceedingly busy. He's as busy as a Texas oil magnate during an OPEC crisis. You give them the impression that Zilch is right now handling back-to-back beautifications, and these people will have to pay through the nose just for the privilege of waiting their turn. But here's the thing, and this is why I really considered myself more than a receptionist from the get-go. Once you delay their procedure, then you start flipping pages of your month-at-a-glance calendar, clicking your tongue against the roof of your mouth, communicating that you're magnanimously brainstorming how to help them with their beauty emergency. Flip, click, flip, click. Then you sigh and realize you have an idea. You don't have an earlier appointment, but you *could* offer them a "little boost" to tide them over. "The latest," you tell them. Sculptra or microdermabrasion, something like that. These procedures changed regularly depending on what the reps brought us. Whatever you have on hand, that's what you offer them and that's what "the latest" is.

No patient would imagine this, but it's the add-ons that actually constitute the bulk of profits for all plastic surgeons. Aestheticians are paid peanuts and don't need to carry insurance. Ninety-five percent of the profit they bring in goes straight to the office; maybe 3 percent for materials, and 2 percent for the aesthetician's cut. Whereas the surgeries carry high overheads—more if Zilch had to rent out a room at Lenox Hill to perform them, which he did for anything requiring full anesthesia, which meant that any surgery that wasn't a simple rhinoplasty (which could be done in "twilight" sleep) involved high insurance buffers and a suite of assistants. Add-ons, as you can see, were the cash cow.

The Sculptra salesperson had given all us front office ladies SCULPTRA™ tee shirts with the words spelled out in rhinestones across our breasts. We wore them to work and—on Dr. Zilch's instruction—to our aerobics classes, lunches, and parents' days at school. We were Zilch's army, he said, and I was especially valuable because of all the contact I had with wealthy former Nazis and royal families in exile. Meanwhile I happened to know that those people had all their surgeries done in Switzerland and sometimes Istanbul, but a *faygeleh* can hope, and hope Zilch did.

Why don't you wear a Sculptra tee shirt? I remember one of the front office ladies—probably Renee—once challenged him. Renee smelled of vodka and body odor, which reflected poorly on the entire office. I told her this once and she did not appreciate it.

Look at this face, Zilch said, swimming his hand up in front of his chin like Vanna White unveiling a letter on *Wheel of Fortune. This face is an advertisement for Sculptra.* He was pushing sixty, but Zilch had that particular dewy masculinity to which every gay man raised on Rock Hudson and cinematic lighting aspired. He was a strangely robust pink, like when a winter sunset flares over a field of snow. His hair was permanently wet with pomade. He wore only taupe Canali suits and Gucci loafers.

Zilch was always going to Stamford, Connecticut, on the weekends to see his "friend" Alan, who was an insurance salesman at Aetna. Alan came into the office not infrequently to take Zilch to lunch. They seemed to exclusively discuss fashion and real estate with each other, and to ask us front office ladies a lot of too-interested questions about our children. You could tell how desperate they were to seem normal, to discuss our normal lives as if they had anything to say on the matter or could offer any useful perspectives. Sometimes they would mention a niece or a nephew and some cute thing they did, like sass them with the latest Valley girl lingo or win a junior tennis tournament. What Zilch and Alan didn't understand was that in America the term "uncle" is an honorific backed up by almost no actual relation. It's not like people still worked farms with extended families all bound together in a unit producing I don't know what. Wheat? Anyway, an uncle doesn't mean anything now, and yet you could tell Zilch and his boyfriend considered "uncle" to be one of their important identities.

Zilch and his boyfriend are another example of how lonely gay people are, even if they are rich.

3 a.m.

It was pouring when I woke up. Lightning flashed purple through the steelgray sky. I had this sinking feeling in my stomach, & in my half-sleep I searched around, trying to pinpoint what it was about.

Usually I don't have to think too hard before my brain hits on "oh right, cancer." But tonight cancer wasn't it, & my mind kept roaming, looking for the source of this unsettled feeling.

Then I realized. I was worried about you! How funny is that? Me, dying in my diaper, worrying about my perfectly healthy "daughter" snoozing away in the next room. I know it isn't rational, but there it was, that unmistakable full-body feeling I used to get when you were little—one part of my brain constantly wondering what could be going wrong at every moment, like I was a wind-up toy constantly unwinding.

I did try to check on you, actually, as ridiculous as that sounds, but I was too weak. Maybe I had taken too much OxyContin again. I kept trying to prop myself up & then my elbows would shimmy & I would melt back into the bed & I'd be drifting off again to the city's muted night honks. As terrible as it was, there was also a slice of happiness in that moment for me. Because it reminded me that, helpless as I might be, & as bad a job of it as I may have done, I'M STILL A MOTHER. And no one—not even you—can take that away from me.

* * *

I was falling back asleep, floating along on this strangely comforting thought, when I was startled awake again. This time, not by the thunder, but a high-pitched squawk, an unmistakably weird & unnatural sound amid the rumble & crash of the storm & the constant cars with their wet wheels blurring down the street.

There was an unholy terror about this noise—a noise that started low & then tore raggedly open into a full-on screech.

 And then a woman—not you, someone else—unmistakably having an orgasm.

What could I do!
 I took another half an OxyContin.

THE HOLY LIFEBLOOD
OF THE PROLETARIAT

AT THE GINGER MAN on sixty-fourth and Columbus, Neil was negotiating at the hostess desk for a premium table.

"We have Nureyev and his entourage coming tonight, sir."

"Well I directed *Once Upon a Goldstein*," said Neil, winking. "See what you can do."

"Oh my mother loved *Once Upon a Goldstein*!" sparkled the hostess with fake obeisance.

I watched Neil slip this girl his phone number on a scrap of paper as she led us up the narrow stairs and into a balcony spot that was a good but hardly premium table.

Shortly after we'd settled into our chairs, Stephen appeared at the top of the stairs, the subway smell radiating like hot iron off his trench coat. Sugar stood up to greet him, pooching his cheeks as one would with a child.

"Look at this man," she said, pooching. A *hamishe* god." She sat again, next to me. "And I have to beg my turtle-headed soon to be ex-husband for sex," she added under her breath.

Meanwhile Stephen, jewel of mild masculinity, sat down, his anxious half-smile pushing at the corners of his mouth.

* * *

Neil ordered "locally felled" venison tartare as an appetizer for the table.

"Do all Marxists dine on venison tartare in fancy showbiz restaurants?" I couldn't resist teasing.

Neil ignored me, clinking the ice cubes in his glass of Chivas Regal. When the tartare arrived, he tucked in, smiling beatifically and murmuring about *how good it is to eat meat that has arrived directly from the real life-and-death theater of the slaughterhouse floor.* He said this as if he knew anything about slaughterhouse floors, inhaling forkful after forkful of tartare like it was the holy lifeblood of the proletariat.

I emitted a half cough, looking directly at Sugar. Our eyes shrieked at each other in ancient female sign language. I took a tiny sip of my wine. Sugar let a giggle escape her closed lips—a little bubble of sound.

Neil looked back and forth. "What."

"Nothing." Sugar swallowed her smile.

Neil went back to monologuing, dropping names like Harvey Korman and Richard Dreyfuss. Neil fancied himself an auteur, but what he really was was the producer of a handful of B-grade Jewish comedies starring second-string actors who all resembled, but were not, George Segal.

Neil droned on as the tartare was polished off, mostly by him, and through another appetizer of duck confit and olives. By the time the main courses arrived, I was getting heartburn. My stomach filled with tiny knives and the waistband of my skirt was digging into my stomach. I bore down through the pain and forced a smile when the waiter set my broiled shrimp scampi in front of me.

"Just imagine the nostalgia of all the East Coast transplants living in California," Neil was saying, apropos of nothing. "I've tapped a real market there. I mean, an artistically degenerate one." He paused, poking at his lamb chop with a tine of his fork. "Well, that's capitalism," he mumbled without looking up, head bent like a coroner making a forensic pronouncement.

Studying his pale orb while he chewed his chop, I reflected that, as regarded his baldness situation, Sugar had not been entirely accurate in describing it as "not a hair left on his head." In fact, it would have been better if he had had not a hair. As it was, a swoosh of straggling amber-colored fronds encircled the lower ridge of skull; it was like Neil's head had an Amish beard around its base. In the center, a furious red pimple oozed quietly.

"What's your latest?" I asked into a silence that had been punctuated only by the bovine sounds of Neil chewing. His prattling had depleted me—and, it seemed, the rest of us as well—of any conversation at all, and so our only option beyond silence was simply more of Neil.

Bending like a soft branch above his meat, Neil swallowed. His latest would be a medical mystery, he said, sawing off another cube of chop. "Like *Eyes Without a Face*, but Jewish."

Sugar set her zinfandel glass down too hard and craned around. "Where's the waitress?"

I nudged my glass by its base in Sugar's direction. The glass was mostly full, though my one or two sips had left a bright lipstick ring stamped on the side.

"Speaking of which"—Neil put his hand up like a school crossing guard.

"Speaking of what?" Sugar had set in quickly on my zinfandel, leaving an overlapping lipstick ring, and now sounded openly belligerent.

"Of Israel."

"Nobody mentioned Israel," Sugar slurred. She was gripping the thin stem of the wine glass too tightly, the pad of her pointer finger ridged pink with pressure. Now I regretted giving her my extra. I reached over and pried the stem delicately from her, feigning the need for a sip just to slow her down. The scent inside the wine glass was sour fermentation, warm breath, and the pencil-shaving undertone of Chanel lipstick.

"You know how I'm always pitching these studios a version of the latest thriller?" Neil was now pointedly ignoring his wife. "They never go for it. They always want me to do comedy. So how did I get this latest one approved?" He was projecting diaphragmatically, enunciating for the cheap seats. "I used *Exodus* as an example. A *thriller*." He banged the heel of his hand against his forehead. "A fucking *Jewish thriller*. Why didn't I think of this before? All these years I've been using every argument at my disposal and it's always *no. No no no.* Then I say *Exodus,* and *boom,* next thing you know I'm doing *Eyes Without a Face* but Jewish."

I shot Sugar a look, boring into her eyes with mine. Neil was behaving as if he had just discovered a gold mine when meanwhile this one had been plenty mined. "What about *Stalag 17*," I asked, fake-innocently.

I was setting up the ball for Sugar to spike. I wanted her to correct him, to unleash her—*our*—movie on him. Instead, she went in a different direction. "But they had Trumbo for *Exodus*," she said, name-dropping a much more famous Hollywood writer than Neil would ever be. I saw that Sugar was going for more than intellectual superiority and knowledge of the biz. She was aiming for total destruction of Neil's sense of self.

"Echhh, Trumbo," Neil gargled out through extravagant chews.

Sugar narrowed her eyes at him over the lip of the wine glass she had managed to regain from me, tapping the dregs back into her mouth. She looked at Neil the way Mickey Mantle watched Sandy Koufax's curveball dive out of range of his bat in the '63 World Series, plummeting from chest- to knee-height, acknowledging with fury and regret the singular direction in which history moves. *There's no going back on life's choices,* said Sugar's eyes. *Strikeout.*

I glanced at Stephen—his face beer-ruddied and smiling, leaning back in his chair with his battered loafer across his knee. It had to be said that I did not regard Stephen with the loathing with which Sugar looked at Neil. There was something tender there, I realized. I had often wondered whether our resentment-laden connection—which often felt like we were aching down a gravel road when everyone else was whooshing by on pavement—constituted a good marriage, but in that moment it seemed our road had been paved without my realizing, and I could not help feeling a flush of superiority.

"Anyway," Neil picked back up, his voice edging toward breaking. "You write comedy. You wouldn't know whether Trumbo wrote a good or bad thriller." He wiped his lips with a cocktail napkin. "You're making claims under false pretenses."

"*'False pretenses'*? Is that your girlfriend's Marxist legalese?"

"Marxist legalese is a contradiction in terms." Neil grumbled. "Marxists are opposed to the law itself, which is an instrument of bourgeois nation-building. Moreover—"

Sugar pivoted, interrupting. "Oh Jesus." She threw her hands in the air. "Talk to *them* about nation-building."

Stephen looked at me with a pained expression, his brow rumpling.

"Fair point," said Neil, stroking his beard. He put his feet on the rung of his chair and leaned forward with his arms crossed on top of his knees like an excited child. The couple had reached a breaking point, but rather than breaking in front of us, they were going to turn on us. "Why *are* you going on this . . ." he searched for a word.

"Look, I have to do *something*." Stephen took a sip of his Carlsberg.

"Something about what?"

"I don't know. The situation."

"Aside from everything else—" Neil began.

"What everything else?" I directed this question at the self-appointed Marxist.

Neil shrugged and turned his hands palms-up.

"Look, they don't *want* to be colonizers," Stephen peeped. "It's an impossible situation. It's not like Vietnam."

"Where'd you read that, *The New Republic*?" Neil waved his empty Chivas in the direction of Stephen. "Tell me you didn't see the photos of the Israeli soldiers eating ice cream and taking donkey rides and actually fall for it?"

"It's a nation struggling for democracy," Stephen said into his beer.

"The democratic occupation of a territory? You'll see, an intifada will break out one of these days."

Neil was flashing around something or other he had heard in one of his Marxist meetings.

"If there was going to be"—Stephen accordioned the wet

label of his Carlsberg beer with the back of his thumbnail—"trouble"—

"An *intifada*," Neil interrupted, "is an uprising." He tipped back the dregs of his Chivas. "The Warsaw Ghetto Uprising is an 'intifada' in Arabic history books. So is Easter Monday."

"No one thinks there'll be an . . . intifada." Stephen's face had ruddied fully.

"Marxists do." Neil crunched some ice. "I mean the real Marxists. Third World Marxists."

I was pretty sure wearing a turtleneck under a blazer did not a Third World Marxist make.

"Are Marxists oracles?" Stephen said.

"Yes," said Neil with total seriousness.

Outside The Ginger Man, the mildewed scent of recirculated water blew off the Lincoln Center plaza fountain. The backlit spout rose out of the fountain's pool and paused with theatrical melancholy, arcing droplets into the night air.

Sugar fussed in her purse for something. She cursed and muttered; shards of receipts and gum wrappers rained from her bag and, blown by the wind, skittered down the sidewalk like mice.

Neil was leisurely clicking open his Zippo and holding the tongue of flame upside down into the bowl of his pipe. He slid the lighter back in his pocket, put the pipe in his mouth and drew hard. A forest scent diffused, thin curls of smoke twisting in the dark.

Sugar tottered over to me, her hand still rummaging in her purse. She seized a pill bottle, uncapped it and removed something, dropping it down her throat.

I pulled Sugar in for a hug. Our spidery bodies twined with a surprising force. Our bodies communicated something to each other. It was not feminism; it was not the moment for that yet, or at least not for us. It was mutual frustration. We were little fury islands, colliding in a pile of bones and joints and wine-breath and Doublemint gum.

"Have a—well, have a trip," Sugar said, against my ear, omitting any qualifier. She leaned back and squeezed my hands in a strangely paternal gesture.

"Come on!" Neil called. He was holding open the door of a cab muttering something about Stephen and me shilling for the imperialist state. Sugar rolled her eyes.

"I gotta go," she said, releasing my hands. "He's going to lecture me the entire cab ride home." Well, like Sugar always used to say in improv class, it was all—and here she meant "life"—one way or another, *material*.

COLD WEALTHY DRIZZLE

THAT WAS THE LAST night I spent with Sugar as friends. Something happened later that evening—I don't want to talk about it now. All I will say is that husbands you *expect* to disappoint you.

Friends, not so much.

Stalag 17's opening shot is genius.

It's unclear what we're looking at. At first it appears to be a skyline—a cityscape in black and white, the shades and geometries of a classic noir layout—but slowly, we come to realize that, actually, it's a bird's-eye view of a POW camp in Germany at night. The moonlight breaking through clouds at the horizon has scrambled the perspective, so it only seemed that we were looking up at a collection of skyscrapers arcing away into the dark.

I've always loved noir voiceovers. The cool tones of Walter Neff's confession in *Double Indemnity*, or Gillis's eerie, dislocated beyond-the-grave narration in *Sunset Boulevard*. But in *Stalag 17*, the narrator, Clarence "Cookie" Cook, delivers his voiceover with comic lightness and a stutter. When I first heard the opening sequence, it captivated me. Normally, noir voiceovers are neutral, clinical. I didn't know you could have textural noir voiceover before Sugar showed me this film. But when I saw *Stalag* for the first time and I heard Cookie's kvetchy narrator telling us that while most World War II movies showcase the glories of battle, he's going to show us the everyday foibles of the POW camp, it all came together. I realized that you could be a real actress and a Flatbushite at the same time. Theater didn't mean you had to shed your identity. Sort of the opposite.

That was the message I took from it then, anyway. Meanwhile, Sugar ended up writing her senior thesis about how, in noir, voiceover is a textual comment on the technical aspects of film itself, highlighting the gap between picture and sound—the fact that the two media are coming from two different locations that get spliced together in the editing process. Like how in *Sunset Boulevard,* Gillis is speaking outside the time of the narrative as it unfolds, because he's dead. And when we watch *Sunset Boulevard,* we just accept this impossible fact. Sugar's point was that voiceover is about how characters escape their contexts and exist in some kind of fuzzy non-space and -time, in between sound and picture. And this space between realms is what makes film work. So voiceover is just a dramatization of the editing process, which is the art of movement across gaps.

Sugar was obsessed with "the editing process," and I thought it was kind of *goyishe* to be interested in technique. Not *goyishe* in a bad way. *Goyishe* in a rich way. And I loved being around it, even if what Sugar loved in movies wasn't what I loved at all. I loved hearing her go on in some ambient manner, her conversation falling on me like cold wealthy drizzle.

In any case the point I am making has to do with *Stalag 17,* and how for me it was about how schtick could be noir, while for Sugar it was about how noir could be schtick. For the longest time, I thought our differences worked to make a complete whole—like one of those prehistoric weapons you whirl over your head and toss, two weights counterbalancing each other at either end of a tether. Two opposites uniting in one dangerously perfect thing. Even as we grew older, and our lives took different shapes, I had been holding on to this image of our friendship. Maybe it was nostalgia about Performing Arts, about high school, and a time when the world seemed poised open for me. Whatever it was, it was bound up with Sugar. Until that night at least.

5 a.m.

It started again. The screech & the soft moans of that girl. My god, how many orgasms can a person have. One is enough. One is a lot. But we were on number two, or three, & after that there was some kind of meandering postscript. I don't know what to call it—a post-orgasm orgasm? A whimpering extension of the entire sordid event that dragged on like a bad jazz solo. The thing just would not end.

This was confirming my sense of lesbians as unhinged.

Finally there was genuine silence from the other room. The storm shifted too. From crackling thunder to a steady, almost rural rain.

Into this quiet came a labored creak as the heavy leaded glass window of your bedroom opened.

Oh, I was very familiar with this noise. When you were a teenager, you had occasionally cracked your window open to sneak a cigarette. Don't think I didn't notice. And so when I heard it tonight I craned around to look out my own window, in a motherly reflex, for the cotton balls of smoke coming from yours, and curling past.

That is not what I saw.

Against the reef of skyline, silhouetted in the purple dark, electric with rain, I saw wings.

* * *

Even I could tell these were not normal wings. They were enormous—the length of a car?—& worse for wear. Bits of dust or dirt (or possibly wing) crumbled off the wings as they flapped, threateningly slowly, ruffling up gigantic booms of air with a sound reminiscent of the Number 2 IRT train rolling into the Beverly Road station.

 As my eyes adjusted to the dark I began to make out more of you. This was the first time you had showed all of yourself to me like this.

You were huge for a bird, because you were a person-sized bird, but you also were not particularly hale or hearty-looking as far as predator animals go. You were raggedy & some feathers were missing in clumps, & what feathers you did have were a very uninspiring taupe color, the color of bargain suits worn by insurance agents & high school principals.

I heard the front door of the apartment opening & then shut. That girl leaving, I presumed. Meanwhile this orgasm-delivering bird was peering in on me with its marble eyes & prehistoric expression. I wondered if you would break the glass with your beak. Just come in & be done with it, I thought. I almost wanted you to. You'd been killing me slowly for so many years with your descent into mannishness. A swift murder seemed like an improvement. Also, I would be vindicated. I had been ringing alarm bells about you for so long!

 I could feel your beak piercing my neck. The

spray of blood. *I saw it all like a film, like the opening of* Sunset Boulevard, *the credits of my life rolling away offscreen while the camera points at the gutter, its nose so close to the ground that the asphalt becomes a galaxy—a slash of deep space, studded with light.*

God I love that opening!

When the camera floats backward from the gutter & peeks up at the road. Then headlights owl into shape. The police are mowing down the camera, zooming past it toward the home of a movie legend & a scandal of death.

Just kill me, *I mouthed at your black eyes.*

You gathered force, pushing more & more air under your wings. Were you going to do it?? I could hear the glass shattering, imagine the feathers of your face ripping off as you hacked your way in to do what you were put on this earth to do.

Apologize! *you shrieked.* I think you added dialectically—"Apologize dialectically!"—*but the word was lost as your shriek dissolved into air. Even your voice was birdlike now, a strangely hoarse, initial gale of sound that burst & then fell precipitously, unnervingly, like a fire engine tearing past.*

I *am* fucking apologizing! *I gargled back, my own voice trembly & weak.*

You pivoted, standing almost upright in midair, & kind of shrugged, condensing into a vampire hunch. It was very hard to read this shrug. It could have meant fair enough. *It could have meant* too little too late. *Then you pointed yourself back in the direction of your own window & shot off, leaving a trail of bird schmutz in the air. A moment later I heard your window ache its way down the soot-clogged frame, & the storm picked back up, wind screaming down the canyon of high-rises.*

AM I RIGHT?

WHAT I REALIZED AFTER this thing that I don't want to talk about that happened between Sugar and me, was that Sugar's attitude—which I don't want to discuss, but trust me, her whole approach to life—was how they *all* were, these daughters of privilege. Like when I heard Joan Rivers, another rich person, say: "But you *must* write down your dreams!"

This piece of wisdom was delivered as part of a longer bit Joan did in 1973 on the *Carol Burnett Show* about how once you're married the only place you'll ever feel desirable again is in your dreams. When I first saw this episode, I don't think I had ever thought about my dreams, but I remember being really affected when Joan sneeringly probed, "How will you ever remember them unless you write them down?" I was affected, to be clear, not with the conviction to begin writing down my dreams, but with the humiliation of realizing that some aspect of the high life has been going on all around me and I never knew. It didn't help that Joan was sitting on a pink stool in the middle of an empty stage like the queen of England, wearing a pink turtleneck tucked into pink satin pants and draped in a fluffy pink boa that hung to the floor on either side. She was ugly in a rich way or rich in an ugly way, and how she said things, it was as if they were so obvious as to barely require mention. I wondered then whether all rich Jews wrote down their dreams (actually I have come to learn that they do).

Joan had been a philosophy major in college and grew up fantastically wealthy. Her entire comedy gambit was a veil under which the absolute fury of her fall from grace from rich philosophy student to wife and housework-doer burbled and stewed. And the way she tossed off this comment, like, *But of course you must!* suggested that we who didn't write down our dreams were basically animals. She didn't do any of her trademark moves to close off the joke and transition into the next one. She didn't point at the audience or say *Am I right?* She left this judgment hanging there for a beat too long, paused, then continued on. That's how you knew she was serious, that she meant to insert a little jab in there about us poor Jews, the non-dream-writer-downers.

Needless to say, I did not heed Joan's advice. But it stuck with me—sort of like a nagging reminder of the thick interior lives of rich Jews, though I had bigger things to worry about, like the thick exterior lives of rich Jews and how they all had Mercedeses while I courted death in a Ford Pinto—and recently I started thinking about it all differently. I guess because I am dying and generally high as a kite, but maybe also because my unconsciousness keeps slipping into my consciousness, I've been thinking, *What the fuck, I'll try it.* And once I started doing it, once I gave the dreams permission, now they come without pause—a gate lifted on a railroad crossing and a jumble of wild animals flooding through in a herd that stretches beyond the limits of sight.

* * *

Being a mother means someone is always asking you: *What the hell went wrong.* Even though the person asking always has their own secret opinion about the answer.

Well, I'm explaining to you what went wrong, and it was before all that.

5:45 a.m.

I would like to point out for the record that it was my decision—not your father's—to raise you to take advantage of everything life had to offer. Your father would have been content to raise you on some nothing street in the nothing suburbs. You should be grateful to me! Growing up in Manhattan where you had the world before you. Fancy schools, fancy colleges, majoring in whatever so-called subjects you wanted, pursuing any interest it occurred to you to have, including many unsavory things. All I asked was that you do something not meshuggeneh with all this education. Just get a job where you can afford two-ply toilet paper, I implored & other such wisdoms. I don't say these things for my own health. Meanwhile, I can't brag of much, but I would like to point out that I've had two-ply for my entire adult life.

But you took to the in-betweens, a life that no one I know would even call a life. I'm not trying to be hurtful, I'm just telling you how it is. One minute I was holding a baby in a green Naugahyde lounger thinking I'd give you everything I never had & still don't, but maybe, through you, I'd get to experience it too. And the next minute, you'd glimpsed some trick of light & taken it for a beacon, a planet. Before I knew it, you had set off in the night with other women, looking to fly into orbits. As if it was enough to love the sky with women. As if a person could do that their whole life.

MEAT AND YEAST

THE FIRST ROSENBERG I ever met was Abe. Abe was the rich Rosenberg, and he never let you forget it. He was short and prosperous and had famously married a shiksa. In his youth he had been run over by a horse cart on Rivington Street, and the unnamed injury (no injuries had names for this generation of immigrants, only consequences) had subsequently stunted his growth but inflamed his ambitions. At nineteen, Abe had founded Rosemere, a trucking company that ferried off-brand trench coats to retail outlets across the tri-state area—first from the sweatshops of the Lower East Side, and ultimately from the lofts of the Garment District. Being run down by a horse cart had fueled Abe's lust for the world of transportation. The whole thing was a not-so-complicated revenge plot. To see Abe perched on a stack of phonebooks, peering furiously over the hood of one of the gargantuan Rosemere GMC Bullnoses was an experience of sublime terror.

Bullnoses were too wide for the narrow streets of the Garment District, but Abe had gotten a deal on two just before GMC phased them out in favor of taller, more interstate-friendly models with sleeper cabs. While the actual drivers took pains to perfect the subtlety necessary for maneuvering these forbidding vehicles, hiccuping down the street around the scrum of other trucks, not *big macher* Abe. On the rare days that he commandeered one, instead of sitting goose-necked over the books in the office, Abe would cram the red snout of the semi down Thirty-sixth Street, accelerating where he should have been hiccuping, tearing the mirrors off rows of double-parked trucks loading or unloading, eyes wide, spinning the huge wheel like he was playing roulette with the barrel of a gun, forever hunting his long-dead equine tormentor.

I am only aware of the Bullnose situation because I was for some time, beginning in 1964, the front office girl at Rosemere, and almost every day at Rosemere there was some incident or other with one of the Bullnoses, the vast proportion of which involved Abe.

I got the job at Rosemere after I graduated college with my degree in dramatic arts. I had been offered a full scholarship at New York University, which I attended while living at home with my parents for four—I have to say—terrible years. All of my cohort lived on campus, had trust funds, and hung out at Cafe Wha? late every night. I commuted under my father's curfew. Meanwhile all of my friends at home had gone on to their jobs and marriages already—Shelley worked at the butcher, Judy worked as a speech therapist at the high school, Diane was married with a kid. By the time I graduated it was clear that the path toward a dramatic career—which would have involved being bankrolled by my parents' nonexistent bankroll—was closed to me.

In fact, a lot of things were closed. I was older than most administrative assistants and had zero experience, so just answering an ad in the paper titled "Front Office Manager

Wanted for Transportation Industry Position" was not so simple. The truth is that I got the job at Rosemere because my uncle Sonny was Abe Rosenberg's bookie. To be more specific, I got the job because Abe Rosenberg wanted my uncle Sonny—an absolute nobody who had suddenly become a somebody on account of being incarcerated at Sing Sing, which, with its proximity to Yonkers Raceway, was where all the high-level trades got made—to be his bookie.

My uncle Sonny was an entirely silent person except for when he was placing a bet, at which point he spoke in a strained tough-guy whisper—as if trying to keep a mouthful of corn from escaping his lips—or eating, which was a grotesquely loud and opposite production in which, without fail, many mouthfuls of food did escape. Needless to say, I neither cared for him nor had given much thought to him. But the fact was that as I had essentially no job prospects, Uncle Sonny—this schlemiel who had gotten picked up for running low-level games out of a garden apartment on Beverly Road, only to essentially matriculate at the Harvard University of betting on horses—was my ticket to a career in the administrative arts whether I liked it or not.

Rosemere employed Teddy and many of the Rosenberg men, including Saul, who had been funneled into working as a contractor—which in the garment business meant he schlepped across the Northeast visiting shop floors, hassling fabric cutters, and buying and pawning off seconds and leftovers.

Stephen, however, was poised to fulfill the promise of skipping the family business entirely in favor of a medical degree, though, as I have already mentioned, he ultimately ended up flushing that down the toilet.

* * *

On the evening I first met Stephen, I was working late in the office—going over the week's receipts for fabric picked up and garments delivered—waiting out a spring storm. My friend Ethel had gotten tickets for a revival of *Exodus* at the Kings Theatre in Flatbush, and I was meeting her there later that evening. But I hadn't had the foresight to wear practical shoes, and I did not want to sit through *Exodus* with wet feet.

The weather tore in that day with a Midwestern intensity, the way I imagined storms fell upon cities that were aberrations within a general landscape of plains. Outside the large windows, from our coveted spot on the twelfth floor of Fashion Tower, I watched rain strafe the Hudson like hooves stampeding across a Missouri meadow.

Not that I had ever been to Missouri. But that's the way I always pictured St. Louis, which for me was synonymous with the Wingfields' apartment in *Glass Menagerie*. The way the play was customarily blocked, you just see this one apartment spotlit against the blackness of the rest of the set. You're supposed to think of it as part of a city block, but when I played Amanda Wingfield I preferred to derive her undercurrent of cruelty and fear from imagining her apartment as a lone outcropping amid vast plains spreading blue and ominous under the moon.

I didn't realize anyone was in the office with me until I heard someone mutter, *Asshole got his license in a Cracker Jack box,* and looked up to find Abe—who not infrequently entered the office midway through a bitter testimonial on the topic of other people's poor decisions and how he had been compelled to hurt someone or damage something because of it—smoldering in the center of the reception area, rain plinking off the lapels of his knock-off Burberry. Here is where I will add that short men should not wear trench coats.

Short men in trench coats resemble underling vampires. You should ideally only wear a trench coat if you are Donald Sutherland.

"Gene in?"

Gene was the mechanic, and this was not a real question because it was past five and no one was in.

I shook my head and pointed at the clock by way of explanation.

"Saul?"

Abe only asked for Saul when he wanted to get into a bullfight. I poked at that day's date on the calendar that lay open on my desk. "Pennsylvania. Stein's."

When a mill was rumored to have a lot of fabric lying around for one unfortunate reason or another, Saul would swoop in, bouncing his cigar between his teeth, and offer to take the material off the guy's hands. All the manufacturer had to do in return was agree to make Rosemere his sole distributor. Saul's job was essentially that of a traveling hoodlum, which I thought suited him fine. But I knew that he had other ambitions.

I knew these details about Saul's so-called interiority because I am ashamed to say I had consented to allow him to take me out to dinner one time, just the previous week, at the Apollo Diner in East Meadow.

Saul had returned early from a trip to a fabric cutter in Niantic. His trip had not been successful, due to a local trucking company having gotten wind of this cutter's extra fabric first, and by the time Saul got up there, a deal had already been struck.

He was in a sour mood and had taken up a post in one of the nubby tweed armchairs along the wall in the reception area that were supposed to be for clients, flicking his Zippo open and closed. I was feeling particularly despairing that day because I had recently been broken up with by my boyfriend of three months, Billy Lipschitz, who drove a convertible and was in engineering school. Billy was charismatic, good-looking, and professional, and I had decided that my life was over when he ended things in order to date a flamenco dancer named Carmen (née Louise) Schnitzer, whom he subsequently married. You try saying "The Lipschitz-Schnitzer Wedding" three times quickly. No one can do it, I had to comfort myself many times in those days.

So Saul, probably because he too felt his life was going nowhere and was taking a stab in the dark, offered to drive me home that day. He was headed to Woodmere for the night because he had to visit a cutter in Nassau County the next morning. Actually asking me out directly was beyond Saul's capabilities. Instead, halfway through the car ride, once we were safely outside of Manhattan and Manhattan dining price ranges, Saul suddenly "remembered" he was hungry and strongly suggested we get a bite. It seemed I was being kidnapped into a date. By that time we were on the LIE, and Saul explained that if we were hungry (I had not affirmed that I was, by the way), we needed to bypass the BQE cutoff to my neighborhood, which was sure to be backed up with traffic anyway, and go eat at the Apollo. I was aware of the calculations going on in his head. The Apollo was three blocks from the off-ramp of Sunrise Highway, and this way Saul could avoid the traffic, and then double back on Sunrise to drop me off in Flatbush by way of Atlantic Avenue after rush hour. He could eat, sort of date me, and not have to sacrifice a great deal of extra time on the road. Saul's entire frame of reference had to do with drive times and shortcuts.

I ordered a Greek salad and a Tab and Saul ordered a hamburger with a side of pancakes. When his multiple plates of food arrived, Saul removed the meat patty from within the toasted bun and rolled it in the pancakes without a word. No disclaimer, no acknowledgment that what he was doing was the work of a child. Not even a sheepish shrug. He just plucked the meat out, threw it onto the round beige pancake, rolled the whole thing up like he was rolling a dead body in a rug, and—gripping it between his thick fingers—descended upon this meat-cake swirl face-first with an absolute lack of self-consciousness. It was as if he had never shared a meal with another human being before in his life.

Throughout, Saul rambled almost exclusively about his gripes with his father and Abe. He wanted to work in the office instead of having to drive to places such as Allentown and Taunton every week. *I could do the books just as good as them*, he said, shaking his head and chewing.

When Saul dropped me off, for reasons that were obscure to me at the time, but with hindsight I suppose actually had something to do with the beastly way that he consumed his food, I invited him to the roof of my apartment building. I had more than once spent time with boys up there, necking in the gravel. But where other boys compensated for their awkwardness—or tried—with a nervous attentiveness to the sexual encounter, Saul was as hapless and cruel as I had ever experienced. He stapled me to the ground at both the pelvis and mouth, opening his jaw so unnecessarily wide—more of a scream than a kiss—that his incisors left red marks under my nose and on my chin. The pressure of his pelvis pressed gravel divots into my ass. Saul had conflated extremity with prowess, or perhaps—I reflected, upon contact with his groin area—he was trying to distract from the fact that while his ass and hips were thick and heavy, his prick was a small, cylindrical afterthought, jiggling in his pants like a loose roll of mints.

Saul's mouth tasted of meat and yeast. He dry humped me until he climaxed in a terrible and sentimental way, wrinkling his closed eyes into bulging prunes while driving his pelvis harder and faster, his thrusts becoming comically short and sharp until he winced out *My angel* and collapsed on top of me.

10:30 a.m.

This morning I was unceremoniously awakened by someone shrieking MOM?

Ahhhmmm uhhhwyyyke. *It was hard to make a sound. I was being rolled around like a piece of dough with my limbs flopping wetly. You were wide-eyed & shouting.*

I'm awake! *This time I got a little more oomph into it. You stopped rolling me.*

Oh, *you said.* I brought you your green shake. *A bad imitation of nonchalance, a performance that would never pass muster at Performing Arts. You were trying to pretend you hadn't thought I might be dead. Like I might not realize I was almost dead, which I found to be very condescending. Most of you, I noted, had returned to human form since the prior evening's escapades, except your fingers, which were feathered at the outer edges.*

I glanced at the shake. Frankly, I did feel a little death-adjacent. It seemed impossible to imagine reaching for it & bringing it to my lips. Beads of condensation slid down the tall Duralex tumbler. These are good glasses, *I said, apropos of not nothing. I meant, don't throw them out when I die.*

Come on, Mom. *You perched at the edge of the bed & brought the shake down to my level, pinching the straw between two feathered fingertips to point at my mouth.*

By the way, *you said casually,* I'm going out for dinner tonight. *I could see you wanted to minimize your plans, slip out the door without me making a fuss. Well, fat chance.*

Nnnn nnnn, *I said, mouth full of straw & green juice, shaking my head right to left. Juice flew out the corner of my lips. I wiped my face with one of the tissues I kept balled in my hands for various wipings of effluvia these days.* You can't leave me here alone. *I'd put an exclamation mark here but my voice didn't actually have that much force beyond a pathetic whisper.*

It's for an hour. I'm taking K. to that Hungarian place around the corner.

The girl who'd been here the night before. Presumably. Or who knew, perhaps it was another one. But you spoke on the phone to K. a lot. One night I heard you telling K. that you wanted to "cum all the way up inside her," a thing that made me retch with a) the concept and b) your deludedness, thinking you could do that. Poor K.! She seemed like a successful young woman who was intent on ruining her life, letting you "cum all the way up inside her." The whole thing was very bizarre, & the proper feeling for me to have about all this was that it was tragic, because my poor daughter, etc. However, due to the extreme disparity in our situations I found myself in fact flush with jealousy, degraded by being left behind here in my bed while you rubbed it in (all the way in?) that you were able to go out, move around, eat at a table, while I marinated in my own malignant sweat.

You were "taking" a woman to the Hungarian restaurant. Oh, I heard the pride in your voice when you said "taking." Yes, you were making it very clear that you were going on a date. And that you were the man. I didn't want to get it, but I got it. I got it.

We fought after that. It was a little bit unsavory, the way I veered between admonishing & begging. I was pleading like a child for you not to leave me. Surely you had stepped out for periods of time before, even recently. But there was something so louche, so cruel about you flitting off for a date right before my eyes, sailing out the door as if you were an actual member of society, instead of sneaking off in the dead of night like lesbians should.

THE OTHER GOON

SAUL, THAT WAS AWFUL, I told him when he came into the office the next afternoon. *We will never speak of it again.* Saul, to his credit, accepted this outcome with a response befitting his station in life. *I probably won't be working here much longer anyways.* He shrugged. *I'm gonna apply for a job apprenticing as a butcher with Ronny Mayer in Bensonhurst.*

I had known Ronny Mayer since grade school, and I was certain that he would not be taking on Saul, as the entire family business was controlled by Ronny's father, who had a deal with the Bensonhurst mafia for keeping an all-Italian workforce.

Well good luck, Saul, I said, extending my hand. He looked at it, unsure what to do, then rowed my hand stiffly up and down before nodding and turning on his heel. Indeed, he did not ever work for Ronny Mayer. But something had been punctuated between us then, and we never did speak of our horrible encounter once, even to this day.

So I was not at my finest when, a week after my unfortunate intimacy with Saul, yet another Rosenberg sought to try my patience after hours. "What about Sidney," Abe asked, pacing around some desks. "Where's Sidney."

Sidney was the company lawyer. And what did Abe want with him this late at night?

I pointed again at the clock. I often had to resort to demonstrating to Abe and the other men in the office the objective causes for things not being the way they wanted them to be.

Abe sat down in Sidney's green vinyl desk chair and began swiveling half-heartedly. He had taken off his hat and was using the felt ridge to mop sweat in a semicircle from his forehead down to his temples and back up again. He put the hat on Sidney's desk and pushed up the sleeve of his other arm, inspecting something. His hand, I now saw, looked battered, and his thumb was hanging limp. He was bleeding a lot, actually. Blood pooled on Sidney's desk, and Abe used his elbow to push Sidney's paperwork to the side, smearing the blood into a calligraphic flourish.

"My hand got trapped against my mirror by one of those double-parked K & J trucks," Abe growled through clenched teeth. "Where the fuck is Saul when you need him." It was not out of the realm of possibility that Abe would ask Saul to attack a stationary vehicle out of pure vengeance.

"Oh, Abe," I said. At work I often played the part of *tsking* lady with a soft spot for buffoons. It was what I thought of as an acting opportunity, and a benign coping mechanism, but this night, following so soon after my miserable date with Saul, it made me feel more trapped in my life than I already did.

"Bastards don't know how to double park." Abe ran his working hand over his sweat-bright bald head, which was a thing Abe did because men in movies did this when they wanted to signal that they were thinking. "Call Teddy," he said after a minute. He had his head in the crook of his arm, and his voice was muffled by his coat. "Tell him to send Steve. He's home for Passover."

I guess I'll finally meet the other goon, I thought as I dialed.

By the time Stephen arrived from Nyack, the storm had intensified, darkening the interior of the office to an oppressive gray. The wind, whistling in around the panes of the giant windows, had shaken loose the metallic scent of old coffee from the pots lined up along the sill, mixing with the dank mildew coming off Abe's imitation Burberry (real Burberrys smell like hot electrical wire). The entire office had taken on the smell of a cross-country bus. I remember it because when Stephen walked in, crunching his ubiquitous chalky Life Savers, the thick air changed, threaded with wintergreen.

Incidentally, it wasn't until after his first heart attack, thirty-three years into our marriage, that I learned Stephen was a secret smoker, and that his Life Savers were an effort to blanket the tobacco smell. Back then I just thought of him as the mintiest Jew I had ever met.

I wasn't concerned that my dalliance with Saul posed an obstacle to my immediate interest in Stephen. In those days, girls circulated between the boys of the neighborhood. To the extent that my neighborhood now included Rosemere Trucking, transiting through Rosenbergs did not appear as a problem to me, though once we were married I did worry from time to time—such as at his mother's funeral—that Saul would get dramatic about it.

What I was preoccupied with, however, was that I had deigned to dally even once with Saul while all along there had been this other Rosenberg hidden away upstate, a med school boy of bright scents.

* * *

Because *Transportation Industry* was a fancy euphemism for *Jewish mafia*, I liked to entertain myself at that time by affecting the attitude of a girl whose job it was to handle subterfuge on a daily basis. That day I was dressed like a gangster moll in a belted mac coat, a mysterious bowler hat, and patent leather kitten heels. This was an outfit Teddy and Abe responded to as having a kind of female authority. When Stephen arrived, though, I suddenly had the completely unprecedented thought—or really, *feeling*—that I would rather have been nude than in this, or any, outfit at all.

"Stevala." Abe opened one arm in a broad, mafia-style greeting. His other hand hung at his side, dripping on the desk.

Stephen glanced at the hand. "We should take you to Bellevue."

I said I wished I had been nude, but it is equally true that I wished Stephen had been nude. In part this was because Stephen was wearing a spinach-green suit. It was double-breasted and it was a travesty. But it was a travesty of the sort generated by men who wanted to signal something about their abstract relationship to a subculture—their ability to take bohemian license with traditional menswear—and to me this bespoke ambition. I ended up being wrong about this, by the way.

The other part of why I wished Stephen had been nude was that I found him very attractive. He was the handsome version of Saul. He had the same immense quantity of dark wavy hair and the same thick beard and mustache. But he had larger, softer eyes. He was shorter but walked with quiet balance. A chain of wooden love beads poked out from under the collar of his white shirt. He was a solid brick of handsomeness, like even his organs were handsome.

"I'm not a doctor yet, Uncle Abe," Stephen added, when Abe motioned him closer.

"I broke it or what." Abe waggled his hand, showing no signs of going to Bellevue to be seen by an accredited physician.

"You did something." Stephen glanced around the office. He smiled at me, sitting at my desk trying to look busy with paperwork. "If you won't go to the hospital I'll need some assistance."

Stephen began issuing instructions in a voice that sparkled with his efforts to keep from laughing. I was trying not to laugh too. Something about being close to each other was making us both giddy. Everything in the world besides us was suddenly our private joke. It doesn't sound nice, but frankly Abe's predicament only added to our joy. We clustered around him like dogs, increasingly emboldened by our competence and youth the more Abe, the aging gorilla, whimpered and bled.

At Stephen's direction I glugged half a bottle of hydrogen peroxide onto Abe's bloody mitt while he cursed me to hell along with K & J Trucking. Then Stephen pulled a clean white handkerchief from his sport coat pocket and swaddled Abe's hand, while I handed him a safety pin from the saucer on my desk.

I did the honors and Stephen slapped Abe on the shoulder and said, "Take two aspirins and call me in the morning." He punctuated this quip with his characteristic tiny *heh* as he appreciated his own wit. When he huffed with pleasure like this, his chest rose and fell, and I had a powerful premonition of its warmth. I wanted to be close to him. And I got that funny feeling in my own chest that I later came to associate with the tiny naughty mini-Stephens I would come to know—the little devils that would peek out quickly before he would snatch them back and bury them inside himself, in order to empty later, privately, into me.

After we took care of Abe's fucked-up hand together, I thought, *I could raise kids with this man. Washing. Swaddling. Sharing little jokes at their expense. How different could it be.*

But dressing a mangled hand is a far safer venture than raising children. Mangled hands don't grow up to become, for example, feet. Or lesbians. Or something else that they are not supposed to be.

P.M.? A.M.? Terrible Day—

Woke up with a fever. But I was fine. I would have been fine.

Instead, you marched in, green shake in hand, all business, dressed like one of those scrubbed-up rockabilly boys from Ocean Avenue in jeans, a white T-shirt & white Converse high-tops. Let me say that none of those boys were nice boys, & you didn't look like a nice boy either. You looked like a person-sized hawk stuffed into a white T-shirt trying to act like everything was normal. But nothing was normal. Your façade had slipped again. I tried to repress my disgust and horror as you peered over me and touched my hand with one wing tip like you were testing a piece of meat. Said we had to go to the hospital. I shook my head no, & a flailing moan came out of me.

I wanted to wait out the fever, but I was too weak and delirious to resist. You flapped at me until I sat up, then herded me out of the apartment, holding me up with one wing in this thoughtless way like a sack of laundry. When we arrived at Columbia Presbyterian I asked you to wait in the car. Neither of us needed to explain why. In the waiting room I sat shivering for hours in a hard plastic seat, brooding about all the people there with their big regular families. Amoeba-people is how I thought of them, individual members making up one entity, one cell, whose limbs reached out in many directions, but all held together by an invisible membrane. I had wanted that so badly for my life. For our lives. And now here I was, waiting for hours in this miserable chair just to have my blood drawn, while a bird in a men's T-shirt sat in a Honda outside, sexting.

After they finally came & drew my blood, I had to wait again while they ran it & read the results. Then the doctors spent more time, endless time, hemming & hawing about whether I needed to be admitted. Several hours in, loopy with fever, I found myself grumbling, This is *fakokta*. I rose from my seat & began staggering toward the front desk. I was possessed by something— I felt like a marionette, utterly unable to do anything to stop my sudden need to register dissent. There was no delay between thought & speech, & I found myself—to my own great surprise—shouting "Attica! Attica!" at the triage station while shuffling forward.

Let me tell you, I was as shocked as anyone else to find myself conjuring an uprising in the waiting room of Columbia Presbyterian, waving my arms at the other patients, summoning them to advance on the reception desk. No one got up, but a couple people made fists & held them in the air as I stumbled past. More shocking, perhaps, was to find myself citing the movie Dog Day Afternoon—the scene where Sonny rallies the crowd gathered around the bank he's held up with the hostages inside.

In Dog Day Afternoon, *Al Pacino plays the lover of a transsexual woman. He holds up a bank in order to get the money to pay for his lover's transsexual surgery. How this movie came to me in that moment I have no idea. I hadn't protested a single thing since 1968 when Stephen and I lived briefly in Boston, where I worked as the administrative assistant to Mr. Noam Chomsky in the linguistics department at MIT, & experimented *briefly with attending demonstrations. I wasn't a leftist, or any political "thing" that I was aware of (though my daughter has called me plenty of names over the years, like "colonizer," "racist," "homophobe," etc.), but everyone else was doing it & at that time I enjoyed method acting the part of a Northeastern radical.*

So I guess that's how berserk I was today in the waiting room. I had been suddenly rewound, like a cassette tape, to my brief life playacting as a lefty in Cambridge, Massachusetts. Meanwhile, my little stunt did not help my cause. I waited for several more hours until I was finally admitted with idiopathic fever, which is where I am now, while they try to hydrate me & bring it down.

ANOTHER DOMINO

STEPHEN CALLED TO ASK me out after Abe's incident. Our first dinner was a double date at Junior's Deli with my cousin Ellen and her boyfriend, Stan, and I don't remember much about that evening except that when Stephen dropped me home, instead of kissing me he looked at me sort of wonderingly and then ran his hand down the side of my ribcage. It was awkward and sweet and also somehow more intimate than a kiss. I can still feel it, the rhythm of his finger over the ridges of my torso.

Stephen and I actually did not have much in common, which was fine. He considered himself a philosopher and had graduated from Cornell, where he had dated *goyishe* girls, and then he went to yet another *yenemsvelt* town and entered medical school at Syracuse. And I was who I have already explained I was. In those days no one expected you to have anything in common with your husband. Stephen was funny. He was going to be a professional. And there was something about him that relaxed me.

Stephen would drive down from Syracuse every other Friday night to take me to dinner or the movies. Steady dating in those days meant dating toward an obvious goal, although there was something about Stephen that danced around the obvious. He was abstracted. He had questions about things—like life, and physics, and how societies functioned. I did not have an interest in those questions. And the night I want to speak of now is the night I think was *really* the beginning of the end, because I think, given the difference in our comportments, things could have and maybe should have gone another way up until this moment.

We were eating a basket of fried clams at Lundy's, the crown jewel of Sheepshead Bay, when, apropos of nothing, Stephen looked at me with his soft eyes, breadcrumbs clinging to his mustache like ants swarming on dried grass, and said, "Barbara, I've been thinking."

A domino was about to fall on my life. On such a beautiful evening, too.

It was an unusually warm April. Brooklyn was bursting in anticipation of an early summer. And Stephen, Nyack Stephen, handsome suburban Stephen, was in his final year of medical school.

"Yes?" I crossed my legs, shifting my weight from one (for some people, maybe too small, for some just perfect—although to the day he died I never really knew where Stephen stood on the matter) buttock to the other. The path to doctoring had finally begun in earnest. Stephen was a man with a tiny, shiny weapon. A scalpel that would pierce the skin of the world and bleed money.

I arranged my face into a marriageable expression. I had, by the way, been arranging my face into a marriageable expression for months now. Nothing to be done about my nose—yet, anyway—but I tried to make the rest of my face soft and open.

"You know that guy Allenson"—Stephen's voice had that

quaver it got when he was simultaneously ashamed and excited, that held-back half-smile that pushed his tone briefly soprano-ward.

Just then sunset dropped like a steel pebble and the horizon went purple-black, the way it does where the outer boroughs meet the sea. A spritz of cooler ocean air threaded through the window screens. I pulled the shawl from the back of my chair and rested it on my shoulders.

". . . Allenson. The visiting professor from Tulane I mentioned?" Stephen continued, in that very specific tone I have just described. "Genteel guy. Tweeds and cardigan type."

I rolled my hand in the air like a film reel speeding up. One thing about Stephen was that he took eons to tell a story. A natural-born narrator he was not. Meanwhile I had learned all about the difference between the architecture of narrative and extraneous details of the sort that Stephen always seemed to latch on to. Not that anyone was asking what I thought of the architecture of a tale; my dramatic career had ended before it began, thanks to my nose, probably, and also my father putting the kibosh on my invitation (not easy to get, by the way) to summer stock in 1961. But summer stock or no summer stock, I knew how to make a story work. And Stephen's love of detail was a flaw—an endearing flaw, but a flaw nonetheless. He compulsively invested minutiae with significance. It was part of what made him sweet, albeit a tiny bit dull. But then again, men were not supposed to be exciting. Not in those days. Not the ones you married anyway.

"Allenson's renowned for his technique," Stephen was saying. His breath over the red-checked tablecloth was a brume of clam and Budweiser. "It's an oblique scalpel angle. He's trademarked it 'The Allenson.'"

Stephen gripped his fork in his fist—a workmanly Poseidon prying a mollusk from its shell. At one point I would have killed to just get one free dinner in Lundy's cavernous Italianate stucco interior from a future surgeon. Now, with the whiff of marriage and techniques such as the mysterious *Allenson* in the air, the restaurant began to strike me as dim and phony.

A series of thumps ran the perimeter of the room—the house manager pushing the soaring colonial-paned windows to their sills. The din of the interior deepened. Overhead lamps clicked on, refracting yellow spiders at the edges of Stephen's wire-framed glasses. Soon this whole borough would be a memory. Stephen and I would bring our children here from Manhattan someday. *Remember when we thought* Lundy's *was fancy?*

"In any case," Stephen continued. "Allenson passed around our instruments, and then he passed around these trays of carrots—our own personal carrot to dissect." He speared and gulped a clam. "You know, to practice the Allenson on," he added, chewing.

"Yes." I dipped my spoon into my chowder. "The Allenson," I encouraged, ladling my soup away from my body.

Unless you want to look like a construction worker, you cannot plow your spoon into soup and drag it toward you. I have always ladled soup away from my body, as I'd once read was recommended by Miss Manners. You must ladle away and then circle your hand back toward your mouth for a sip. This move will feel awkward—sort of like being a conductor of soup—but I have always firmly believed this was how Audrey Hepburn ate soup, and so I was then, and I remain now, committed to the pomp and circumstance of it.

When my hand arrived back in the vicinity of my face, I opened my mouth with my lips curled back, so as not to muss layers of taupe lipstick and liner, and tipped the soup in. Boy, did I eat soup like a pro. I am pretty sure that if a blindfolded person had been sitting at the next table, on hearing my teeth click lightly against the silverware (as I closed my teeth, but not my lips, and swallowed), they would have sworn they were hearing a WASP eating soup. *Swirl click. Swirl click.* Soon, I would be out having soup at a ladies' lunch with new Manhattan friends while Stephen would be *Allenson'ing* some poor schmuck who had the misfortune of ending up at Montefiore Medical Center with an Allenson-able ailment, whatever that might be.

"To make a long story short," said Stephen.

"*Shortish*," I said, promenading my spoon on another 360-degree tour of the soup.

Stephen smiled. "There I was," he pressed on, "standing over my carrot, looking down at it, preparing to Allenson it. And at that moment I suddenly couldn't help but think about all the world's barbarity. Could I heal such barbarity with single incisions, one after another? What could *I* contribute with but one scalpel?"

My heart began to thunder in my chest.

"The answer," Stephen continued, waving a finger in the air, "quite simply, was: Nothing! I can contribute nothing this way. And, knowing this, I had a realization. I need to help *more people* at once. More people than you can help as a physician. And, as I had this realization, with my scalpel grazing the peel of the carrot"—and here Stephen's finger joined the rest of its cohort into a cupped palm, and then he upheld both cupped palms, saying, "I felt the world open. And just as quickly as I felt it open, I felt the world close. A darkness fell." He clenched his palms into fists and looked deep into my misery-filling eyes. "Babsie," he said. "I fainted."

This was the moment I should have left, and yet this instant, when I watched Stephen rip in half like a movie poster of Stephen, and my carefully constructed image of him was left curling on the ground, while the actual Stephen was a tiny astronaut hitting eject on his birthright of becoming a surgeon, shooting instead into the non-surgeony nothingness of space—this was the moment when I found myself unaccountably, counterintuitively, and in a way that I would come to rue, saying, "Do you want to see *Exodus* at the Kings after dinner? They're reprising it for a second run."

Not forty-five minutes later we were on Flatbush Avenue parking Stephen's Plymouth Savoy, an ungainly thing the bright bronze color of a bad dye job. The car was long—like a giant stepped-on cockroach, its rear end arching up at an unnatural, broken angle—and Stephen was making a grand effort to conquer a too-small but well-situated space with this behemoth, inching back and forth with the patience and devotion to ritual of a monk. Never before in the history of mid-level Plymouth Savoys had anyone so gingerly handled a Plymouth Savoy; never had a parking job commanded such love. This was a gentle man, I thought. Maybe a lackluster salary was less important than gentleness?

But this, of course, was an utter guess, because I did not know from gentleness. My father, as I have already suggested, was not the kind to get mushy over much. Papa was and would forever be a hump-busting vacuum salesman as likely to be found on the road as off. In fact, given Papa's overly *physical* manner of expressing his frustrations, I had come to feel that it was better when he was to be found on it.

* * *

In the neighborhood they used to call me Princess Horowitz of Ocean Avenue. Not to my face, of course. But I had heard more than one boy refer to me that way—when the wind changed direction and I caught scraps of conversation down the block—and frankly it was true. So what. I ruled those streets, standing on corners with packs of friends, slugging back sodas, trading photos of Elvis and James Dean like baseball cards. But I wasn't going to stop there. Soon I was taking the IRT into Manhattan to sneak into matinees in the Theater District. Before long I had established a foot in each borough, and I had become lore. For I had evaded Erasmus High, where everybody who was nobody in Flatbush went, and instead won a rare place at and matriculated to the legendary High School of Performing Arts.

When I met Stephen, I had already burned through every boy from Parkside Avenue in the south to Bedford Avenue in the north (if we take the summer season into account: from Parkside Avenue in the south to the SGS Bungalow Colony at 261 Mount Hope Road in Swan Lake, New York, in the north). None of them were good enough for me. I broke engagements, broke hearts, even turned down Ronnie Mayer, who stood to inherit three butcher shops, and did: one in Rego Park, one in Bensonhurst, and one in Forest Hills.

By 1963, I had sampled all the rough boys from Flatbush, and what I wanted for marriage was a boy who carried the lawns of Nyack in his heart, a soft boy whose father had done all the clawing for him, who didn't prowl Brooklyn apartments in A-shirts and anger. A boy who had sipped the air of true assimilation. WASP neighbors. Clean lungs. Leisure sports.

It wasn't, of course, exactly that simple. Saul, I now came

to realize, had been the family's sacrifice to the gutters. Saul was the one who absorbed the trauma of history, took on its heat like a spoon in a glass mug of hot tea. And meanwhile Stephen had gone on to become the long-jump champion at Nyack North, emerging from his childhood with unflappable optimism.

The family had invested all their hopes in Stephen—and the rest of them, Teddy, Saul, and Blanchie—had pyramided themselves for Stephen to climb up. But something had gone wrong, and now words like "neighborhood health" and "free clinic" were coming out of Stephen's mouth as he inched the car interminably into place. I studied his teddy bear cheek puffing with air as he squinted out the window and slowly rolled the steering wheel this way and that. He was a chemist of parking—a chemist assessing the contours of a parking space with no less a sense of solemn responsibility than that with which one would parse the contents of a petri dish. Not—it seemed—that he would ever work with a petri dish. Such things were for *clinicians* and *researchers*. Doctors who *doctored,* who didn't faint at the sight of a carrot laid out in a surgical theater. Perhaps it was impossible to find kindness and a salary in the same man. I had been foolish to imagine I could have both. I saw that then, and I saw that I would have to make a choice.

People began streaming into the theater. Stephen wasn't going to be a surgeon, I silently repeated to myself. I had put time in on this man, from enduring his unaccountable green suit to saying nothing when he had "needed" to take an internship in St. Thomas the previous summer, during which it seemed he had dated god knows how many local girls. Men required cultivation just like the flora of a petri dish, and so to be fair both Stephen and I were chemists—he of parking,

I of husbands. I had cultivated my petri dish with patience, with strategic lookings-away (both from the suit and the extracurricular dating), and now it seemed this petri dish just wasn't going to produce what I thought it would produce. In fact, it was possible—no, likely—that Ronnie Mayer would be making more off his butcher shops than Stephen would doing god knows what. *Helping people.*

I couldn't have said then quite what bothered me so much about this formulation, but I understand it better now. Stephen's drive to "help people" seemed to bear no relationship—or even a negative relationship—to helping *me*. This service to an abstraction was, I suppose, his secular religion. Which is another thing that Marx talks about. How some people, aka "liberals" (which is not a word we ever used until my so-called daughter started uttering it like a slur, and I realized Stephen was one and I was actually just a bigot, but according to students at Wesleyan University both were equally bad!), think relationships in the world can be the embodiment of abstract ideals. Liberals think that living in accordance with these abstract ideals makes them good people, and Marxists think that's bullshit, and actually this is one thing I really agree with Marxists about.

The line was inching forward, having extended back all the way to the thickening trees of Beverly Road, running nearly to my parents' apartment. Our apartment was *right there;* I could simply leave. But then something about the desire to avert the outcome I saw unfurling before me was exactly what paralyzed me. I was in the grips of history—or God, or fate, or the beige leather expanse that constituted the Savoy's front seat. I had done the very best I could to change my course in life, first with Performing Arts, and then with Stephen. Nothing ever worked. And I realized in that moment, it wasn't because I hadn't tried, and it wasn't because I was thinking about things wrong. It was simply that I was in the grips of something tragic and bigger than me. Destiny was driving me toward disappointment. I did not move.

A few more bumps forward and back, and Stephen shouted a triumphant "Yeah!" as he turned the car off. He looked at me, beaming with the sheer heroism of having parked this bronze schooner in an impossibly tight aperture, and embraced me with all the pomp and circumstance of Odysseus arriving back in Ithaca. His arms and beard were Greek-god thick. Then he murmured into my hair, shrugging his shoulders up while hugging me, and thus shrugging us both up, "I mean . . . I could go into public health. You know, work for the city. A municipal servant." And even then I didn't extricate myself. I sank deeper into the hug, and into Stephen, and into tragedy, and thought: *I'm fucked.*

By the time we finished the parking project, the towering white stone façade of Kings had fully digested the line. The street echoed with the emptiness of its sudden desertion. I grabbed the loose wrist of Stephen's jacket and whisked us through the hushed lobby until we reached the threshold of the massive theater. Almost the entire 3,000-plus-seat room was full, but even this considerable quantity of buzzing humanity was dwarfed by the Bourbon gigantitude of Kings. The sight of this temple of movies never failed to inspire the deepest thrill in me. Massive columns loomed in the gaping hollows along the sides of the room, lit by art deco light fixtures the size of rhinoceroses, flanked by floor-to-ceiling red velvet curtains.

* * *

Stephen poked his elbow into my ribcage in that way he thought was funny. A sheepishness edged around all his actions, an air of discomfort with adult masculinity. At moments like this, I felt a particular tender frustration with Stephen, who seemed still a boy who could only enact romance under the aegis of mocking it.

The only seats together were in the very back row, the "make-out row," the row patrolled by Kings' aisle matrons, who, if they suspected funny business, would point their heavy steel flashlights in your face and shout "Hands to yourselves!" It was not an honorable row. Stephen turned to look at me, his forehead knotted in question, and I nodded minutely.

This would not be my first time in the back row. It would not even be an exaggeration to say that I *liked* the back row. My friend Howie from theater class used to say, "Cinema—which is to say, the general umbrella of 'drama' and everything that comes under it—*is* my sexuality." For a while I thought this was just a way to get out of saying he was a *faygeleh* but then I realized that it applied to me too. I could get halfway to orgasm by someone onscreen storming into or out of a room in a floor-length silk robe, dangling a cigarette while her suitor drained a tumbler of brown whiskey. So, unbeknownst to Stephen, I was no stranger to the make-out row. But I allowed him to sweat it out about our sordid seat selection.

"Is it really okay?" he asked, his face a rictus of concern.

"Is what okay?" I teased. A shroud of righteousness, an aura of diasporic virtue had descended upon Stephen. I had seen it congealing around him at dinner, and by the time he had made his announcement about *Social Work*, he had achieved a combination of glow and remove, like a museum piece under perfect gold lighting, posing with quiet significance in a glass case. Stephen had seized on the meaning of himself: he wanted, more than anything else, to be *Good*. But what I knew from Flatbush Avenue—not to mention Tennessee Williams plays—was that nobody was just good. And watching him try to maintain his newfound Goodness while also wanting to exploit the back row with me was a convulsion of subjectivity to behold.

"What do you mean 'Is what okay?'" Stephen bugged out his eyes and swept his hands open, gesturing at *the make-out row*. The entire back row, in fact, was largely empty, as it seemed no one else wished to broadcast to the neighborhood that they intended to make out during *Exodus*.

"It's fine," I said. And then, just for the fun of watching him fully dissolve in guilt: "At least we got a good parking spot."

Stephen laughed then. He laughed—as he always did—with the delight of someone surprised and slightly embarrassed to find they liked the feeling of being momentarily not in command of themselves. A couple peeps of clandestine delight, and that was it.

The lights dimmed, and *Exodus* began. Ernest Gold's score thundered to life as the monumental illustrated flames of the title sequence shot orange tongues toward the top of the screen. Eyes fixed to the screen as the score boomed, Stephen's hand crept to the left over the armrest and missed its mark, arriving at the un-erotogenic location of my knee. His hand fluttered for a moment like a manta ray rising to the ocean's surface; his hand was acting out a small skit of indecision—should it course-correct now that it had landed, or embrace the current coordinates as if they had been intentional? The hand seemed to settle on the latter and began squeezing my knee awkwardly, in a half-hearted attempt to suggest that knee-palping had been the hand's intended target all along.

I tried to bracket the entire hand situation and focus on the movie. I was exhilarated by the technological marvel and artistry of *Exodus*'s title design. No sooner had the name of an actor or director or member of the crew flashed onto the screen than it was engulfed in bright cartoon flames rising from the bottom of the frame. Even before the movie had begun, the names themselves had become dramatis personae in their own right—tragic Joan-of-Arcs of the alphabet, bravely shuffling onto the screen with the flames licking at their feet.

I too, I thought, as the palping continued, was in a tragic situation. Stephen's palping of my knee had transformed itself into a doctorly kind of knee-assessment, as if I'd come into an office complaining of problems with my tennis game. Technically this was a fantasy that I might otherwise have indulged, but for the nagging realization—an intensifying background hum—that Stephen would in fact never see a patient in an office once in his life.

4:27 p.m.

The doctors & nurses come in & out all day, & I've developed a cheeky stock opening line to explain the fact of the bird, who sits with me now, reading its book, my shame visible to all. On some level I would love to clarify to the personnel of Columbia Presbyterian Hospital, "This is my incredibly disappointing daughter." But that's just not an objectively verifiable claim anymore. So, helpless in the face of the non-language available to me to describe what this creature is, whenever anyone comes into the room, I throw my hands in the air & shout, "This is Jordana. She's a Marxist!"

THUS ARE OUR FATES SEALED

THE MOVIE BEGAN, BRIGHTENING the theater with a sweeping view of the Mediterranean as seen by Eva Marie Saint aka Kitty Fremont, in cat-eye sunglasses and a platinum bob. Stephen used this opportunity to flinch his hand back onto his own knee, as if the sudden brightness was a rebuke for deeds far more sordid than he had actually accomplished.

Cyprus was a place of tragedy, Kitty's Cypriot tour guide was saying. Endlessly conquered, endlessly colonized. Still, the Cypriots loved everyone, even the British, he assured her, just in case she was British. And Kitty *did* look British—cold, emotionless, palely surveying the landscape. Then she took off her glasses, in a dramatic gesture meant to showcase the American sincerity of her eyes. "I'm American," she said, not looking sincere in the slightest. "We love Americans, too!" the Cypriot shouted.

I was surrounded by tragedy. Was I really going to stay the course with Stephen Rosenberg—this high-minded Jew? Now Ari Ben Canaan as played by Paul Newman was emerging, shirtless, from the nighttime Mediterranean Sea. I feasted my eyes on Newman's wet, moonlit physique. Newman who undoubtedly had a mansion on upper Fifth Avenue; Newman with whom it was so easy to fantasize a life—so glistening was he, so intimate, so almost-naked. So much easier than trying to picture a future with Stephen now that my fantasies would require replacing the images I'd had of a classic pre-war six in the 10028 zip code with something more modest. Something that would have to be east of Third Avenue. A wave of anxiety blossomed and took root in my body.

A thing I hate is when anyone uses the word "sweating" to apply to me. Or, really, to women in general. "Men sweat," I have found myself having to explain on more than one occasion. "Women *perspire*."

It has to be said, however, that I was in that moment perspiring so profusely that I briefly considered the possibility that my bodily effluvia had crossed the gender line.

Onscreen, the film had pivoted from nearly naked Newman to Kitty, who had been recruited into serving as a visiting nurse at Karaolos, the Jewish internment camp. Outside a medical tent, Kitty had stopped to argue with the baggy-suited ancient Dr. Odenheim over the proper treatment of a child's case of facial impetigo. *You need medicine for that,* Kitty said, appalled, as medicine-less, interned, wrinkled Dr. Odenheim, formerly head doctor at Vienna Hospital who had fallen so far as to have to cheerily make do with a folk remedy, held the child tenderly and wiped at the sores with nothing more than a washcloth dripping with soapy water. *This works just as well,* Odenheim asserted with the fanaticism of the desperate, exposing the child's gleaming pus hollows to the supposedly healing sun, and Kitty backed away. *These poor, jailed Jews,* she might have been thinking. *Oh, the pathos of a people who lacked both cat-eye sunglasses and actual medicines. How terribly sad it was and yet how strangely thrilling to observe these bereft weirdos and their unaccountable faith in dubious Old World rituals,* Kitty thought, as she tripped off into the medical tent to dole out actual medicine to someone who would accept it. Except that no one would accept it; they would have none of her *shiksa* nursing. Not even Dov Landau, who definitely seemed en route to dying of his own British-police-induced infected wounds. It appeared everyone on Karaolos had an infection, and Kitty was stumbling from patient to patient in a sea of pus-crusted refugees—lunatics who wouldn't accept the charitable ministrations of an American blonde.

And why should they? Hadn't Kitty just moments earlier been telling the British commander that she felt "strangely" about the Jews?

Thanks but no thanks, lady, multiple infected Jews who would rather die than indulge Kitty's genteel bigotry informed her.

Ten minutes later, Odenheim and the rest of the camp had boarded the *Exodus* only to be detained at the harbor by the British police. Now they were having a hunger strike, and five minutes after that, Odenheim—after having waved away Ben Canaan's concern over how he was holding up with a martyrific "What does it matter how an old man feels?"—had dropped dead of a heart attack on the deck.

Stephen, I realized, was like Odenheim. A man who was willing to sacrifice his life for abstract principles like *goodness* and *helping*. Well, let me tell you, goodness buys you what. Rhinestones and bupkes. According to the *Today* show—a very reputable source—80 percent of people can't tell the difference between a rhinestone and a diamond at a distance of fifteen feet. Any closer than that and the jig is up. Was this going to be my lot in life, I wondered. A rhinestone-crusted faker attempting to maintain a fifteen-foot perimeter around myself at all times in the zoo of humanity that is every avenue east of Third? *I should break up with him*, I silently scream-thought. I had other offers. Boys from the neighborhood. Hard boys who chewed gum, slicked their hair, drank liquor, and incubated the pool-stink of fresh semen in thin wool trousers. I could have any of those apes destined for jobs in butchering, or finance, or the Diamond District. Why bank on a philosopher type, this boy with gentle eyes?

I had thought I'd be the first to make it out of Flatbush. But just that month my cousin Ellen had shacked up with Stan, and the two of them piled into his MGB and sped off with the top down all the way to Ardmore, Pennsylvania, for Stan's job managing the Philadelphia Macy's. The most modern couple ever to have emerged from Flatbush. Second in line was my sour grapes to bear. And not only would I be second, but I would not be able to choose the carriage of my conveyance, which I had thought would be an apprentice surgeon's Cadillac. No, it seemed I'd have to swim for it, brave the waters and fling myself upon the shores of Manhattan—a female Ari Ben Canaan materializing out of the East River onto the glistening black pavement.

A sensation of constrained fury descended on me, something like how I'd Method acted Amanda Wingfield. When playing Amanda Wingfield, I used to imagine all the muscles of my ribcage were made of water, seizing up at a freezing point. If someone were to put an ear to my ribcage, they would hear the pop of ice furrowing into solid form, splitting against the walls of a tray. I had always been able to summon Amanda Wingfield-ness at the drop of a hat. I was proud of being able to project silent rage. But here I was being Wingfielded by some force beyond my conscious control. In the back row of the Kings Theater, I was Method acting against my will.

Almost as if guided by the unbearableness of this feeling itself, powered by pure misery at my helplessness to fate and my anger at Stephen for being the accomplice of my destiny, I now found *my own hand floating* to the right over the armrest, tracing Stephen's hand's path in reverse, except I actually hit my target, arriving plumb in his lap, where I proceeded to unzip, and then remove, his prick from its pants—this prick that had been nudging itself warmly, insistently against my thighs for months of goodnight kisses. This prick that was so forward and un-Stephen-like. This prick that, it now occurred to me, was the only truly ambitious part of him.

I could not allow this prick to follow Stephen down the path of meek liberalism. I began to pump his prick in earnest.

Thus are our fates sealed. Not when our hearts open to another person, but when we are confronted with that aspect of a person that is most intolerable to us, and we foolishly believe that we can fuck that intolerability away.

Meanwhile, Ari and Kitty had started on a road trip to one or the other of the kibbutzes where they coincidentally happened to be staying within miles of each other. They'd stopped the car, and now Ari was romantically dragging Kitty up a hillside to survey the landscape. He asked Kitty if she knew her Old Testament, then he spun, giving the camera a long, lingering view of his ass, and promptly settled in to explain the holy book to her. It was an uncanny echo of the opening scene with the Cypriot tour guide, only now Kitty was with a proper love object and they were viewing the vista that the entire audience had been waiting for: the glorious land of Palestine.

With the theater in this reverential hush, I ministered to Stephen's prick, with Stephen gasping—*Babsie, really?*—alternately whipping around to see if anyone was looking and then staring back at me with incredulity as he fell deeper and deeper into his own body. I grew annoyed by his alternately squinting and then staring expression of sheer wonder at the joys of his own fantastic prick. I needed a break from this look, plus I was missing the movie. I laid the side of my head against his chest, watching the screen out of the corner of my upturned left eye while I pumped.

The camera panned over the landscape. Ari was going on about this or that supposed ruin that lay below, and I did to Stephen's prick the things the boys on the corners in the neighborhood mimed doing to their own while I walked by; I did that monkey thing they liked to show me. I did this thing to Stephen while I could feel him shifting and straining with the uncontainability of such wonderful sensation delivered to him *at the hands of a woman*. I felt his body stiffening—his thighs contracting, his abs bunching—as he disintegrated into frozen ecstasy while Ari began to explain biblical history to Kitty.

Although Ari was explaining history, he wasn't looking at Kitty. Instead, he had turned to look at the camera, with Kitty gazing at him in wonder. I knew about breaking the fourth wall, and this was more like a small fracture. While we sat and were taught about the Bible by Ari Ben Canaan, Ari's sapphire slit-eyes peered meaningfully toward the audience without seeing us, so beneficently clouded was his vision with the dream of Palestine. Kitty, meanwhile, was verging on rolling her own eyes and smirking behind his back. *These Jews were so serious about Palestine!* she communicated silently to us, as Ari gazed out over the landscape and pattered on about whatever archaeological discoveries. Ari and his family—his father, the Haganah leader; his uncle, in love with his samovar and bomb-making; and his sister, Jordana Ben Canaan, the horse-riding female head of the Palmach. Kitty's expression conveyed that it was okay if the audience couldn't keep all the military factions of the Jews straight in their heads—neither could she! *Just focus on Ari's transfixingly blue eyes...*

Stephen leaned down and kissed my cheek. "I love you," he croaked out through a throat constricted by the proximity of ejaculation. He sounded, in that moment, disturbingly Saulesque, with the slight difference that *my angel* had been replaced with *I love you.*

"What just happened?" I waved his head out of the way of the screen.

"Kitty said something about how people are all the same, but Ari said people like being different," Stephen garbled. His hand moved down toward his lap, almost clenching mine in his own. It made a pumping motion in the air, the international adolescent sign indicating *faster.*

"People *are* different." I nodded against Stephen's chest, pausing the hand job for a moment. He emitted a kind of whining wheeze. I put a hand on his thigh, shushing him. I felt renewed in the power of filmic bibliomancy. Was *Exodus* trying to communicate something to me? Was the movie laying the groundwork for dumping him? People *were* different. I felt my anger at his public health pronouncement dissipate into a removed, almost orbital calm. Stephen and I were different—just like Ari Ben Canaan said—that's all there was to it. Arriving at this simple conclusion, I relaxed, sighed, glanced down at Stephen's burgeoning cock, and settled myself into stroking again—more quickly now, thus to bring things to a conclusion. Yes, people were different, I thought "at" Stephen's cock, willing it to give over its contents.

Maybe I could leave him—find another Manhattan-bound boy? There was a kind of cinematic pleasure to considering the finality of this hand job. I'd do this thing to him one time only, and I knew from the look of wide-eyed panic-stricken joy I'd seen on his face that it was good. Let him try to find a Nyack girl who'd be fast with him in a movie theater. He'd be miserable over me, remanded back to the goody-two-shoes of his youth. I savored the thought of his impending melancholy as his prick got hotter in my hand and began to near its punctum—swelling to a previously unforeseen and unanticipatable girth, mottling and spiking up toward the Kings' filigreed ceiling. (And here I have to note that I was surprised to find that, unlike the many surprisingly shy squeakers of pricks that belonged to the rough peacocking boys of my block, Stephen's prick was an entity of actual power, a kind of straightjacketed beast shaking its head in the back reaches of a prison cell, a beast with a frenzied cranium reddening like a hanged man's face until it burst with all the fury of the condemned.)

Thus did his prick announce its momentous climax.

Stephen, however, announced his climax with the characteristic soft humph with which he punctuated his other mild assessments of reality. Stephen's prick was a brutal, wealthy cardiologist in Pompano Beach, a thick golfer in polo shirts and gold chains. But Stephen—the actual Stephen—humphed softly like a deck of cards was being shuffled low in his throat, looked mildly at me and, with a sheepish half-smile, while stuffing his exhausted noodle back in his pants, whispered, "So, what, you wanna get married?"

White noise filled my eustachian tubes. I ought to have known this would be the outcome of my actions—and perhaps on some unconscious level I had—but the articulation of the actual question threw me into a swirl of wordless dread. Stalling, I reached into Stephen's jacket pocket for his handkerchief, which I used to fussily wipe down my sticky palm and thumb, scrubbing the crevices between my fingers, swabbing under my nails. I took a long time with this, the meticulousness of my display suggesting I had jerked off an atom bomb leaking nuclear goo. I needed to think. I had just been proposed to from the make-out row of the Kings Theater by a man who was pursuing a "career" in public health. Moreover, *I* had precipitated this proposal by my own actions, undertaken as an ambiguous, perhaps-goodbye gift to Stephen. I had thrown a kind of gauntlet. But Stephen had thrown a much more momentous one.

"Let's talk about it after the movie," I managed, replacing the limp handkerchief in his jacket pocket.

"Okay," Stephen burbled happily, throwing his arm around me and pulling me back to his broad, slowly rising and falling, post-orgasmic chest. The aggravating thing was that he settled in without a shred of anxiety as to the outcome of my determination. It was not that he couldn't imagine me saying no—I'm quite sure my stricken face when he'd announced his carrot-fainting episode had told him a lot—

and it was not even that he was entirely unambivalent about me—this I knew from the cavorting-in-St.-Thomas episodes. It was simply that nothing bad had ever happened to Stephen, and his suburban-bred optimism about life extended to all possible forking paths his life might take.

Onscreen, things took an unexpected turn.

Kitty, with the wind poufing her platinum hair to a beatific shiksa halo, began telling Ari that, actually, it was *he* who was wrong. People weren't so different after all, she said. By which she meant either that she no longer found Jews "strange" and that she'd come to peace with her own unaccountable hunger for Jewish bizarritude, or else that apple-assed, blondie boy Ari was kind of a shiksa in his own way—and maybe it was actually the latter, because, in a shocking gender reversal, especially for the über-feminine Kitty, she now lurched toward him, grabbed him around the back of the neck like an alleyway rapist or Fred MacMurray swooping in on Barbara Stanwyck in *Double Indemnity*, pulled him toward her, and kissed him.

This precipitated a shift. Some wave of emotion came over me, and continued to come as the movie unfolded. Here was Kitty enduring a terrible dinner at Ari's parents' house, replete with political shouting and a very palpable scorning of Kitty by Ari's horse-riding, Palmach-leading sister, Jordana.

Here was Kitty breaking up with Ari—a man with political convictions that made no sense to her—and pursuing a comparatively boring life on her own kibbutz. And here, finally, was Kitty meeting up with Ari again, and coming around to planning an exciting prison break. Here was Ari getting shot, and here was Kitty saving his life with some home surgery (finally a Jew who would let her operate!) thus winning the approval of the hard-line Jordana Ben Canaan. Kitty was falling back in love with Ari just in time for the British to leave Palestine and the State of Israel to be founded.

I had not given much thought to "nations" before. But a nation combined with Paul Newman was another thing entirely. Ari's hair goldened against the night sky of Palestine—now Israel!—and I put my arm around Stephen's torso and hugged him.

2 p.m.

"This is Jordana, she's a Marxist!" I shouted at one of the midday nurses when she poked her head into the room. She ignored me the way you ignore a crazy person on Lexington Avenue. She glanced at the beeping monitors, took a hasty note & left.

This hospital, if you can believe it, doesn't even have cable. No Food Network, no Turner Classic Movies. It's like the Soviet Union. I am limited to a roster of early morning shows, then The View, *then an afternoon dead zone of nothing, then Judge Judy & Ina Garten &* CSI *& god willing at that point I pass out.*

During the dead zone I am susceptible to whatever mishegas *the bird has on offer. Today it was that book again.*

> *Chiasma felt Litotes hit the Idle switch. The ship exhaled, nuzzling into the ground like a lion cozying after eating an entire antelope. Then Litotes re-upped on the Torpor handle, and the ship's motor wound down to a distant grumble. This was terrible for the transmission and the sensors and the wiring and the ship's self-diagnostics. If they even were able to launch now they'd run out of gas halfway and have to stop at a way station—probably that decrepit one at Moon's half-perigee; the one with no windows or vents and the bathrooms that incubated that overly sweet zero-gravity smell—and this would have to all go down on Chiasma's launch report, too.*

> *But then, with barely a tremble registered in the body of the vehicle, the engine purred up, and the ship was rocking and seemed like it might lift. Little spheres of crystalline exhaust that had condensed with all the on-off idling rattled in the thrusters and were blown hard, down into the grit. Chiasma got those familiar little butterflies in her throat as she anticipated lift-off—*

Is this entire book just about lesbians trying to get a ship off the ground, I shouted.
No, *the bird said, poker-faced.* Later they're going to kill a bunch of people in a revolutionary uprising.
I did not care for where this story was going.

THE CHOSEN AUDIENCE

AFTER THE FILM WAS over, we stayed in our seats, winded with excitement over *Exodus*. Additionally, we were avoiding running into any neighbors who would identify us as occupants of the make-out row. We slumped against the red velvet cushions, turned toward each other like mirror fetuses.

"What did you think?"

"Uncle Abe said it was the greatest Jewish epic ever committed to film." Stephen wrapped one hand around a tucked-up knee.

"My uncle Jack said it 'glorified Jewish terrorism.' "

I actually didn't agree with or understand my uncle Jack's objection, even though I adored him because he gave us Mary Jane candies and took us to Coney Island. I didn't agree with my uncle Jack because there was something that set him apart from us. He was childless and busy all the time with people who were always mimeographing things, working together on making something happen, the contours of which I never understood, but which felt strange and urgent to them, I could tell. My parents told me he was "in the party," which they said while shaking their heads, like he was incorrigible, and I guess on some level he was. My uncle Jack was the secretary for the American Jewish Committee, and he and my mother had had an argument after they had seen the movie the previous year, about the fact that the AJC had come out strongly against the film as "Zionist propaganda."

But I mentioned my uncle Jack's take on the movie to Stephen because I didn't want to agree with Stephen's uncle Abe, and I hadn't heard any other objections I could recall. I was trying to have a debate, I suppose, maybe something along the lines of Stephen's own interests in politics and philosophy.

Why I was doing this I didn't even know. I guess there was something in the air, a *zeitgeist*, that had made us all feel at the time that it was urgent to know where people stood on the issue of this movie specifically.

"But," I continued, "I want to know what *you* thought."

"Well, I thought"—Stephen reached the palm of his hand out across the armrest and I tickled it with my fingernails. "*I* could go there."

"Go where?" I was not being coy. I genuinely needed to understand where he wanted to go and where it fit in with his "helping" plans. For all I knew he meant Cyprus. Or "refugee camps" in general.

"Israel. To work. An internship in public health. Or a residency with the Health Ministry? I heard they're looking for American doctors." He contracted his palm, closed his warm fingers around mine. "*We* could go there."

And suddenly I saw it—I could see us in my mind's eye in a filmic way again. And this movie was better than Ellen's Flatbush-can-go-fuck-itself move to Ardmore. It was even better than a pre-war classic six, this movie. In this movie, I would be wearing a khaki gauze blouse like Kitty, and Stephen—not so nice, after all; a junior colonialist with a shy smile—would be in a smart linen suit. We'd eat dinner on the terrace of the King David hotel.

As the white stone mouth of the Kings disgorged us into the honking and tumult of Flatbush Avenue, everything seemed sharper and more momentous. The chatter gargling out of popcorn-greased throats, the shuffling as people shook out their jackets and put them back on. The whoosh of hats being replaced onto heads. The stray *oy*s as moviegoers stretched their legs.

All of this was suddenly wonderful to me. Perhaps the rest of the theatergoers were there because they too had not managed to get advance sale tickets the first time around, when the movie opened in 1960. We were all, perhaps, an audience of latecomers, very latecomers, who had nodded and pretended while the rest of the world saw, and debated, and denounced, and devoted themselves to, and became possessed by *Exodus* fever. And we had all felt, separately, like schmucks—the only humans on earth who had not seen this film. But now suddenly, with the enormity and pomposity of Kings as our backdrop, and the enormity and pomposity of the film, we realized: Actually, we were not schmucks, *we* were the ones who had suffered. We were the ones who had experienced the shame of not knowing what the hell *The New York Times* meant by a "massive, overlong, episodic, involved and generally inconclusive 'cinemarama.'" We were the ones who had had to sit quietly during epic family screaming matches about whether we were pro or con "Jewish terrorism." We were the ones who had had to sit and suffer these debates in shameful silence, being sprayed by errant pellets of *kasha varnishkes* flying from the mouths of hotly contesting family members as they railed about this film for hours on end until the buckwheat went cold and the bow-tie noodles hardened and yellowed along their edges. With the closing score still ringing out from inside the theater's deeper reaches, I became possessed of a conviction: To hell with all the people who saw the movie the first time around. We, this evening's theatergoers, should embrace our identity as latecomers, for it was *we* who had longed for this film, we who had suffered for it, we who had nourished the dream of *Exodus* in our hearts for years. Really, it was *we*, I realized, who were the Chosen Audience. We who had been possessed by this movie to enter history.

Yes, *Exodus* had made me feel that I, Barbara Rosenberg née Horowitz, was a part of something much larger than me—but also something that was entirely *about me*. Something that had unrolled a carpet from ancient times to arrive at my feet in the present. And I wanted that something. Wanted it to the exclusion of any other consideration. In fact, if someone had asked me then, what about the Arabs who already lived there, I would, like Rhett Butler, have said, "Frankly, my dear, I don't give a damn." Well, the bird has told me my whole life I'm a bigot, and for all I know it'll put it on my headstone: *Barbara Rosenberg, An Ordinary Fascist.*

"I'll walk you," Stephen said, inclining his head in the direction of my apartment. He placed his hand in his trouser pocket, this time without the ribcage nudge. He was possessed of an unusual confidence.

Perhaps it was the hand job. Or the film. Or both.

I took his arm, fluttering my long beige fingernails up his biceps, and leaned against him. Walking like this, I felt a general love of men well up in me. Something that was not desire so much as a kind of mania for gender itself.

We headed down Flatbush in a tributary trickle of other

theatergoers who were heading deeper into Flatbush or toward the train. The sound-speckled air of the theater's immediate surround dwindled as we turned right on Beverly, where couples descended into the IRT station, its lettering lit up in soot-stained gold.

We still hadn't spoken about the proposal.

"And what do *you* think?" Stephen said, as we rounded Ocean Avenue.

"About what?"

Stephen shrugged mildly. "Any of it?"

We had arrived at the entryway to my parents' building. The red brick façade cluttered with fire escapes descended to a long tongue of chipped concrete that rolled out past a small collection of brick planters to the sidewalk. I could see my parents standing at our second-floor window, their faces like pink lollipops against the glass. Across the street, a nighttime Prospect Park clotted into prehistoric denseness, heads of trees elongated with shadow.

I considered this Israel proposition. We would be a couple. An *international* couple. A safari-gear-wearing couple. It was British. It was cinematic.

Stephen half sat against a planter. I stood, facing him.

"I think," I said, "that if we have a daughter, we should name her after *Exodus*."

I saw myself walking hand in hand with a little girl in a taffeta dress, visiting Flatbush from Manhattan, or Israel, or wherever. Running into neighbors in *schmattes* sitting out on stoops smoking and arguing. *Who's this little angel*, they'd cough out through smoke-damaged tracheas. *Kitty*, I would say, looking down imperiously at these Brooklyn-mired relics of my youth. *Kitty Fremont Rosenberg.*

6:15 p.m.

Today the fever has come down, & I guess they don't care much about to whom they release you, even the custody of a giant bird. You don't have to go home, as the saying goes, but you can't stay here.

On the FDR Drive, I started thinking about being driven on this highway with my parents when I was young. Sometimes we used to visit my aunt Pearl in the mental institution in Spring Valley or my uncle Sonny upstate in jail. My father would lecture us every time about how a portion of the FDR Drive had been built from concrete & brick chunks, piles of debris brought in after World War II, detritus of the Luftwaffe bombings of Bristol. My father considered himself knowledgeable about the underbelly of the highway because my parents had even gone with everyone else to East River Park to watch on the day the Navy ship carried these giant mounds of wreckage into the harbor. This was before most people had TV, so it was the closest some of them had come to seeing the war itself. The park was shoulder to shoulder, but my mother had been pregnant with me, & they had been able to get a front-row viewing. My father always said, crackling with pride, You were so big! Everyone just parted when they saw you coming through! Like my mother had been a battering ram he built out of his own semen to steer through throngs of onlookers. My mother would force a half-smile that was all grimace & say in a feathery *voice*, Well, and I stank too, from the morning sickness.

I don't think my mother had even wanted to go watch the ship come in, but my father was a bull who only cared about keeping up with the other bulls of the block, & everyone was going into the city. There's this one curve in the roadway as you rise up onto the skyway at Fifty-second Street, & when we'd go around it, my mother used to whisper over her shoulder to me in the backseat, "That's your curve," because the combination of me jostling in her stomach & the way my father gunned the accelerator too hard had caused my mother to vomit out the passenger side window. This was the beginning of her labor with me, but she wouldn't realize it until later that evening when her water broke.

For a long time I always felt a little nauseous myself, & guilty, when we would drive down the FDR. Even if we were nowhere near Fifty-second Street, I always felt responsible for "my curve" & for having made my mother sick. But somewhere along the way, the whole association began to fade. I think, for a time, I allowed myself to believe that Stephen & I had escaped my past—my mother's misery & my father's gorillic furors. The FDR wasn't the place where I made my mother vomit after all; it was the moat that kept non-Manhattanites flowing on the outer perimeter, & us—who had made it into the borough—safe inside.

Today, though, maybe because I was nauseous myself, I remembered how part of it was actually rubble. And as the sports dome of Asphalt Green & the graffitied retaining walls of the highway blurred by, I was struck by the ridiculousness of life. Here we were, me still with my hospital bracelet wilting on my wrist, & this hooligan of a bird, rumbling along the roadway my parents used to promenade our old Buick on, my father shouting about American power & my mother faking a smile.

I got the crazy idea to tell the bird about "my curve." Maybe I wanted to reminisce, for lack of any other conversation. After all it was the bird's family history too, much as we might both like to deny it. But the bird, noting me swallowing & getting ready to speak, flicked the car radio and an audiobook came on.

> Briefly Watford City turned to a golden palette of circular launch pads ringed round with mid-range hotels for the pilots and techs. Chiasma watched the ancient, automated sky train snaking above the tent towns sheltering under the elevated cement tracks. The ship tilted right over Watford Tor, then wheeled further, too hard, and stuttered. A squealing sound ripped through the ship, which hiccuped, leapt vertically, and began to drop. Chiasma was tossed to the floor. She clawed her fingers between the holes in the grate and pressed her cheek to the cold metal while the vehicle careened like a ride at a county fair.

I had been very close to falling asleep. The sun was beating through the window of the car, & I'd closed my *eyes. But then I realized, with a jolt of furious bewilderment, that yet again nothing had happened beyond these lesbians trying to launch a spaceship! I was filled with anger at the absolute travesty of story arc (or lack thereof), which (this lack thereof) seemed, in its structure, very "lesbian" to me. No goals, no raising a family. Circling the drain if you will. It defied all the rules of three-act structure. There was barely* one *act* here! *Achh, I grumbled. And just then I saw myself almost from above—saw myself as I really was in that moment—& actually had to burst out laughing. America had ascended on the shards of old Europe, & for what. For what? Here I, a dying woman squired around by a demonic bird in a Honda coupe, was being subjected to erotic gay Marxist science fiction as we drove down a loop of old Holocaust asphalt stitched onto the edge of Manhattan like a mitten clipped to a child's sleeve.*

What are you laughing about? *the bird asked.*

I could not even begin to explain the pathetic turn that both my life & history had taken.

No more story! *I shouted.*

Oh sorry. *The bird shrugged fake-innocently.* I thought you liked it as a kind of bedtime routine. You always fall asleep right away.

Well, it's not my bedtime! *Now I felt suspicious in addition to irritated.*

It was rush hour & traffic had slowed on the Drive. One of those beautiful ragged Manhattan sunsets had begun, clouds torn open in a deep pink sky like clots of fat bubbling to the top of a chicken soup. The bird was driving slowly, ignoring me while weaving in &

*out of other cars, wing over wing on the wheel,
a driverly paternalism patient to the point of
infuriating.*

*Every time the bird had to look slightly to the left
or the right to change lanes, it was turning its entire head
instead of just moving its eyes. There was a robotic edge
to the movement, & it was making me nervous. The
sunset was becoming a deeper & deeper pink, & the bird's
sunglasses—which it ordinarily wears, often even inside,
because the bird is always worrying about getting
migraines—sat unused on the Honda's dusty dashboard.
The bird wasn't blinking in the sun, or shielding its eyes,
although the sky over the East River had become a
pulsating bright magenta. Then, while I was studying its
face, a thin opaque film flicked down & quickly retracted
over the lens of the bird's eyes.*

*This for some reason was the final straw to me.
Honestly it was a relief. When I saw the eyelid, I just
felt myself stop the mental gymnastics of trying to
dance around everything that was happening, stop
trying to repress & normalize all of it. Who knows
why it was the eyelid that did it. So much had already
gone off the rails. But there was something about the
effect of seeing this bird eyelid, this milky wet curtain
that looked like an internal organ falling out of an
orifice it's not supposed to fall out of. It was like a
prolapse. The prolapse of a hellish, surreal underworld
into this one.*

Hello, doctor, it's Joan Rivers. I've got a prolapse.

What kind of a prolapse?

Well, doctor, the apocalyptic destruction of all my hopes & dreams has just *prolapsed* into reality. [Pointing at the audience.] Am I right? Am I right?

I know I've said that I felt worried for the bird, & it's true; at other moments I have felt worried for it & its well-being. But not at this moment. At this moment I was just overcome with the desire to free myself of the bird, to disassociate myself from it. Simply put, there was no way the bird could be a part of me.

I looked at the bird blinking its weird wet lid & said—(Actually, I want to preface this by saying that I didn't plan *to say this, these words just* came out of me. *I had what you might call a case of a* prolapsed unconscious. *My unconscious* prolapsed itself *into speech.) Anyway, I said—I am sorry, but I did say—* I didn't give birth to an ugly freak. You're the biggest mistake of my life.

I do regret saying this. I do. Sometimes when you're a mother you just get outside of yourself, & words & actions take on lives of their own.

The bird looked punched. It had that stillness it has always gotten when I've told it the truth along these lines. That way it has of just staring quietly & trying to unhear things. But the bird did hear it, and I guess on some level I really did mean it.

A surfeit of clarity swelled over my consciousness, & the next thing that happened was that, watching the white lines whip by on the road, I had this other unmistakable thought—*why wait to see what death is like!*—accompanied by an exhilarating desire to merge with the pavement. Why not kill myself. No more having to write an epic apology to a Marxist bird. No more lying helpless in bed, waiting for scraps of information from the outside world, which, because the bird's interface with the world is through the sad marginality of lesbianism, are always scraps of information I would have preferred never to know about in the first place.

One fling—I thought—& the increasingly unbalanced ratio of my real life to this degenerate coda would be halted in its tracks.

I have to say, I felt proud of myself as I took matters into my own hands, slipping my fingers into the handle & throwing my shoulder against the door, fully prepared to tumble out into the wind.

A thing I had not anticipated, however, was the pressure from the air as we moved through it. I got off a couple failed attempts of projectiling myself out the door before the bird glanced over, sighed, leaned across me & pulled the door shut. Then it secured all the locks with the push of a button on the driver's side. Instead of saying anything, or trying to comfort me in my moment of existential despair, the bird kept driving, looking straight ahead in total silence the rest of the way back to East Sixty-ninth Street. The bird parked the car illegally in the post office loading zone & ushered me in the back door of the building & upstairs, where I *immediately collapsed in bed. Moments later the bird was back with a green shake & a pill. Who even knew what this pill was. I didn't care. Maybe the bird would poison me & I'd just die. I swallowed it & sank into sleep.*

RIGHT BACK TO BROOKLYN

"SO WE'RE AT *EXODUS*, is what I was trying to say, and we're fooling around in the back row"—I had called Sugar to update her on my evening. *Exodus*, the marriage proposal, et cetera.

"During *Exodus*?"

"What's that supposed to mean." I moved the phone from one ear to the other and ashed into a saucer on our dining table. Charcoal flakes drifted onto faded pink and green roses.

"Nothing," Sugar said. "It's a little blasphemous don't you think? But it's good stuff. I'll mention it to Lenny for a bit we're working on."

Lenny Bruce, whom Sugar referred to by first name only, had been one of the first guests on *The Tonight Show* when Sugar had begun there. Maybe they had fucked; I often wondered, given how often she brought him up. Whatever the encounter was, it had started her on a path to realizing she needed to be au courant with politics in order to write good bits. Sugar wanted to pivot from Carson to *Saturday Night Live* (and eventually did), and so she began hanging out with more bohemians, experimenting with edgier material and perspectives for her sketch packets.

"Well it *is* kind of a sexy movie"—I ashed again—"once

you get past the Holocaust part." I was trying to earn Sugar's approval by being edgier, too—and was rewarded with a nasal snicker.

"So we're fooling around in the back row, and then, right after he, *you know*—"

"Uh-huh." I could hear the snap of a lighter.

"—he looks over and goes, *What. You wanna get married?*"

"So? Marry him." Sugar drew hard on her cigarette and exhaled. "What's the problem."

"The problem is, right before the movie, he announces—get this—*he* doesn't want to be a practicing physician after all. He wants to be a social worker with an MD! To work for the city, investigating insurance fraud for three dollars an hour."

"Well, on the bright side, you'll never get busted for insurance fraud."

This was a moment where Sugar could have acknowledged the real differences in our stations, the seriousness of the crossroads at which I stood. But instead, I heard she had calculated my realistic chances of ever actually changing my own station, noted the fact that Stephen had essentially committed to keeping us in place, and determined on my behalf that that was fine for me.

Meanwhile, we didn't name her Kitty. And maybe everything would have been better if we had. But something happened to Stephen after *Exodus*. He developed "tribal attachments." And we ended up naming our girl after a real *farbisine* Zionist, a horsey minor character instead of the WASPy heroine. Look how that turned out.

* * *

We didn't make it to Israel back then, either. After the movie, when Stephen first insisted we go. Well, to be precise, we *made it*—we were there for approximately twelve hours in 1967, long enough for me to write my parents a postcard from Ben Yehuda Street, telling them that Israel in the '60s was like Brooklyn in the '40s. Looking back, though, I actually don't know if I meant the 1940s or the 1840s. The Israelis were not modern at all. They had been infected with a daguerrotypism. They wore khaki colors and had fixed, solemn expressions as if waiting for a half-hour flash sequence to capture their important images.

This, in any case, was my very brief impression. That, and that Stephen had rented us a room with only a single bed, which was either a very high compliment or a very big *Fuck you*. But before I had a chance to work up a head of steam about our lodgings, the first planes screamed across the sky, and we were informed in a rush of broken English from our Ukrainian landlady that the war had begun. It took us a while to understand what she was saying, and in fact I think I didn't fully realize the seriousness of the situation until she came rushing at us with a broomstick, shooing us toward the door to the apartment, then locked it behind us. We took a taxi back to Ben Gurion, and a day after we'd arrived, we were right back to Brooklyn.

3:27 a.m.

I know I am sick & losing hope by the day.
Things I still want to do:

1) Walk in a spring rain
2) Play mah-jongg
3) Meet my friends for lunch
4) Eat real food
5) Be a mother (good or bad)
6) Be a grandmother (good)
7) Do my own shopping
8) Sit & eat at a table
9) Enjoy (?) holidays
10) Have flanken, chicken, matzoh ball soup, mushroom/barley, health salad, Orwashers challah
11) NOT WRITE THIS BOOK!

But what can I do.

LIKE WOLVES

SO IT STANDS TO reason that when we finally returned to Israel, in 1983—shortly after Blanchie died, after things fell apart with Sugar—I had my trepidations.

Though by 1983, Israel had entered not the twentieth, but the twenty-first century.

The Health Ministry had arranged for us to be put up in a small dwelling they erroneously referred to as a "townhouse." Really it was a squat little prefab cement square attached to three other such squares on the campus of Tel HaShomer Hospital in Ramat Gan, which we quickly realized was first and foremost the location of a major army base and only secondarily a hospital. Everything in Israel was something and also an army base. The wards at Tel HaShomer were white-domed bunkers scattered among arid fields. Everything was yolk-colored sand and scrub. I had imagined that the desert would be rolling and Sahara-like. But it was burnt and old looking, absorbing light.

Our townhouse was outfitted with terrazzo floors, Israel's ubiquitous flooring equivalent of parquet, and brown velour couches. To sleep on, we had cots instead of beds—folding metal cots that had been dragged from a storage area full of hundreds of these collapsed iron spiders, as I learned when I vociferously demanded a "real double bed" from the grounds manager, and was wordlessly taken to the door of yet another bunker. The manager unlocked the door, did a little ta-da with his hand in the air and walked off, leaving me staring at a mountain of single cot frames piled in the dark.

Still, the air conditioning was powerful, fueled by the hospital's fleet of generators that lived underground, emitting blasts of hot air through grates that peppered the dirt walkways between bunkers. The townhouses were their own outcropping at the perimeter of the wards, surrounded by scrubland and across from an unused cracked clay tennis court. There was nothing else nearby, and the rest of the townhouses were unoccupied for the entirety of our stay. For amenities, we had to walk twenty minutes along a network of interior roads past the bunker-wards to get to an area that wasn't a town but more like a military commissary complete with a bus stop, a small bank branch, a supermarket, and a stall selling candy, gum, and newspapers.

In the back, the houses overlooked the scrub, and beyond that, the highway to Jerusalem. Yellow headlights rose through the hills all night in a constant biblical trickle. Sometimes the scrub would catch fire and release curls of smoke. I knew nothing about wildfires, and so it was like watching a painting of a wildfire on the frontier prairie of yesteryear. I didn't know whether we were supposed to be concerned, so I wasn't particularly. *Aysh!* I would announce, a little excited, ducking back inside the townhouse, like a child triumphantly translating an index card with a drawing of fire on it. I enjoyed using Hebrew words for things, as it made me feel very of-the-land. I used Hebrew for the strange diminutive Israeli appliances, the cans of olives and pickles that accompanied all meals, and the fires, which drove out the large black iguanas that ordinarily scuttled amid the underbrush. When the desert burned, the iguanas would lumber up the stucco walls to the roof, where they looked out over the landscape like wolves.

None of this sounds very twenty-first century, I know. But there was something about the combination of warlike backwardness and the neon busyness of Dizengoff Street in downtown Tel Aviv that was ahead of its time. America didn't reach this schizophrenic situation until after 2001, when we drank black smoke from the burning rubble for months and the citizens of New York were given the gun of shopping with which to murder terrorists. Bloomingdale's was a weapon in a holy war in 2001, but in Israel you could do that in 1983, with Dizengoff all lit up like a carnival, soldiers choosing from fifteen different flavors of frozen yogurt with their guns slung over their shoulders, laughing in the heat.

I tried to forget about Sugar and what happened. I tried to forget about a lot of things.

For the first few weeks we were there, Sugar sent postcards to me at the townhouse, none of which I responded to. She had gotten the divorce and moved into an apartment on Fifty-seventh Street, overlooking the horse carriages and the park. Neil had gone back to L.A. Sugar was dating a semi-famous dentist whose patients included Molly Ringwald. This boyfriend had a stereo system in his office and played Duran Duran while drilling and filling.

Sugar had found work in the writers' room on *The Edge of Night* and was excited to be writing a noir show. Sugar felt that she had been neglecting her skills at "serious narrative composition," she said, and *Edge* provided an opportunity for "dramatic expansion."

Barbara Rosenberg had disappeared abroad without a trace, opened Sugar's last postcard to me. She was trying to make me laugh, to minimize what had happened between us, our break in communication (the reasons for which I still don't want to talk about). But she was being cinematic, too, trying to flatter my cosmopolitan ambitions. Someone else might have regarded the postcard as an actually vulnerable, last-gasp attempt to get in touch. Not that she'd admit it, but clearly Sugar must have realized what happened between us, although I never mentioned it because I'm not that kind of a person. Anyway, she must have realized at this point and was probably scrambling to figure out how to make it right. And yet the barrage of postcards, and this one in particular, served to aggravate me further.

Because with every word she put to paper, I suspected Sugar was trying to kill two birds with one stone. Sure, she was expressing feelings, beseeching me, in a way. But really, she was experimenting with her writing. This last postcard's darkly comedic tone was a draft, for all I knew, for some scene that ended up on the cutting-room floor.

That said, in my time at Tel HaShomer, I did feel as if I'd disappeared without a trace. Israel was not anything like what I'd hoped. There were no glamorous drinks on the terrace of the King David Hotel with upper-echelon bureaucrats. No rumbling through the cobblestone streets of Jerusalem on the back of Paul Newman's motorcycle. It was just me and Stephen—who in his forties had begun to take on a potbelly that sagged roundly against his polo shirts—and my pre-teen daughter, permanently attached to her Walkman, warbling out the Madonna album from the back seat of rental cars or from her bedroom cot. Most days, Stephen worked in a nearby bunker on questions of epidemiological concern of which I was not apprised, as the iguanas marched from scrub to roof and the headlights paraded endlessly into the hills, and occasionally some part of the landscape would light on fire.

One afternoon at the bank, I left my daughter in the townhouse on her Walkman and walked into "town" to do my weekly exchange of dollars into zillions of shekels. There, I saw a mother and two children depositing money at the teller, dripping wet in their bathing suits. Nobody raised an eyebrow about this dripping and that was because no one in Israel had any concern for decorum. Bodily fitness was paramount, and so if you were Jewish and it was for the purpose of fitness, you were allowed to drip anywhere you wanted like a barbarian. I waited for the mother and children outside the bank, near the candy and gum kiosk, the sun pouring its golden heat on the small shops and bustling soldiers.

The mother spoke English, as most Israelis did, although when Israelis spoke English they spoke it with a hauteur and an intentional obnoxious intensification of their Israeli accent. They were being cheapened by their contact with diaspora, and so they drowned their words in tonality and mystique like it hurt their mouths to speak English. I asked the mother if there was someplace to swim nearby. The words sloughed out of her mouth like she was coughing up marbles; there was a community pool in Ramat Gan, she hacked, just beyond the border of the hospital grounds. It made no sense to me that no one had thought to tell us of this resource, but then again our only introduction to the immediate environs had been conducted by armed guards.

Later that day I walked my daughter through the immense heat, past dirt yards with occasional, for whatever reason, donkeys, to reach this secret oasis. After plodding through over a mile of sand-coated, largely deserted streets, we arrived at a throbbing playland of chaise lounges furled across Astroturf and a giant shimmering pool full of crystalline pale blue water. I had previously wondered why there were no children on the streets of Ramat Gan during the day, and had surmised something about the heat, or summer school. But no, it seemed the youths of Ramat Gan spent entire summers here, glued to their plastic-tubing chaise lounges, or lining up at the kiosk at the edge of the Astroturf for massive pitas stuffed with hummus and, as was their fashion, french fries, or attempting to drown one another in the pool. We began attending daily. The other children turned dark in the sun while Jordana snuck her chaise repeatedly into the shade to read. I would march over and yank at the corner of the chaise until my daughter disembarked so I could move the chaise back into the sun. *You look more beautiful with a tan,* I would say over my shoulder while yanking. I understand this is yet another thing that sounds cruel, but my daughter seemed to have no clue about the stakes of looks, and how things would pan out for her if she kept up her level of dis- (or strange) regard. I never felt like more of an animal than when instructing my daughter about the necessity of looking good. To my mind the question was literally one of life or death. As a woman, there are things you need to do, things to which my daughter was just frolicking through life oblivious. So yes, I was an animal, showing my wayward child where to forage for berries and roots. The situation was urgent. I conveyed this in throwing my weight against the resistance of the chaise lounge, scraping it with a cascade of sparks across the concrete and back into the sun with my daughter perched atop the whole time. On strict orders to tan, she would crisp and scowl in the torrential Mediterranean light, squinting miserably at her book. It actually amazed me that I still had such power over her at thirteen. Whereas when I was thirteen, I was drinking Harvey Wallbangers on dates with boys at Coney Island and puking in my parents' linen closet. But that was me, I guess.

When I wasn't schlepping chaises to and fro, I read magazines and was roundly ignored by the Israeli ladies who were busy swimming laps and organizing throngs of children. In the evenings, when Stephen returned from his day at work, we would travel as a family into the city—goggling from the bus at neighborhoods thick with Hasidim—to eat a new flavor of frozen yogurt every night.

We did this drill every day and night for four months until Stephen had completed—what? He said he was conducting a study of drinking water purity and infant mortality in different areas of Tel Aviv. But then, remember what I said about everything in Israel being something and also an army base. So what was his actual job I never knew. I had met Stephen's boss—an older woman who resembled Julia Child, with wide, Frankensteinian shoulders and a dollop of gray curls—only once. She took us to dinner at an outdoor restaurant in the slummiest area of Tel Aviv, where she was proud to introduce us to "Sabra cuisine," which excited Stephen very much, especially when we were served grilled turkey testicles, which were laid down at our table in a glistening wreath. There must have been twenty separate pairs of testicles, which Stephen gobbled down, following them with huge swigs of his Maccabee beer. His eyes gleamed with adventure. His boss was cordial but removed, uninterested in women without professional credentials.

That was another thing about Israel. Women were in high-ranking positions of power and had taken on the dry authority of men—even the beautiful ones, which Stephen's boss incidentally was not. The point, though, is that Israeli women seemed just as capable of emotionless murder as the men, and were practical, clipped, and condescending.

In fact, no one was nice to me in Israel. It was made very clear to me everywhere I turned that I had no status there. I was a hysteric, a yenta, a diasporic mess. But the thing was that, however punishing the adult Israelis were to me, the adolescents were many times more unrestrained in their feverish frontierism, and there was an aspect of this, I must admit, that I admired.

The Israelis loved Stephen. He was an athletic beacon of handsomeness. An American star, a success whose piddly New York dollars were worth zillions of shekels. He, actually, was the real Kitty Fremont. And the Israelis responded to him with reverence and the zealous will to assimilate him into their roving band. Jordana, however, they pounced on immediately as a dangerous aberration, no matter how tan I tried to get her. *Why are you wearing that—nobody wears that!* I overheard a muscular Israeli pre-teen shout at my daughter regarding her mannish polo shirt. By "nobody" he meant no girls wore that, which, hello, had been my point umpteen times. *They don't like your braces,* said another one, apropos of nothing—a gangly outcast boy who took himself to be doing my daughter a favor by cruelly informing her of what was wrong with her. *Maybe when you get them off the boys here will like you.* My daughter was a dog who had rolled in the wrong smell.

The Israeli children had a comment on every single aspect of my daughter's face, hair, body, and apparel, even her bronze jelly sandals, which I had bought for her and actually thought were chic.

Apparently not. The standards of beauty of the Israeli youth were even higher than mine, and I suppose I ought to have protected my daughter from this brutal hazing but to be honest it was a relief to have my convictions not just verified but glorified by an entire junta of Israeli pre-teens. The chief antagonist of my daughter's life had briefly shifted, and I found myself rooting for this throng of bullies. Without having noticed it, I had indeed found my own private *Exodus* myth. Where I had once thought the transition from the United States to Israel would be seamless—and maybe it is if you go directly from Ben Gurion to the Tel Aviv Hilton and spend your days drinking Coca-Cola with other tourists from Rockland County and Bergen County and Woodmere, Long Island—living there had clarified to me the immense disjunction between the Israelis and us.

However, this gulf, while it initially bewildered me, gradually came to infect me with desire. Israel was working its violent magic onscreen. *Remake my daughter,* I silently begged the adolescents of Ramat Gan, *in your own image.*

4 a.m.

Tonight I lost control of my bowels.

There are only twenty-nine steps from my bedroom to the kitchen, but I hadn't made it farther than the bathroom—which is just four steps from the bedroom door & eleven total steps from my bed—in weeks. In fact I had been en route to the bathroom when this event occurred. It was maybe six p.m. I had just woken up from—I want to stop calling these things "naps"; it wasn't a nap. It's more accurate to say that, multiple times a day, sleep grabs me like an angry flower & I put my head on its breast and die. Anyway, I had just woken up from one of these spells & was wobbling, slowly, toward the bathroom. I've gotten used to this routine, this circumscribed life. On some level you just do. Moving past each little nub of carpet is a world of effort. You see textures & details. You dwell on things. That indented rectangle on the carpet where Stephen used to rest the four feet of his briefcase every night. The black & pink blotch where Jordana ran by & spilled my cup of makeup brushes when she was young, grinding blush & mascara into the shag.

    I was crossing my hurdles—briefcase nubs, makeup bruise—& then, all of a sudden, I felt an urge. And as quickly as I felt the urge, I realized that there was no way to communicate anything whatsoever to my rectum about how to respond. The line of control had been snipped, & I could only watch in horror as my panties heated in a quick flood.

I had been quavering & weak before this happened, shimmying at the speed of a snail over the carpet, but once my panties filled with sloshy shit, a jolt of adrenaline ran through me. I needed, in that moment, to spare my child (whatever might be left of her inside the bird) this sight. But also, & maybe more importantly, in this moment of crisis, I needed to not need the bird & all its fake ministrations. Or, I needed it not to know that I needed it.

I ducked into my bathroom, stripped off the shit-filled panties, threw them in a plastic bag from under the sink, & wrapped a towel around my waist. From there, I headed for the kitchen & the washing machine.

The bird was standing in the living room, its wings folded, blocking my way.

What's this? *the bird interrogated without uncrossing its wings, pointing its elbow (?) at the bag I was holding.*

Move, *I whined, making brushing motions in the air with my free hand. It did not budge.*

Mooooove, *I mewled. Very childish tones were coming out of me. The bird glared at the bag. My scent rose up between us.*

Come on, *I pleaded. We were doing a dance, each of us hopping from foot to foot, as I tried to get around it & it tried to confront me.*

You're incontinent! *it fumed, as if I were doing this on purpose.*

I darted around the bird, shit-bag flapping, & made a beeline for the little washing machine stacked under the dryer in the dining nook. I popped open the lid &

tossed the plastic bag of shit panties inside. Then, grunting & heaving, I began my effort to dislodge this machine from its location & pilot it toward the kitchen. My arms were shaking with effort, & it seemed I was not strong enough. The little wheels stuck & jammed in the pile carpet.

Errrrgh! Arrrrgh! *I whelped.*

You need help, *the bird intoned from behind me. It didn't mean with the washing machine, it meant with my progress toward death.*

With my hip I began banging into the washer repeatedly like a deranged dancer conducting a macabre Lindy Hop, until lo & behold it nudged a bit, then a bit more, & I was able to pull it out from the wall, turn it, &, with a final series of Lindy-bumps, crest the inch of molding that separated the linoleum floor of the galley kitchen from the dining nook. The wheels landed with a short bang onto the comparatively slicker surface, & from there I was able to sort of rest my body on the washer & half walk, half ride the washing machine the ten feet across the galley kitchen & park it in front of the sink. Panting, I collapsed my upper body across the washer.

The bird had watched this entire display standing behind me with pursed beak & folded wings. Now that it was done squinting at my plight, it was back to yelling.

I can't do this! I can't do this alone! *Actually, it was shrieking in a very high-pitched way. It would not have enjoyed how feminine it seemed in its extremity. I comforted myself with this fact as it shrieked on.* We need help! *it shrieked.*

It meant a home health aide, a nurse. A hospice nurse. It was practically shoveling me into my grave.

I untangled the hose from the back of the washer & wrestled it onto the faucet, ignoring the bird. Turned the faucet on & opened the lid of the machine with one hand while reaching under the sink for the slim bottle of Woolite. The room was spinning. I righted myself effortfully, untwisted the panty-bag & began shaking the panties out. Comically, they resisted, having become mortared to the inside of the bag with my own shit. I shook them violently, beeping & caterwauling with frustration & strain. Finally the panties crawled down the side of the bag, like a Slinky meandering down a flight of stairs. Toward the end, the shit-filled panties built enough momentum to free themselves from the plastic bag & plopped into the machine. I tipped in a capful of Woolite & slammed the lid shut, then stepped with a shaking foot onto the garbage pail lever, tossing the bag in.

When I turned around, the bird was still looming in the narrow entry to the galley kitchen. With the drama of the panty-quest having ended, my legs were giving out. I leaned back against the machine & sank to the floor.

The bird used this not as an occasion to extend help, but to hop further into the kitchen & lord over me.

I'm going to call Jewish Family Services tomorrow. First thing. We don't have a choice.

Frankly the bird looked insane. Its marble eyes were wide & darting around. Its feathers were staticked in a million directions.

Maybe I deserved this. To have a lunatic bird judge

& belittle me while my panties burbled away in a shit bath conducted by a $150 piece-of-junk, tenement-style washing machine. The bird bent down, put its wings under my armpits and hauled me to my feet, then walk-dragged me back to my bedroom.

I don't care what you think. We're getting someone in here. *It was breathing hard, recovering from its scream-fest. Both of us were shaking—me from dying, it from lesbian fury & lack of life purpose. It got me back to my bed & kind of dumped me down onto it. Then made a little show of caring by placing the pilly yellow blanket over me.*

Okay? *it said, regarding what I had no idea; nothing was okay. It raked a wing through its feathers.* I need to take a shower, *it said.*

It *needed to take a shower? How about me? I was covered in shit. But apparently that was my problem. Or a problem for Jewish Family Services, which was going to come tomorrow—I could see that now—& wash & morphine me, & boom, I would be gone by the end of the week. That's how these things worked. I wasn't stupid.*

LIKE A WORN-OUT TEABAG

WHEN WE RETURNED TO the States six months later, Sugar called me occasionally. I didn't return these calls, and eventually she stopped calling. She knew what she'd done.

Meanwhile despite whatever gender policies had been drilled into her in Israel, my daughter's affair with the corduroy blazer resumed, unrelenting, and I was steeping myself in regret like a worn-out teabag.

Maybe, I began to consider, if we had brought my daughter up in the suburbs as Stephen had wanted, but which I had strenuously vetoed long ago, it would have been possible to steer her away from developing attachments to items of clothing that were not meant for her. But in Manhattan it is easier to escape the weather than to escape window shopping. My daughter had simply been exposed to too many blazers growing up, and it was not possible to shield her from developing certain louche desires. What was I supposed to do, walk this girl around the city with blinders on like a Central Park buggy horse? I should add that I never liked a corduroy blazer on Stephen either. I didn't marry a man with an MD so he could apparel himself like an editorial assistant at Doubleday. But fate has its way with us.

10 a.m.

That was not, however, how this thing ended up working.

I woke up expecting Nurse Ratched with a syringe full of morphine. Instead, I was alone, drenched & exhausted, practically fermenting into the linens.

In our entire forty-seven years on it, Stephen & I had never once replaced our mattress, & the formerly smallish impress my body created over the decades spent on my half, having deepened since my illness, now engulfed me with heat. I'd always thought we'd buy a brand-new mattress & a headboard. But here I was, game up, dying on a worn-down pallet on a bare metal frame ringed by a green gingham dust ruffle.

Stephen had long ago accepted (embraced?) that people of our station did not buy furniture more than once in their lives. When the mattress first started to sink, instead of replacing it, he slid a plywood board under the boxspring. I'd hated this bed for decades, but since Stephen's death have found myself sanctifying his half. Now the bed has an aspect of a pita, the heel of which is Stephen's unused area, which I do not disturb, slipping in & out of the pocket of blankets. Raw plywood peeks out along all four sides.

This morning I was even more delirious than usual. I knew I was in our bedroom, but I could not get a handle on *where* in time *I* was. The light had that Sunday morning 1970s quality—Second Avenue growling outside & bars of sun throbbing through the thick venetian blinds. On mornings like this my daughter used to play at the foot of our bed while we groggily woke into that sharp peculiar scent of a family: the animal musk of two mouth-breathing adults, the sweet synthetic lemon of Jean Naté After Bath Splash evaporating off the night-cooled flesh of my arms, my daughter's wet cornflake breath, & the smoky off-gas of the cracked rubber feet of her pajamas.

I could have sworn I saw my daughter's head peek up from the foot of the bed. *Jordana*, I said, waving my hand to summon her up to me the way I used to do. The head did not move. *Jordana*, I summoned again. I blinked & the head disappeared; a rumple of yellow blanket took its place.

Stephen, I said, turning to my left. Air was where his body should be, the sheets smooth & tucked.

I remembered then what year it was, & how bad things were. I was very thirsty. I called for the bird and no one came.

Later—

When I awoke again, I was on the floor.

I must have slipped off to sleep or overdosed. Who knows. Who the hell even cares. I was much worse off than before. More confused, hotter with fever. Very very weak. My stomach was a screaming knot of pain. Urgency of the bowel variety had returned.

Much as I did not want to request help from the bird, I also did not want to beshit myself & repeat the foibles of the night before, further solidifying the bird's conviction that it was time to euthanize me. I called again for the bird. The apartment thrummed with an ominous quiet in reply.

I rolled myself to the right, though my legs were so trembly I could barely get them to the edge of the bed. I snaked closer, then sort of dropped them off the side, hoping that I could use the momentum of my falling legs to pivot to a stand. But this was insane, given my condition. I see that now.

My legs descended—very quickly, as it turned out, because there's no muscle left to ease them to the ground—&, with a sickening lurch, I realized they were going to pull me along with them. A horrifying feeling, to experience the gravity of your body as a thing. I simply could not transform falling into standing. The physics of the situation were beyond me.

I made an effort to follow my legs with my torso to streamline the descent, but immediately began to flail & crumple. I grabbed for purchase on the dresser & my fingertips landed on my open notebook, which whizzed like a shuffleboard puck across the oiled mahogany surface, banging into the rotary phone, & together they flew toward the edge. The notebook, phone, & I fell in a series of thuds & clatters. I hit the floor on my knees, then bobbled like a dreidel at the wild end of a spin, landing sharply on my ass with my shoulders shoved up against the dresser, the rest of me splayed out like a discarded Raggedy Ann doll.

My arms were jelly, my legs were jelly. Even my hands were jelly. The only saving grace of the situation is that, whether from the event of the fall, or the sheer fact that I had already shit my entire brains out last night & hadn't eaten since, my guts at this point went into some kind of stasis & the intestinal pain abated.

I pulled the rotary phone to my side & dialed the bird. Perhaps it was simply ignoring me from its childhood bedroom. As was its wont.

"I'm on the floor." I dispensed with introductions or pleasantries. It knew who was calling it. I was unnerved to hear how thin my voice was—I sounded much more dying-er than I ever had.

"Mm-hmm," the bird said.

"I was trying to get to the bathroom & I fell. I can't get up."

I could hear the whir of traffic in the background. The sound of deceleration & the beeping alert of an engine going off.

"I need help," I whimpered. Where was this bird? Undoubtedly embarking on something sordid.

"Dr. Norman told you at one point that you would

deteriorate slowly over a period of time & then you would enter a 'rapid decline,'" the bird said after a long sadistic pause. *"This may be that."*

"Please," I whined. Who did this bird think it was, a medical doctor? Fuck it for deciding when it was time for me to die. *"I must have taken too much Oxy earlier this morning. Plus I didn't have my green shake. All I need is a hand."* I paused, made a concession. *"A wing."*

"Mm-hmm," the bird stalled. *"Mmm-hmmm."*

"Mmm-hmmm what."

"Jewish Family Services will be there by five," it finally said.

"No!" I shrieked. As I've said, the arrival of Jewish Family Services is the universal sign to an apartment building that the resident is dying. An entire machine rolls into action. First the doormen alert the management company. The management company starts salivating over the property value of your rent-controlled apartment. Then the doormen start scheming about how to abscond with your knock-off designer purses, & everything goes to hell. People are allowed upstairs without even alerting you—the doormen know you can't make it to the intercom anyway. Things disappear. I already explained what happens next. *"No Jewish Family Services!"* I screamed again.

The bird was silent. Then, in a very low, cold tone, *"They'll be there at five."*

"What time is it now?" I had not had my watch on when I fell & I could not reach the dresser top. I hated having to ask the bird questions, to accord it any authority whatsoever.

"It's"—it paused. *"Almost that."*

"Where are you? Just come get me." I was full-on begging.

"I'm far away," the bird said. Its refusal to elaborate was maddening. Why could it not just tell me where it was? It wasn't like I was in any position to hunt it down! Wherever it had gone, the fact remained that this bird—my child!—had simply woken up & abandoned me in my sad state. My mind boggled.

"I'm sorry, Mommy," it said. It had not called me Mommy in decades, & it didn't sound warm or familiar when it used this term now. It sounded like a dot matrix printer printing the word Mommy. Its voice was clinical & blank.

"It's fine," I said, convincing no one. "It'll be fine," I repeated, & hung up.

I lay there, foot-level with the furniture, the dust of our forty-year-old carpet a strange comfort in my nostrils. I dialed 411, then Jewish Family Services. I would cancel the morphine-givers myself.

"Ma'am, you authorized this morphine directly by phone earlier today," the sour nurse on duty informed me with the vacant air of a maître d' discussing a menu item.

"That wasn't me!" I shrieked. "That was the bird!"

The nurse sighed a deep, world-weary sigh, the sigh of a person who has become indifferent to the identical, delusional high jinks of women at the end of their lives. "Second-guessing is common. Trust me, you & your family will be relieved once JFS is there." What family? I felt very sad for myself, unbearably sad, actually. Phones rang & buzzed in the background. A symphony *of other dying Manhattan yentas.* "It's the close of the day," she graveled, "and I'm sending our nurses across the borough now." *She made it sound like a wartime armada of beneficent women in starched uniforms were fanning out to deliver hand jobs to soldiers in traction at some field hospital, when in reality squadrons of death-dealers were closing in on their unfortunate prey.*

I could, I contemplated, just die here, sucking in Stephen's and my forty years of ground-in carpet dust. Before JFS came. Before the doormen & the management company began glorying in my impending end, I could get a jump on the whole thing. But how? My Oxy was out of reach. Perhaps I could strangle myself with my own hands, had anyone ever tried that?

Unfortunately, my guts had begun to recover their motility & were making it clear that they needed to empty themselves come hell or high water. I became possessed of an idea. If I could make it to the bathroom, I could prove to JFS that I was capable of taking care of myself. It had all been one big misunderstanding, I was fine & they could go home. I began to crawl.

There was a lot to navigate to get from my bedside to the bathroom, I realized, as I dragged myself along the carpet, twisting & turning around the enormous mahogany bedroom set we had for some—what seemed to me now, insane—reason stuffed into this cookie-cutter post-war dollhouse of an apartment. How had I never noticed before what an absurd situation this was.

In addition to the large dresser across from the foot of the bed, Stephen's armoire squats hugely in the far corner. Another massive dresser, which serves also as a night table, looms over my side of the bed. Because it is considerably higher than the mattress, & because I am now so weak, I have to reach up & hook things like my ChapStick using an outstretched finger or a pen, pulling the item tentatively toward me & tipping it off the dresser like a cat poking trinkets off a ledge. I had not anticipated such a situation for myself when we inherited these hulking gargoyles from my parents, whose Flatbush rooms were pre-war sized.

In fact, on the day the movers paraded this furniture in like a string of giant circus animals, only Stephen was concerned. These are large, *he breathed*, as an elephant-sized armoire creaked past on a dolly. A procession of interlopers had arrived to mock the meagerness of our abode. But Stephen & I had been using cardboard dressers from Kmart, so I saw this as a major improvement. *No one bought furniture back then. No one I grew up with anyway.* They're solid wood, *I said*, possessed of the belief that the room would somehow grow, like a womb, to accommodate its new occupants.

I was wheezing & perspiring like a pig as I rounded the bed corner & snaked down the runway between the bed and the dresser. When Stephen had been alive, he had had to turn to the side and crab-walk down the passage between the Scylla of the bed's foot & the Charybdis of the dresser to arrive at his armoire. When I first became ill, I would wobble to the bathroom, stabilizing myself with one hand on the foot of the bed & one hand on the edge of the dresser, like a set of gymnast's parallel *bars, & shuffle through. But today I was crawling, inching & huffing like an elderly Taliban at boot camp.*

At the end of the runway I paused, in the carpet, trying to catch my breath, which was not really catching. I sounded like a lottery machine rattling Powerballs around. When I exhaled, it was like a whale breaking the surface of water, a ragged whoosh. The bathroom was what I knew to be eight steps away in ordinary times, but I was beginning to doubt my ability to make it. I got no farther than the dressing table chair. What poetic justice. This chair on which the bird sits & reads & sends sex emails to whomever. Flattering itself that it is "keeping me company."

Part III:

Vogelfrei

Afternoon—

One glimpse of Sugar standing in her Burberry trench in the doorway of my bedroom emitting the scent of Diorella perfume (which to me has always smelled like candied violets mixed with the coffee breath of a handsome man), & it all unraveled before me like a film running backward.

At some point in the distant past Sugar Becker had been born Jewish.

That's what I thought when I came to and saw her, like an apparition in my room.

It would have made a great opening line for a novel, but unlike certain people I'm not writing a novel.

The second thought I had was that I was no longer lying face down on the carpet, my nose mashed against one of those little plastic carpet protectors that cradled the foot of my dressing chair. I had no idea how I had removed myself from that situation, but I was now sitting on the floor with my back against the bed frame, the plywood edge digging into my spine.

I set this unnerving lapse aside. What was Sugar doing here, after so many decades?

Thanks to my time working at Zilch's, I could reconstruct at a glance what had happened to her face. I had a gift for this kind of discernment, & in fact had saved many of my friends money over the years by doing ad hoc phone consultations regarding their plastic surgery needs, that's how good I was. And yes, it did *gall me that I possessed all the elements of a profession, yet lacked the accreditations & the technical training, which had never been an option for the likes of me, while Zilch, one of a slew of middle (to lower) strata Manhattan plastic surgeons, slept on a pile of money at his Sutton Place apartment.*

The whole megillah must have begun with the nose job. Severe thinning of Sugar's nose produced something that had length but not width. This much I remembered from the last time I had seen her. The rest required the reconstructive precision of a noir detective, which, as regards the world of aesthetic enhancement, I am. Things had clearly gone haywire from the nose. The thinning itself may have inspired cheek implants in the hopes of balancing out the pencil-like result of the nose, but the top-heaviness that the implants contributed to the face must have served to accentuate the (what quickly became apparent) nonexistent chin, and chin reconstruction would have become at some point the obvious next step. Most people would opt for lip injections to infuse fullness into this landscape & yet for reasons unknown she had left her lips inchworm narrow, so that once her chin was lengthened, her lips and nose looked now even more out of proportion to the overall situation of her face, which was increasing in the vertical direction as it decreased in orifice size. An eye tuck had dragged the ocular area up & back, but this tends to create a walleyed effect, which, when it occurs, can only be counteracted by time & a little snippy reverse procedure to give a little motility back into the skin. But that is evidently not what Sugar had elected to do. Judging from the whole situation, she must have been administered an ill-advised neck suck instead. This had heightened the strangeness of the entire vista of her face, which now poked out from the neck in an unnatural layering effect, like an actor filmed against a green screen.

It's not the nicest thing to say, I guess, but I was relieved that the years (and the doctors) had not been kind to her.

We're looking at each other in total silence, & then Sugar goes: What.

That's her opening gambit. After thirty years, on encountering me collapsed on the floor of my own bedroom. This is what she says to me. What.

Frankly I had to respect it. I had seen some yenta high dudgeon over the years. God knows I had delivered some high dudgeon. But this offhand what *from Sugar had to be the highest.*

I think you know what, *I said.*

Ech, Barbara. It was such a long time ago.

Sugar twirled the sash of her trench coat, pantomiming the lightness with which I ought to apprehend the accumulated weight of history. As if time had ever really healed a wound between friends.

You want to at least attempt an apology. *I omitted any hint of a questioning lilt.*

You want *me* to apologize? *Sugar poked a thumb at her sternum.* Barbara, please. With yentas, as you well know, there's no defense, only offense.

She unshouldered her trench & draped it over the back of my dressing table chair. I could see that she had lined her Burberry with an old mink. *This was what they all did now that mink put a target on your back for paint-wielding PETA loons.*

Who called you, *I said.* Was it the bird.

She squinted. You called me.

I most certainly did not. *But when I looked down, I saw that the phone receiver was in my hand.*

The empty dial tone blared through it. I dropped the receiver, & the cord recoiled along the floor, dragging the handset back to its base.

You were barely coherent, ranting something about Jewish Family Services & how I had to come get you.

I tried to process this information. Sugar would have me believe that, in an OxyContin haze, I had crawled all the way back to the phone, undoing the progress I had made toward the bathroom, dialed a number from memory that I had not dialed in decades, & then dragged myself again to the dressing table, there to await my salvation in the person of Sugar Becker?

Who said that thing about yentas, *I said, changing the topic.*

What thing.

"Only offense."

You said that! The time your mother caught us playing hooky from school. We were going to sneak into a matinee of *Raisin in the Sun*, we had just run out the doors of the school, down the street, into the subway, & voilà, the first person we see is your mother. We see her before she sees us, & you say, in my ear, Don't make excuses, don't apologize. With yentas there's no defense, only offense.

I don't remember. *I sort of shrugged. What actually happened was that I tried to shrug but could only get my shoulders to flinch against the bed frame. I should point out that I was still propped in a puddle of my own legs between the bed & the dressing table while Sugar remained in the doorway. It occurred to me that she might be afraid to come closer.*

You said she'd never make a scene in public, so we should go right up to her & before she even got a chance to interrogate us, we interrogate her. Ask her what the hell she's doing on the IRT in Manhattan during the middle of the day.

How did that go, *I laughed, & realized with immense sadness that I could not remember the last time laughter had bubbled up in me in that particular effortless way.*

Not well. She had come from Barney Greengrass with a smoked sturgeon for the High Holidays, which made us feel pretty guilty. And when you got home she grounded you for a month. But we did have a very peaceful IRT ride, so you were right about that.

Sugar took in a large breath—I could see she was steeling herself, & it did make me wonder just how fucked up I looked—then she blew it out & grapevined elegantly around the edge of the dressing table like she was in a slow-motion aerobics class.

My daughter's a bird and it's trying to kill me, *I blurted as Sugar bent down & put her hands under my armpits. I hadn't planned to say anything about this, but as Sugar came closer, my mouth and mind betrayed me. I could feel my body succumb to reality as words slipped out of me like a shit I didn't mean to take, & I threw appearances to the wind.*

Most of them do, *she groaned, meaning "children"—completely ignoring the bird part—& heaving my torso face down onto the bed.*

Sugar farted a little from the effort of picking me up, a dry little toot underscoring her groan. We did not comment on it. I began worming myself the rest of the way up the bed, trying to wriggle under the blankets, but soon realized I wasn't making any forward progress. I turned. Sugar had a fistful of my nightie in her hand, reining me back.

Barbara, *she said in the gentlest voice I'd ever heard from her or any yenta.* I think we should get you in the bath first.

I could smell it too. But I had hoped perhaps my own proximity to me meant that I was privately experiencing the potpourri waft of dried human shit. How I wanted to just crawl into my own bed & sleep, shit & all, but Sugar had the upper hand, so to speak, & was preventing me from moving any further & thus soiling the sheets. She had a point. And yet, as I reviewed the geometry of getting into the bath—not to mention lying there when it was done, buck naked, with my arms outstretched, waiting for Sugar Becker to raise me like an infant from the tub—I realized it was too much. Even if we could manage to get me in, Sugar would certainly be unable, even if my waning shred of propriety would allow such a thing, to get me out of it.

I can't make it, *I said, knowing in that moment what the next step on this flowchart would be. I had crossed yet another existential threshold.*

There's a bucket, *I sighed,* under the sink in the kitchen. And washcloths in the linen closet in the hallway.

We made quite the pair. Sugar reappeared a few minutes later, listing heavily to one side against the weight of the full bucket in her hand like a Minsk peasant schlepping well water. I was still on my stomach, half on, half off the bed, like a whore waiting to get fucked. Sugar set the bucket down on the carpet, then plopped her pocketbook by the foot. It was a Bottega Veneta Hobo Bag in dark burgundy leather, soft & wrinkly like an over-stewed prune. Okay, Barbara, *she said, & I put my head down on the sheets & closed my eyes, trying to pretend this wasn't happening as Sugar lifted my nightie & folded the hem onto my lower back.*

The first thing I felt was heat. A wonderful wet heat across the backs of my thighs. Almost immediately, the bright scent of rosewater body wash came into contact with the agricultural pungency of dried shit & filled the air with a skirmish of odors. I balled the sheet around my nose so I wouldn't have to experience the indignity, but I could not fully block it out. Sugar splashed the washcloth over & over into the bucket, & finally the air cleared of shit. Just roses predominated & I relaxed a little, melting into the bed with what I must frankly say was the startlingly animal pleasure of being bathed.

Sugar was so painterly. She washed me in long, slow strokes, careful, soft & firm. It did unnerve me that Sugar felt licensed to just go ahead & caress me after not seeing each other for decades. But what unnerved me more was how desperate my own body was. I think I might have emitted a moan. Not in a sexual way! I'm just saying it was nice to be touched. Never in my life had I imagined Sugar Becker bathing my naked ass, but frankly it was sublime.

I'm in an urgent situation of impending murder, *I found myself growling into the sheet, probably to avoid murmuring "This feels so good."*

Being impendingly murdered is what it means to be a mother. *Sugar said, standing. Next a big towel wrapped my legs from behind & Sugar was rubbing, the friction creating a new layer of delicious heat.*

What would you know, *I said,* you have sons. *I was practically crying from the joy of being touched, being cleaned.*

I wanted to say, You have sons, not birds, *but I barely had the wherewithal to say anything. Also, I could see that Sugar was going to pretend she either didn't hear it or I didn't say it. Well just wait till she saw this bird.*

Sugar removed the towel from my legs & began shimmying a pair of lounge pants up them.

Sons shmons, *she tossed off blithely. Sugar refused to understand the gravity of the situation, & moreover was going to keep issuing abstract sayings about parenting for whatever reason. Maybe she was writing a parenting book. My lounge pants had reached my waist, & Sugar gave my ass a little "All done!" slap. I shimmied up the bed & this time—washed & floral— I was permitted to move freely. I rolled over, sliding my legs under the sheet. Sugar sat down at the edge & pulled the pilly yellow blanket up, smoothing it over my shins.*

Meanwhile, at this point Sugar could have confessed that one of her sons was a gambler who worked at Legoland & the other was now a Jehovah's Witness living in Kansas City. It's not as bad as a bird, but it's not great. I knew about Sugar's children's fall from grace because once I asked the bird to help me google Sugar's children & the results had been very satisfying indeed. In fact, I would say that the bird & I had kind of a fun time that night. Anyway, it would have been fair for Sugar to divulge her own details of dreams dashed, as there can be no trust between old friends without mutually confessing the indignities that our lives had been dealt.

Humiliation & regret washed over me, & I searched for something else to say, to pretend that none of what had just happened had happened. As if we had been at Le Pain Quotidien this entire time eating poached eggs.

Though honestly, Sugar said, I think my boys will let me rot when it's my time.

So Sugar was going to trade indignities. I pulled my hand out from under the covers & patted Sugar's hand, which was in the middle of patting my leg. It was like that child's game of hot hands, where one kid tries to slip their hand from under the other's, each kid whipping their hand out & slapping it on top of their friend's. Our play of sympathies had taken a new twist, I realized as I patted. Poor Sugar, *I made my hand convey to her hand. Now we were getting somewhere.*

No they won't, *I lied. Meanwhile, I could tell from the google search results that her boys were more or less letting her rot right now.*

There was a light knock at the door. JFS liked to knock so low that you couldn't even hear it. This way they didn't have to wait for you to stagger to the door. So they tapped like little mice & then barreled right in like bulls, claiming you didn't hear their knock.

That's them! *I shrieked.*

Who them?

Jewish Family Services. Like I told you, it's part of the bird's murder plan. Please, Sugar, go out there & tell them it was all a big mistake. And say you're an immediate family member, otherwise they won't listen.

Sugar tossed her head back in that way she used to do when she was expressing hauteur. It worked back then. Now, though, it made the tendons bulge in her freckled neck. Barbara, *she said,* I was born for this.

Sugar stood from the bed & left the room. Next I heard her speaking to the nurse in a hushed voice— a voice which I knew she knew would be inaudible to me. This I did not appreciate, & it began to concern me the longer it went on. Sugar & the nurse were having quite the extended conversation.

Sugar's voice was nasal & pinched, a constant electrical whine. All she needed to do was say, I'm the sister, I'm here, & I'm handling it, then send JFS on their way. What was taking so long? I wondered if she was really doing what I had told her to do or if she had in actual fact been summoned by the bird & was in cahoots. For all I knew Sugar was a double agent.

Pieces began falling into place. I could imagine a scenario—not impossible!—in which Sugar & the bird had found me unconscious on the floor & staged the whole thing, placing the phone receiver in my hand where I would find it, like a planted gun, when I awoke. A horrifying twist. Cold overcame me & I began shivering.

I heard the door open & close & the locks clicking.
Don't worry, Barbara, *Sugar said as she breezed in,* she'll be back.
Who? *I asked, my chest tightening.*
Sugar patted my hand and gave me an odd smile. She was back to having her hand on top. This could only mean that indeed the JFS nurse had left to gather supplies and a stretcher for god's sake, to schlep my morphined-unto-death body out the door & down the hall & down the freight elevator & out the back door of the building & into some nondescript van. A mad bird would conduct my funeral.
Sugar was patting my hand an overly long time. It seemed like a goodbye pat & a victory pat & the hint of being on the verge of physically restraining me should things come to it, all in one. Her hand was kind of massaging my hand while it patted. Then the patting and massaging stopped & turned into a warm but very firm clasp.
This was it. The end was nigh; it was presaged in the now undeniable transformation of Sugar's pat into a balmy embargo on movement.
You lied to me! *I yelled, pulling my hand free. It was wet with our combined perspiration.* You're going to let them do it!
Do what? *Sugar looked genuinely confused.*
The JFS nurse. She's coming back to kill me!

For god's sake, she's bringing a bedpan and diapers! *Sugar smiled a strange impish smile, her lips pressing into a little duck bill in one corner.* I told her I was in charge now & that you were my wife.

You what, *I choked out.*

If I'm going to act, I want to really *act,* you know. *She said this with a British trill.*

I gave a stunned cough. Well when the bird returns I'll have to deal with this whole murder situation all over again, *I grumbled, trying to compose myself.*

Sugar waved me away. Clearly, Sugar was as repressed about the bird as I once had been. And why not. I flashed on a memory of visiting Sugar and Neil in Laurel Canyon when the kids were small. Sugar's boy Timmy, all of three, standing in the open doorway, stubby in his overalls & bare feet, saying "Come in, make yourself comfortable," to my daughter, sweeping his arm like a small earl. Right then & there I could see them developing a lifetime of sweet memories, kisses, dating, getting married. But instead Timothy became a Kansas City nutcase, & I got a Marxist bird. In the end, all Sugar & I had ever really had in terms of parental naches *were a couple brief moments when we had stood in delighted awe at the gallantry of toddlers.*

All it does is sit in that chair glowering & planning. *I gestured toward my dressing table chair. Then I had the sudden thought that if Sugar hid in the closet, she could tiptoe out at an opportune moment when the bird was deep in texting & tie its wings to the armrests.*

Is it there right now? *Sugar asked, absurdly.*

Don't be ridiculous! I'm just saying that, when it is there, it lords over me in a creepy silent way.

She was always kind of quiet, the way Stephen was quiet, *Sugar offered, sort of changing the subject. It did give me a little enjoyment to know that Stephen was still her point of reference for stoic masculinity. Let her yearn. Wait till I told her he had had a thick fluffy head of hair until the day he died.*

Most men, except the gay ones, spend their entire lives in a fog of things unsaid, *Sugar went on,* so why I couldn't find one such fog-bound man I have no idea. You were lucky.

I could see she was winding up to go on her own rant about something or other.

I don't know anymore what lucky is, *I said. I reached up & waved around for the warm glass of seltzer on the dresser. Sugar leaned in & handed it to me, the straw bobbling weakly against the rim.*

Lucky, let me tell you, is avoiding a talky man.

I really needed us to extrapolate an approach to the bird's return, but between the stupefying bed bath & the stressful events of the JFS nurse's visit, a heavy exhaustion had begun to set in, & I could see that I was submitting to Sugar's pivot to monologue whether I liked it or not.

You never met Mark—*Sugar looked at me pointedly.*

I did not say, "Yes Sugar I know that I never met him because I had stopped speaking to you." *Instead, I said,* What, *and managed to sleepily raise one eyebrow with a slight cock of my head. I could still* what *with the best of them.*

But he ended up being talky too, *she pushed on.*

I had not asked her to account for the missing years,

& it did bother me that she felt she could just supply these details without comment, as if we had lost touch for no reason at all.

At first I thought he was the opposite of Neil. A quiet, hirsute capitalist. I was intrigued by the whole boring scene of his life. There was something about the DDS after his name, & the lab coat, & the 9–5 that made me very amenable. Every time I saw him he had just come from handling another urgent dental happening, which he loved to recount in some detail. Mark seemed like an adult, is what I'm saying, after Neil & his Hollywood parties & his Marxism. I had never realized the importance of teeth. *The gateway to the soul*, Mark liked to say, which was not a good line & maybe I should have paid more attention to his lack of rhetorical skills, but again, the DDS, & his Audi, & his utter normalcy had drawn me in. The next thing you know I'm installed in his Sag Harbor shiplap contemporary, the kids are in public school, & Mark's working in the city during the week. He commuted out to us on the weekends. It was great. I had time to myself during the school days. I started writing novels.

I saw.

Some of them did good.

Mmmm, *I said, deliberately noncommittally, though some of them were indeed good.*

But then Mark came out for the whole of August that first summer & oy. Without his dentisting he was an empty cup. Sitting there all day, desperately hoping to be filled up by our goings-on. Every time I turned around, there he was, blank as a page. At least Neil had opinions about something other than teeth.

Don't tell me you miss the Marxist.

One day a year, yes I do. I permit myself to miss him on May Day.

I had a hard time imagining Sugar parading in Neil's honor, swarming down Fifth Avenue with all the other sad sacks carrying banners & shouting.

May Day! And how do you observe?

I go to the Lower East Side & buy a coat on sale, *Sugar said, without missing a beat.*

On all other days I pay full price, but on this day I pay wholesale, *I managed back.*

Sugar laughed while reaching a hand behind her. She slowly pulled a notebook from her purse. Did she think, in addition to dying, that I was blind too? After everything, she was doing it again, & right in front of me. Time paused. There was a moment of dead air in which things I wanted to—but couldn't—say poured through my brain.

It all flooded back to me. That night at The Ginger Man. The way Stephen & I had sighed with relief as Sugar and Neil's taxi joined the clamor of taillights heading down Broadway. And then the hostess calling to us from the entrance.

"Your friend." *She pointed to the sidewalk at a small dark shape I couldn't make out.* "Dropped something."

She leaned out of the doorway, holding the sill with one hand like a trapeze artist, & stretched toward the object, plucking it from the ground. I walked toward her.

The hostess was holding out Sugar's notebook toward me. It must have fallen from her bag when she was rifling through. I took it & slipped it into my own.

Later that night, by the time I'd applied my creams, changed into my nightgown & come to bed, Stephen had fallen asleep with his paperback filleted open on his chest. I was about to start my crossword when I remembered the notebook. I felt a strange combination of compulsion to read it & inexplicable trepidation. Like I said, it's easier to imagine living with a husband after discovering his secret life than it is to imagine going on with a friendship after a betrayal.

I still have the notebook. It's in my dresser drawer, right under my pile of panties. Why I even saved it I don't know. Once in a while, I guess, I'll take it out when I feel myself slipping back into the desire to call her, & read it again just to remind myself that I haven't invented the whole thing. There's no need to, though. I've memorized the page.

If found, please return to:

Sugar Becker
4775 Laurel Canyon Boulevard
Los Angeles, CA

CHARACTER STUDY:
FAWN DUSHOTSKY (aka Barbara)

- Neighborhood Jew

- "Thwarted potential"

- Fawn's demeanor as she ages: tight and disappointed.

- She tries to mask it with a calcified smile, which only has the opposite effect.

- It's envy—or, more precisely, the poisonous grain of an unadmitted sadness: the rigidity of someone who has reconciled herself, without being reconciled at all, to shifting the mental category in which her dreams have lived from the aspirational to the purely fantastical.

- Fawn has encased herself in a private mythos in which she can perpetually visit and water her now-fantastical dreams. She has grown a glass membrane between herself and the world.

- From afar, one might be forgiven for thinking Fawn Dushotsky has something of Barbra Streisand in her, specifically the nose. And yet, while her nose may be Streisand-esque, the overall effect is not as Streisand-esque as one might hope.

- *Rather, it is as if Barbra Streisand had been tragically prevented from becoming the star that she was meant to be, and is consigned to starring only on the stage of a small rent-controlled apartment overlooking an exhaust shaft.*

- *Or, it's as if someone has taken Streisand and wiped that peaceful expression of a multimillionaire living her dream off her face and replaced it with an undertone of unquenchable frustration and white-hot rage. <u>Fawn Dushotsky is Barbra Streisand if Barbra Streisand were played in a movie of Barbra Streisand's life by Joan Crawford.</u>*

That, for me, was the end. All along I had thought Sugar & I were each other's secret voices—each other's Belle Barth. Until I opened her notebook & realized that actually it was just me.
I was Sugar's secret voice. I was her material.

And now here she was, picking me up off the floor, washing my ass, sitting at the end of my bed as if none of it had ever happened, chatting to me about bargain hunting.
You deign to shop on the Lower East Side?
Well it's very different now, *Sugar said surprisingly defensively.* Very hip. Haven't you been?
Not since—*I stopped myself.* I'm very tired, *I said.*
Of course.
Sugar capped her pen & ratcheted to stand. As she bent over the bed gathering her things, I saw that, with age, she had developed a projecting vulture neck & accompanying hump that swelled under her cashmere sweater like a hillock. Sugar had married another man after Mark, a publishing mogul named Howard who eventually left her for a cantor at Wilshire Boulevard Temple who had a Dorothy Hamill–style bob & about whom no one could understand the appeal. I saw now that Sugar—frail as a baby giraffe, all bones & neck, swaying slightly as she placed her items in her big soft expensive purse—was not going to have any further husbands.
I brought some matzoh ball soup from Bernstein's, *Sugar said. She went into the kitchen. Almost immediately I drifted into a half-sleep through which I*

heard beeping that felt as far away to me as if it were in a movie of someone using a microwave.

Next thing I knew I was smelling the dirty dishwater scent of hot chicken soup & Sugar was placing a bowl next to me on my dresser. I'll come back tomorrow. *She peered at me, petting the back of my hand through the yellow blanket so lightly it almost tickled. Her nails traced a thin line down the ridge between the tendons of my own, massaging in a sort of absent way, the way you might when you touch your own child. I supposed that was what illness did, too—flay you open to your friends like a newborn.*

As I started down the ramp of sleep, I could feel my mind begin to unravel, like a piece of knitting being pulled out to correct a slipped stitch. What a day of learning things I never wanted to know! Such as the odd and unnatural feeling of being touched by a woman. The touch of a woman felt so familiar that it made my stomach turn & I found myself wondering, I guess for the first time, how the bird stood it, let alone had sought it out for all these years. And if this was how unnerving it felt to be touched by the fingernail of another woman, what would it be like to kiss one? Nauseating surely. It had to be. Sugar's skin was so soft, so much like my own.

But then again maybe after a while with women, kissing men would feel unnatural, like kissing a stucco wall or an old shoe.

The Morning—

These days I lie in bed for a long time before I get up. And I wake up with this drained feeling in my limbs, like a wet piece of paper that's melted into the bed. I don't know how to explain this. My body is trying to become something else.

    Sometimes when they're exploding out the tunnel underneath the transformer station on the corner, I imagine how deep into the rock they're drilling, how far down, & it seems so peaceful.

    I guess when I say "sometimes" I mean times when I am high as a kite on OxyContin, which is most times, but sometimes higher than others. And I know when I'm really high because the drilling won't bother me then. I imagine the cold dark dirt & I find myself thinking: What would it take to get out of this bed, down the hall, down the elevator, out the back door, sneak into the construction site, lie down & just bury myself. It's terrible what happens to minds left all to themselves. Then I turn on the Food Network & try to remember about eating & get reinvested in life. But my efforts lack oomph.

When I heard Sugar opening the door I understood the doormen must have given her keys. I hadn't thought about this before. I see now that everyone is starting to arrange things without consulting me. I don't like this feeling. And it makes me think maybe my dirt daydreams are just that—fantasies. As if dying could be as easy as going downstairs & lying in the dirt.

Instead I am going to have to suffer god knows how many indignities before I get to that part.

You left your coat here, *I said, when Sugar appeared at the threshold.* I woke up in the middle of the night to pee & your coat was thrown over the back of my dressing table chair. It startled me because it looked like someone was sitting there—the bird, I thought, waiting to murder me. But then I remembered: It isn't here—it's wherever the hell it says it is, doing god knows what—and I realized it was your trench with the fur inside.

Part of this was a lie. I hadn't gotten up to pee. I'm wearing a diaper. I peed on myself last night in my diaper.

But I had woken up & noticed the coat over the chair. That part was true.

Oh that. *Sugar glanced at the coat.* It's never really fit me well, & I just thought maybe you'd want to keep it. For when you're feeling better & we can take a walk around the block.

I would have preferred a coat with the mink on the outside, I thought.

What else do you want to do when you're feeling better? *Sugar asked.*

God how I wanted to play this game. My body had a really hard time believing it though.

I want to walk to Googie's Diner on 78th & York & eat the seafood tower, *I said. I didn't want this at all, but seafood seemed like the kind of thing people who were relishing life would want to consume.*

Well that's what we'll do, then. We'll do that in our mink coats. *Sugar came over & put an iced tea in a* lidded clear plastic cup down on my dresser. She pulled the cap of paper off the straw, crumpled it & dropped it in her purse. She picked up the untouched cold matzoh ball soup with the practiced ease of anyone who has ever been a mother &, without comment, turned and brought it into the kitchen. I heard the water running, & the dishwasher open & shut. Then Sugar was back. She sat down on the bed again & took out her pen and notebook.

I brought you some SweeTango apples too.

I didn't know what a Sweetango apple was. It must be a new kind. They're always coming up with new apples these days. I thought about all the apple varieties that would stretch into the future without me & felt very sad.

They're hard to get, *she added.*

We'll cut them up for lunch later with cottage cheese, *I said. I would have to explain to Sugar where the candied ginger was. I like my cottage cheese dotted with candied ginger.*

So, *Sugar said, reviewing her notebook,* you haven't been on the Lower East Side since when?

Why was she so fixated on this? Sugar was parked on the bed, shuffling her hand around in her mammoth Bottega Veneta purse. Then she pulled out & laid on the bed another notebook—a battered one with some mail & papers jammed inside. But this one looked old. One of those black-and-white marbled ones, now yellowed, like a composition book from decades ago.

What's this? *I said.*

Just my notes—I'm working on a horror film if you can believe it. Jewish horror, who would have thought.

Sugar laughed in her worldly, jaded, not-open-for-further-questions way.

You're telling me, I thought but did not say.

No, this, *I said, & indicated the composition book. I recognized it but couldn't place it.*

Oh, I was picking up in your daughter's room in case there were any stray dishes, *Sugar feigned, & her simultaneously guilty & delighted affect made me realize what she'd found.*

What was I supposed to do, *Sugar said.* I couldn't help but peek. It's some kind of teenage diary. Your daughter's.

I was astonished at Sugar's lack of guile.

The bird's, *I said. My guts gripped with the realization.* It's the bird's diary, *I repeated. I affected a blasé tone, as if I was deeply bored by this document.*

I picked up the composition book & put it on my dresser.

Oh, you want its story, *I said.* I'll give you its story. The bird was born & raised in Manhattan, on the Upper East Side, but east of Third Avenue, which is basically a slum where only single people & third-rate accountants live. It grew up mincing around trying to get its hands on menswear, playing softball, reading god knows how many books. It attended college— a barbarian school which did not deign to have a "curriculum" though certainly deigned to charge for one—where it proceeded to fuck every drunk bisexual sorority girl that Wesleyan had on offer, most of whom went on to marry men, which just adds to my general thesis about the tragedy of lesbianism. At some point, the bird & I parted ways. Well, who ever thought we would get along in the first place? Where is it written we should have liked each other? That's what I have to tell myself.

I had been thrown off by the diary, and now I was telling Sugar more than I wanted to. I attempted to stanch the flow of information by sipping my iced tea at length.

And the Lower East Side? *Sugar gently prompted after some silence had passed.*

I really didn't want to get into it about the Lower East Side & what happened that day, but I hadn't expected to be in competition with the bird for an account of our lives, & now Sugar was in possession of a rival set of documents.

Not since the Soviet Union started to go kaput, *I sighed. I put my iced tea back down on the dresser & settled myself against the pillows.*

We were on the way to the Apollo Diner for an obligatory lunch with Saul, who was in Woodmere for a job. Myself, Stephen & the bird. The bird had recently learned of its acceptance to Wesleyan University, which I don't know if you know, is a not-so-elite place populated entirely by lesbians. I think—*I paused & affected thinking hard*—the bird had just returned from visiting the campus for a pre-enrollment orientation. Yes, it must have just returned from that visit, *I said, as if I was reconstructing these events in an ad hoc way, & with effort, when really they were burned on my brain, because it was the first time I had really registered a major transition was happening in our family life. It wasn't that I was melancholy about the bird leaving home. It was more that, without my even noticing, our entire story had been written. It wasn't a good story, but somehow I'd clung to the idea that I still had a chance to change things. But now the narrative arc of our family tale was closing. The bird had one claw out the door of our lives. One claw out the door & straight up the vagina of some lesbian at Wesleyan.*

There was nothing I could do about it. The bird had received a scholarship. Why not Cornell, or the University of Pennsylvania, where lesbians inhabited a miserable shadow life. But no, Wesleyan it was. Despite my overriding dread about this, I had resolved that day to try to go ahead with the façade of a nice family weekend.

So we're heading off for this family trip to Long Island, *I continued,* & it isn't until we get to the car that I realize Stephen looks schlumpy. There's a whole day planned & Stephen throws on an old ski jacket without any thought to it like he's going out to muck horse stalls—

You've mucked a horse stall? *Sugar asked.*

I'm saying he looked like a mucker of something. And thinking about it started to aggravate me. I just couldn't get over it. It signaled how clueless Stephen was about the stakes of family get-togethers. They're judging us, I'd always say, & he'd say no, no, no, it's just Saul. And I'd be like, right, Stephen: It's Saul! Saul! All Saul cares about is who's doing better than whom. That's Saul's life.

And Shira—you remember Shira? Saul's wife whom he was in the process of being divorced by—was just the same, which was a pickle because someone was always going to be doing better than her. Actually, as their marriage progressed, Saul had softened a little into the self-satisfactions of fatherhood, while Shira—whose life revolved around watching Saul watch football every night while the boys tore each other's hair out brawling in the basement—became more desperate. So, no, no one could be more miserable than Shira. But she held on to hope that someone was worse off, & would try to find some clue as to my own misery on every visit.

This reminded me of something.

Sugar, *I said,* do not allow Shira to come to my funeral or shiva.

The ex-wife? You're making the guest list already? *Sugar was being nice. The guest list was long overdue.*

Listen, one time we had Saul & Shira over for a poker night &, can you believe, I found her rummaging around in my hall closet inspecting the tags on my coats! To see if they were real fur! I told Stephen about it afterward & he came up with every excuse under the sun. Something had spilled at the dinner table, so maybe Shira had been seeking the Dustbuster? Or she was looking for something in the pocket of her own coat & got confused about which coat was which? But her coat was linen, a thin linen coat!

I had no coat that even came close to being like Shira's. No equivalent garment of clothing whatsoever. But Stephen needed to believe that an equivalent coat existed somewhere in our closet, because life was a bowl of cherries to him & everyone was good.

Anyway, I'm looking at Stephen driving happily along to the Apollo Diner in his shitty ski jacket of which, if she heard about it from Saul, Shira would instantly & triumphantly take notice, & the next thing I know I'm tapping on the steering wheel with my nail, saying "Get off at Houston"—

At that time the Eastern European animal hide markets were in the toilet. Which I happened to know because the Bratva mistresses were dealing sheepskin coats out of the trunks of their Lincoln Town Cars. When they came into Zilch's for their appointments, they would try to sell us these coats, & Renee—my co-receptionist who reeked of vodka and cigarettes & BO & for this reason was never going to get a man—had bought one. I, however, could not give the Bratva mistresses the satisfaction. On the other hand, I did want to parade Stephen around in a resplendent Stasi-style coat.

 So as we were about to pass by the Lower East Side on the way out to the expressway, I realized it was the perfect moment to buy sheepskin.

"You need a new coat," I say. "A sheepskin coat." Stephen, in that quiet way, without taking his eyes off the road, mumbles—you remember how he used to mumble?—"I don't need sheepskin." Well, this was insanity. Who doesn't need sheepskin at a cut-rate price?

 Sugar nodded, although I doubted she had ever bought anything at a cut-rate price.

 "All the stars are wearing sheepskin," I say, & Stephen obliges, gliding the Oldsmobile across the chaos of the FDR Drive toward the exit like he's rowing a boat across a pond. The fact of the matter was, Stephen's experience of his own body was not admissible evidence in my style court.

Meanwhile, when I say "All the stars are wearing sheepskin" I can feel my daughter silently burst with excitement in the back seat, seeing herself in one of those big bulky communist men's coats. I turn around & bark, "Not for you." Why could I not put a stop to this thing between she & men's apparel.

And get this, she cracks open a copy of Marx's *Capital* like a real college snob & mutters to herself, but loudly enough for me to hear, "What the fuck is her problem."

That's how I knew the tides had turned. My meek daughter, giving it right back to me. Here I thought we were in a classic Cold War détente, & that I could stave off my daughter's lesbianism with the nuclear threat of my raised eyebrow alone. Meanwhile she had correctly assessed that in the impendingly-post-Soviet free-market chaos, sheepskin coats were up for grabs by any gender person whatsoever, like pellets out of a Pez dispenser. Here I had raised this girl among the New World blue bloods, & the elitist schmuck I had so hoped she would become was entitled enough to believe she could do whatever the fuck she wanted with her life.

Sugar laughed at this. I could make au courant jokes as good as an SNL writer, despite what Sugar thought.

En route to Orchard Street, we stop off at Russ & Daughters, where I bargain over the price for a pound of sour prunes on the reasoning that it ought to be a crime to charge so much for something that essentially is used for medicinal purposes. I would like it to be known that I got half off.

Sugar's pencil had stopped.

Are you writing that down.

Yes.

But she was not writing it down. I squinted at her. The space between Sugar's eyebrows creased the tiniest bit, straining against Botox. A thin line rose to the surface of her skin like a pencil tracing across onionskin paper, then vanished.

". . . believe she could do whatever the fuck she wanted with her life," *Sugar read back to me.*

No, the thing about the prunes.

I'm lightly editing, *Sugar had the gall to say.* We don't need that detail.

It's character though.

Sugar wrote something down. Whether she was heeding or overriding me, who knows. The line flicked up again between her eyebrows.

I wasn't going to haggle over every line with Sugar; I had plenty of good ones.

On Orchard, *I continued,* no one has sheepskin, but everyone has a story. "Sheepskin shmeepskin!" "Not until October do we get our big run on sheepskin!" "What good is sheepskin if your underwear has holes!"

At Manny's we get a "You want sheepskin?" & bald little Manny lures us back into the bowels of his store. "I got better than sheepskin." He gets out a stepstool & pulls an item out of an upper rack. "Cor-du-roy!" he says, like he's presenting a debutante at a ball.

"You want *him* to wear corduroy?" I point at

Stephen like he's the Prince of Wales. Manny didn't need to know how much corduroy Stephen actually had. It just galled me that we had been sized up as corduroy-level shoppers.

"Lady," he says, his forehead wrinkling, "this is a nice coat."

Stephen, the good cop, pokes around the sock area for an apology-purchase. "What about these? Do these have good elastic?" He's holding a limp pair of ribbed brown dress socks.

"Yes, yes, the best elastic," says Manny, dismounting the stepstool. "The best! It's what I wear myself. The very best!"

Stephen nods. "Coats I have enough. But socks you can always use."

"If the elastic is so good," I slide around the side of Manny like a commando, "then why are your *own* socks hanging around your ankles?" I point at the baggy material pooling in the space between Manny's pant leg & the top of the foot disembarking the stool.

"These?" He looks down & shrugs, not missing a beat. "To get these down I had to pull them down myself!"

Tremendous bullshit.

Somehow we settle on a mid-thigh-length tan corduroy overcoat with leather elbow patches. This thing makes Stephen look like a downwardly mobile Jewish lumberjack, but at this point I don't want to leave the store without buying anything lest Manny think we don't even have money enough for corduroy. Meanwhile, as we're paying, my daughter beelines for the boys' section, toward a junior version of this coat.

Right in front of me she's shopping for men's apparel! I whip around & tunnel my way through a sea of *schmattes*. "Absolutely not," I blare. "That jacket is for men."

My daughter looks at me, not letting go of the coat, shrugs & says, "What."

She *"what'd"* me. Can you believe. She actually looked sorry for me. Apparently it was pitiful I was not aware of the fact that in 1988 you didn't need to be a man to fuck cream-of-the-crop genuine beauties at Wesleyan University.

"Ultimately," I say, trying to contain the situation, "you could use a new pair of dungarees. One of those semi-flared styles they're wearing in *Vogue*."

Manny, on cue, pulls out a pair of dusty 1981-styled Sassons with zippers at the ankles from behind the counter & says, "You want dungarees, we got dungarees. Take a look at these—the latest."

"We'll pass," I say, holding up my hand. "What is this, the Iron Curtain?" God forbid I should be buying seven-year-old denim. I give him the arched eyebrow & whisk us out the door, issuing the coup de grâce. *"Gey gesund a heit,"* which technically means "Go in good health," but because it's Yiddish, actually means "Fuck you."

I thought Sugar was going to scratch through the page with excitement as she scrambled to phonetically spell out the Yiddish.

The flared jeans idea, *I continued*, was sort of a Lauren Hutton thing, an androgynous concession. An attempt to make lemonade out of lemons. A desperate last gasp to sculpt the oncoming tidal wave of lesbianism into someone I could still drag to Bloomingdale's to collect my free gift with purchase at the Clinique counter. Someone that some man somewhere someday maybe would touch, if he had low self-esteem, or was a bottom, or a little bit gay.

Sugar glanced at me.

I know what a bottom is, *I said.* I watch cable television.

As Stephen's pulling away from the curb, my daughter looks at me in the rearview mirror with an unreadable expression. "I think I'm gay," she says.

Heeeeere we were. Finally.

"Yup," she elaborates, and cracks open Marx's *Capital,* "definitely gay."

"I'm nauseous," I say.

"Nauseated," my daughter corrects, like a real Wesleyan schmuck.

And now she starts reading out loud. "The wealth of societies in which the capitalist mode of production prevails appears as an 'immense collection of commodities.'"

What else is new! I tell you, Sugar, if this line had been embroidered on a gold brocade throw pillow I would have showcased it on my slip-covered couch next to the one that says "My Other Apartment Is in Paris."

I heard myself slurring. "Paris" *had come out* "Parish."

Sugar nodded. I used to say to Neil, when he got all high-and-mighty on his Marxism: It doesn't take a rocket scientist to know that the commodity is the appearance of wealth, but is not itself wealth.

Here I balked. Was this "not a rocket scientist" me? I didn't really feel like hearing this from someone who had a lot of what is indeed "itself wealth."

If commodities were wealth, I said, I'd be fucking rich. *I tried to make myself sound jokey but my voice was trembly with exhaustion.* Alas, *I soldiered on,* capital is not a throw pillow.

Capital is value that moves, *Sugar added, sounding show-offy.* It sheds one body & takes on another. Production, exchange, consumption. It's got to move through those cycles otherwise it's just a worthless pair of Sasson jeans sitting on a shelf. That's the whole point.

That was not the whole point, I thought. First of all, it was all too obvious. These cycles were something anyone who had worked the front desk of a trucking company would know about. Despite the bird's conviction that you can only learn Marxism from lesbian professors at New England colleges—& Sugar's that you only learn these things writing sketches in Hollywood—you can ask anyone from the streets of Flatbush what Marxism is. Growing up, what were our options for life? Trucking thug, fabric cutter, or Marxist. My uncle Jack, for god's sake, was in the communist party & he made a salary of exactly bupkes unionizing elevator operators, & he had a lot of aggravation. He died young—of Marxism, if you ask me.

Suddenly my throat was so dry that it clung to itself. The energy had run out of me like I was a tub of bathwater & someone had pulled the stopper. Also, I was becoming increasingly distracted by the notebook emanating next to me on my dresser like it had a pulse.

It had been how many years since I'd last seen it? And I was starting to realize something; I needed to be alone with the notebook.

I have to stop, *I managed.* You can go. *I waved Sugar toward the door.* But if I happen to drop dead tonight—*I gesticulated with my chin to the jam-packed little closet next to my dressing table*—everything in there is for the bird. I forgot to make a note about that in my will.

Why would you drop dead tonight? *Sugar asked in a very poorly acted performance of everything being fine.*

Just make sure it knows everything in the closet is for it, *I rasped.*

I knew it didn't want them & couldn't use them. I did know that. But a mother can dream.

Around Midnight—

For years, whenever I used to go out window shopping, I always remembered to pick something up. *The first time it happened, I heard myself pretending to be the matriarch of a normal family.* This is for my daughter, I said, fingering a necklace of chunky, multicolored stones. *And after that I just kept doing it.* Ooh, my daughter would love this, *I'd say, smoothing an oversized velour turtleneck at Eileen Fisher, or a pair of bobby socks at Socks on Lex. Sometimes, more recently, I'd mention a granddaughter too.*

My closet is stuffed with unused bags of costume jewelry, washable silk blouses, Bebe sparkly leggings, semi-flared jeans. Everything brand-new, if decades old. There are off-brand cashmere cardigans, wrap dresses from Bolton's, slips & nightwear. Several Pierre Deux zip totes stuffed with the fruits of my free gifts with purchases—tiny John Frieda shampoo samples, Thierry Mugler mini perfume spritzers, one ping-pong-paddle-sized NARS eyeshadow palette I scored in a coup.

This actually is the whole point.

Because I'm asking—my dear torturer, my terrible baby bird—if commodities on shelves are valueless, then what is all that?

12:30

My skin is crawling with fever & pain. I'm in too much pain even to watch television. I can only watch the sky, the one sliver of moon that keeps disappearing in clouds tinted violet with light pollution.

I'm being sliced from the inside out.

12:45
———

I think maybe I believed if Sugar left you would come back—that you would know I was utterly helpless now, truly without hope.

Well you're not back but I'm your mother, and I can still hear you, wherever you are, threatening me in that obscene, unearthly voice. "You're not done yet. Keep writing."

THIS WEAPON,

MY DAUGHTER

LATER THAT DAY, AFTER we'd settled at the Apollo Diner—Saul, myself, my daughter, and Stephen in his new corduroy coat—Saul announced, "I'm joining the Israeli military."

"They take sloppy, *farbisine* fifty-year-olds now?" was what I managed, incredulous. The Intifada had started, though, so who knew. I turned to Stephen as the waitress tried to find space for our menus among the paperwork and brochures Saul had strewn on the table.

"It's a volunteer unit," Saul said, rebuking me with strange cheeriness. He handed me a mimeographed two-page pamphlet with the words "Sar-El. Service to Israel" in heavy block lettering across the front and a grainy black-and-white photo of someone in a military uniform saluting the Israeli flag.

"So they'll take anyone," I said.

Saul ignored this. "There's a push," he said, "because of the 'conflict.'"

Saul had become a military history nut. An Israel nut, too. That day of Blanchie's funeral, he had kissed the photo of Leon and Ari at the Wailing Wall and slipped it back into the coffin, proclaiming dramatically that he would soon be traveling to Israel with the boys to plant a tree in Blanchie's honor. *They plant the tree for you, Saul,* I said. *You don't need to go all the way there to stick it in the ground yourself!* What kind of an idiot was Saul. But no, he says, he has to go in person.

Of course it was all a charade. Leon had not been accepted into any American pre-medical program. Leon had been accepted to a made-up institution, "The College of Judea and Samaria" in a *yenemsvelt* settlement in the West Bank, a handful of broken-down trailers plopped on a scrubby hilltop surrounded by garbage and chickens and managed by sandal-clad frontier loons with dirty hair.

So Saul's trip to Israel had nothing to do with planting a tree. He was escorting Leon to this *fakokta* settlement, which he'd been too embarrassed to admit at the funeral. It galled me, though, that Saul was heading to Israel at the very time we were embarking on our glamorous leave-taking for Stephen's posting at the Ministry. I was so annoyed, in fact, as well as bitter over the unjust accusations of photo-absconding, that I refused to see Saul during the entire time we overlapped. I didn't permit Stephen to see Saul in Israel either, even on his own. And I knew it pained him, but as far as I was concerned, that was what marriage was. A show of loyalties at the point of a proverbial gun. I'm sorry but it's true.

When we had all returned to the States—Saul after several weeks; us after several months—we made a great effort never to discuss it. So I'd had no idea that, over the years of Leon's attendance of his "school," Saul had gotten himself involved in this Sar-El venture.

Saul unfolded the pamphlet and tapped on it, leaving a small cluster of burger oil fingerprints. The brochure explained the importance of diasporic service to the homeland,

and introduced readers to the glorious directorship of Sar-El by some general or other "who's also in charge of the Logistics unit of the Israeli army," Saul woofed around a mouthful of food. "So essentially, the volunteers are part of the Logistics unit too."

What did I care about who was in what military unit. Saul, however, cared an immense amount.

When Saul said "Logistics" it was as if he was saying "sex." I had not seen him so excited since he ejaculated into his pants that evening on my rooftop long ago. Hamburger and pancake flecked the table as he spoke. Saul was a piñata of military history, bursting.

The Logistics Corps, Saul foamed, had once been the Ordnance Unit of the Haganah. Saul loved saying "Haganah"; the word shot out of his mouth like a phlegm-greased cannonball. In fact Logistics, Saul explained, was the heart of the Haganah, because the whole operation would have gone nowhere without gunrunning. I actually knew this, or had intuited it, from *Exodus*, because in that movie, characters go to ports to pick up illegal weapons—as well as *Judith*, which, if you think about the scene of Sophia Loren emerging from the smuggled crate into the port of Haifa, is also, in a way, Logistics.

"Israel only fights offensive wars!" Saul went on, his face purpling. "Israel is too tiny to even consider for one single second being invaded. No, being invaded is totally foreclosed!" Logistics was key to this whole never-being-invaded thing because Logistics, according to Saul, was the science of storing equipment in a state of constant, clean readiness to move onto a battlefield. Apparently this Sar-El general had been such a famously good weapons storer, cleaner, and mover that they gave him Sar-El as a little present, so now he had a whole battalion of volunteers to help with all the storing and cleaning.

Unbelievably, Saul was one of the regional coordinators for Sar-El through an American wing of the operation called "Volunteers for Israel." He had gotten Abe into it too, and the two of them worked out of the back of Abe's pool and spa supply store in Sloatsburg, which Abe had opened when the garment industry went kaput. The back room of the store was now the recruitment center for the Eastern Tristate Volunteers for Israel. (New Jersey had its own center in Bergen County. We didn't know those people.) The back room at the store was a small "interrogation" area, as Saul called it, where Saul would discern the sincerity of the Sar-El applicant, and, if found adequate by whatever Saul's standards could possibly be, inform them of the details of daily life on the army base such as how you got to wear the uniform, sing the national anthem, and clean the toilets and dry the guns of the soldiers.

You could see that Saul was dying to go dry some guns in Israel, but Shira had him tied up in court. He was seething about everyone trotting off to Israel while he twiddled his thumbs in Nyack. Abe, it turned out, was over there already running the volunteer coordination at a base outside Jerusalem. "I'm gonna go this summer," Saul bragged, "after the divorce is settled."

At some point in this song and dance about Sar-El, an idea began forming in me. When Saul would infrequently pause to chew his hamburger-pancake concoction, clawing down his meat roll like an aging panda, I started putting two and two together.

I remembered the fierceness of the Israeli youth—their total commitment to the commandments of gender—and I began to think about who else could go on this volunteering mission besides Saul. More precisely, who could be mandated to go on this mission before her unfortunate matriculation at Wesleyan University. We had spent our time in Israel going from waterslide parks to frozen yogurt shops and being shat on by the Israelis for not being Israeli. But, silly me, you could just *become one*. So I decided. No way was Saul out-Israeling me. I would send my daughter to this army camp too. In Israel—land of rigor, gender, and brutality—they'd take care of the gayness, the mannishness, the whole bit. My daughter would come out of it cured and boyfriended. Plus, I can't say that the idea of helping soldiers in their struggle didn't appeal to me too. Was I living through my daughter a little bit? A lot bit.

Next thing you know I'm signing her up. She was seventeen, too young to go on her own, but also too young to have a say in whether or not she was going (she resisted mightily, which was a pain in the ass). She would join Saul and Abe's "squadron" (which was Saul's term) or whatever they called these volunteer groups.

Life takes funny turns. I had spent my entire adulthood keeping my daughter away from the lowlifes of our family, while trying to use her as a ballistic missile to puncture the carapace of New York High Society, and it had only backfired. Years of girls' school in the bosom of the bourgeoisie had left my daughter with nothing but a hatred of capitalism and a love of women. And meanwhile Saul's son had gone from a

Nyack basement to pre-med at "The College of Judea and Samaria," and then medical school in Serbia. Soon he would be returning to the United States in Gucci wing tips. I had been pointing this weapon, my daughter, in the wrong direction the whole time. I was rerouting now.

2 a.m.

What is happening to me? I can barely move. I am lightheaded, like I might faint, just lying here, which is a terrifying feeling. The room keeps growling & lurching, getting larger & smaller around me.

 I'm thinking again of Marx's damn French Preface & its fatiguing summits. Have I summited, fatiguingly? And if so, what comes next.

LIKE JUDITH

THE THIRD TIME I arrived at Ben Gurion, I was cloaked in such an aura of purpose. I did, I suppose, feel a bit like Judith, released from her hellish transit into the glow of the Holy Land. My own hellish transit had consisted of managing my daughter's relentless sobbing the entirety of the flight—she had gotten close, I suspected, with a woman, and was dramatically displeased to be shipped off to the Israeli military. Plus, she had developed let's say a critique of the whole thing—a vague "anti-war" stance of which she could not be disabused. Stephen and I practically had to strong-arm her onto the flight.

But then the vast Arrivals building gleamed through the sliding doors, backlighting passengers as they moved like shadows through the hall, and I burst into a spontaneous warble of Milk and Honey's 1979 Eurovision hit, "Hallelujah," which I had blaring out of the earphones of my Walkman as we waited for our luggage. Several people joined in to my warbling, clapping, and swaying.

By the way, I have come to think that my attachment to noir films about World War II spies comes not out of a particular militancy, or even a love of the Jews and a compulsion to save us, but out of an enchantment with the route by which World War II entered mythology: the stylization and submission of catastrophe to the ethereal classiness of thriller. What I learned at Performing Arts but didn't realize until later was that the alchemy by which the chaos of history had been emulsified in silver halide and projected onto a screen in three-act structure shaped my whole outlook on life. Or, as I've always said: If you look good you'll feel good. Out of the muck and mundanity of the world of cottage cheese for dinner, and pungent holidays with food that smelled indistinguishable from the muskiest breath, might come sharp-edged performances, dramatic lighting, and that specific noir gender that wears its femininity like a robe of icicles.

Outside, in the wet heat, a soldier with a Sar-El placard paced under palm trees across the drop-off lanes. We rolled our wheelies toward the crosswalk and I noticed other volunteers making purposeful beelines from a variety of positions. They moved with a serious-faced, martial aura, flocking wordlessly with us toward the placard. As we accumulated, however, I soon ascertained that no group could have looked less battle-ready than this. We were joined by two retired ladies in *schmattes,* purses overflowing with knitting, and three men my parents' age, all with a haunted, New Jersey–widower look, button-down shirts tucked hopefully into pressed polyester pants. A couple of other stray young women, presumably also looking for a man.

The soldier—whose ridge of sparse red curls wrapping around the base of his skull did not in fact give the intended effect of hair—waved us onto the school bus, where another soldier waited, smoking, in the driver's seat.

My daughter threw herself sorrowfully into a seat across the aisle, next to Stephen, and I was left with one of the silent widowers as we began snaking through the rusted-out husks of tanks and convoy vehicles along the highway shimmering in 110-degree afternoon heat.

"Battle for Jerusalem," the soldier, who was now a sort of tour guide, proclaimed. He hung on to the handrail at the top of the steps, swinging as the bus wheeled and shook around curves. "We leave them there to remember Israel's permanent victimhood and its permanent invincibility at once. A contradiction?" He paused. "No!" he answered himself, without explaining further. The retirees and knitters delivered a volley of appreciative coos—an aviary of excited patriotism—as my daughter leaned over and glared at me.

I ignored her, watching the landscape as it flashed by. Israel was a religion of its own miraculous impossibility. It had been squeezed like a blackhead out of a pore of history in a once-in-the-universe set of colliding circumstances.

Now the soldier launched into a series of endless bitter references to the Intifada while he drank profusely from a water cooler stashed next to the driver's seat. Many minutes passed as he grumbled and drank. Finally he began making his way down the aisle with little cones of the water, bragging that it was Israel's finest—"direct from the Cretaceous."

Filtered through chalk, he elaborated. The Cretaceous-period limestone and chalk that made up the aquifers. Everything in Israel was about ancient times or the future.

The water had a bright, sweet undertone and left a gin-like residue in the corners of my mouth that I licked at between cups. I saw other people licking too. When we arrived at the destination—we had risen to the hills of Jerusalem and came down the other side, but where exactly we were I had no idea, and still don't; we were never told the name of the base, or given any coordinates to orient ourselves—I had recovered from our flight, hydrated by the milk and honey of the Holy Land.

We disembarked at the base of a dry riverbed at the bottom of a long ravine, near a set of unmarked gates in salt-dusted steel with a padlock hanging open like a cracked jaw. These were guarded by three more soldiers, all coated in an angry, overheated sheen. A tall one, pacing with his assault rifle perched on his shoulder, scuffing his boots at the creeping sand; a soft pale one squatting glumly, resting his rifle on an outcropping of rock; and a trim third one with a shiny rifle, wearing a uniform that appeared freshly pressed. The bus soldier with the rind of red curls handed us over to this third one. He was our guide now, and he brought Stephen and me to the dimly lit mess hall, and the volunteers to receive their military uniforms in their barracks.

Shortly the entire motley crew joined us, straggling in like a bunch of mallards. An additional volunteer—a brawny Brit in his early twenties who actually properly filled out his uniform—seemed to have arrived on an earlier flight, and was already peacocking with the soldiers, flashing machismo. I perked up, imagining a variety of marital (and martial) scenarios for my daughter.

Though when she slunk in at the tail end of the group and made her way over to Stephen and me, she looked troublingly mannish in her uniform. Why did she keep ruining this for me. I took off one of my own silver bangles and clamped it onto her wrist. *You need a little something,* I said. She fidgeted it closed but did not resist.

Dinner was thin pucks of schnitzel piled on faded blue melamine plates that were dropped down at the center of the table by soldiers, along with canned olives, pickles, and slabs of tinned halvah. Glasses of warm Sprite were passed around.

I had been hoping we would be seated next to the brawny Brit, so that I could finesse an introduction, but instead we were trapped between a *schmatte*-wearer—now officious in her military uniform—and Abe, who had been on the base for weeks in his capacity as the point of contact between the volunteers and the Sar-El program. He thought even more highly of himself than he had before, you could tell. Abe was Israelifying, tanned to a crisp, thirty pounds lighter than I'd last seen him, in sandals and a dark olive army uniform. He settled in next to me like a baggie of toothpicks.

You know who's got a million other places to be, he said as an opening salvo, pointing a thumb at his chest. *This guy. Did you know that my daughter, the lawyer, invited me to come with the family on vacation to Costa Rico?* Abe paused to sip some Sprite. *They went to Costa Rico for vacation, they rented a big condo, and they invited me. But I said no, because of what's happening here. I had to be here! Costa Rico! Monkeys, spa pools, great food. It would have been my first time in Costa Rico, and I wanted to go, but you know what, Barbara, what could I do. I'm a military man now.*

*It's Costa Ric*a, *Abe,* I said, my explaining tone coming back to me from my time at Rosemere. Abe looked at me and frowned. Outside the mess hall a general mauveness glowed from behind a blanket of clouds. Floodlights clicked on, and crowds of large gray moths began to gaggle around the windows.

Moths are drawn to the light, Abe said, changing the subject, interpreting the world to me as if women were Neanderthals who didn't understand why anything took place. *They cannot resist!* He flung his hands open in exasperation at moths and their stubborn inability to be better than themselves.

Well, he said suddenly, folding his napkin, *I've got work to check up on.* He wandered off through the dim mess hall with his hands clasped behind his ass like a Vichy general enjoying a constitutional on the Champs-Élysées.

After dinner we were taken on a tour of the base by a rawboned soldier with a pronounced stoop, to whom the others had given the nickname "Chicken Man" because of the chickens his family kept at home. He was a Mizrahi Jew, dark and hated by the Ashkenazis. He did not know any English, which had the effect of preventing him from having to answer any questions.

Chicken Man drove one jeep and the Brit drove the other, having already been vested with authority and keys. We left the mess hall in a caravan and started up a large hill pocked with outcroppings of various buildings—the barracks where the volunteers would sleep, and the bathrooms, long sulfurous trailers, covered with graffiti proclaiming the excellence of Pink Floyd, Led Zeppelin, and the Rolling Stones. Partway up we arrived at a gun storage room, a cavernous hall with floor-to-ceiling racks of machine guns surrounding us on all sides, their butts facing the center. The light inside was gray and grainy, and the room smelled powerfully of grease. Chicken

Man slid a rifle from its slot and broke it open, fingering the barrel while looking at us meaningfully to indicate that the volunteers would be cleaning these. Everyone in the group except my daughter, who sulked and scuffed around in the doorway, emanated excitement—especially the post-menopausal knitters, who clearly could not wait to get their hands on guns.

Next we visited a large barn, the size of a circus ring, housing thousands of duffel bags lined up on shelves. Chicken Man brought one down and pulled out some items—rolled up underwear and a packet of dried fruit—then dramatically put them back in, nodding at the group about their other new task, packing and readying the bags.

We ascended farther, twisting around switchbacks as the sun dropped behind the hills. As the jeeps crested the top, we found hundreds of tanks lined up in rows across a vast lot, huge piles of metal darkening in the gloam. Chicken Man marched us through the rows for what felt like hours. At each tank he stopped and pronounced a different unintelligible word in Hebrew—the name for a specific type of tank, presumably—then opened his hands to the group, egging us to speak the equivalent word back in English. "Tank?" we replied over and over, shrugging at one another. At each helpless iteration of "Tank?" Abe yelped the specific English word—Sherman! Patton! Super Sherman! Centurion! M48! AT-3! Mark II! Mark III!—patting each machine on the nose familiarly, like a Bullnose parked on Forty-fifth Street.

Chicken Man brought us to a set of massive canvas-wrapped hoses projecting from a utility shed and coiled in the sand. He pulled one hose from the dust and aimed it at the tanks in a mimicry of the volunteers' tank-washing task.

* * *

Night had fallen. It was very dark. Thuds began to sound in the distance. Stephen and I were leaving in the morning. We piled back into the jeeps, which descended through the dry chilly air along the switchbacks. The sky was a dome. Stars laddered into blackness.

I would not see my daughter again for a very long time, though I didn't know it then.

Part IV:

Papers and Communications:

J. Rosenberg,

Abe Rosenberg, Sar-El,

San Francisco County Records

ADDENDUM # 1:

DIARY FRAGMENTS,

J. ROSENBERG, APRIL 1988

April 4, 1988

S. PRESSED SUBLIMITY INTO my mouth with a warm tongue last night. My first kiss. My first everything. In her room in an expropriated fraternity house at the top of a hill overlooking frozen margarita Fridays sparkling in the deindustrialized valley below.

S. possesses an adult's grace and air of unspecified tragedy. She is of some Nordic heritage, with translucent blue-white skin that gives the impression of being permanently chilled, and a thick wall of hair the deep dirty red of ancient stained glass. S. is a senior whose plan is to move to San Francisco after graduation to be a yoga teacher and avant-garde dancer.

S. is from the Pacific Northwest. There is a lot it seems she can't say that has to do with her past.

A lot of S.'s personal anecdotes involve being on a road. My creative writing class taught us that it's not necessary to show how a character gets from point A to point B. Unless something happens on the journey, you should definitely cut out most if not all roadside A-to-B from your narratives. But S.'s stories are all road. She is so completely American. You can taste it on her cold white skin. S. comes from a place of brightly lit gas stations and low-lying fog twisting through forests.

I had noticed her right away, lounging on the library steps amid a crowd of Wesleyan students drinking beer and smoking. My student guide had brought me, because it's where everyone hangs out at night. Patches of old snow lingered in the crevices of the stairs. S. was optimistically dressed in tight leggings and a tank top, her shoulders red with cold.

You're new. S. beckoned me into a cloud of Body Shop mango body butter and Drum loose tobacco, and delivered an interrogation in a voice that was lower than anticipated, almost stern. *Adorno or Benjamin.* This was a love cry and the only right answer was Adorno. I was mostly guessing, based on the fact that it seemed anyone could love Walter Benjamin—even a "Madonna Studies" person, of which, I had noticed in visiting classes that day, there were many.

Adorno, I said, my heart pounding.

Trick question, S. said. *The right answer is Trotsky.*

She made some comments about Adorno's theory of atonal music that I think were not favorable, and some friendly assessments of Benjamin, which surprised me. I had pulled a pen from my pocket and was writing notes on my hand. She dragged on her hand-rolled cigarette, watching. *The reason Trotsky is the right answer is because Trotsky is the Marxist who attaches us most concretely to history, and to struggle.* S. punctuated every iteration of "Trotsky" with her cigarette. *You shouldn't need to write that down.* She gestured toward my graffitied hand.

* * *

Things happened quickly. S. brought me upstairs to her dirty-laundry-littered room in the expropriated fraternity house on promises of showing me her copy of *My Life*. She immediately flopped on the bed and began orchestrating a series of seductive flicks through the book, which she had produced, along with a packet of Drum rolling tobacco, from a green backpack.

S. gave special emphasis to the pages that concerned Trotsky's mockery of his city cousin who comes to visit, enamored of Trotsky's family cows.

Look, almost everything is bound up in Trotsky's asides about cows. They are an animal, first and foremost. An "insignificant" animal to country-born Trotsky, such a part of the metabolism of daily life as to be unremarkable. But in the cousin's eyes they are exotic, novel creatures. Auratic. For Trotsky, the hopes of the revolution rest on reckoning with this gulf of perception between himself and the cousin—that is to say, on making politics *in the relationship between the country and the city. Trotsky did not skip over the mechanics of this, as Engels later did, however right he might have been in suggesting abstractly that communism meant the "abolition" of the distinction between the city and the countryside. Trotsky was strategic, and moving too quickly to the abolitionist horizon made no sense to him. For him, these country-city dynamics were the revolutionary context and needed to be lived granularly.*

S. explained that the urban and the rural poor developed, together, out of feudal serfdom. Capitalism began by forcing serfs off common lands on which they used to forage. A free but rightless proletariat was born. "Free" of feudal overlords, but "free" also of any means of support or access to land, and so unable to make a living except by selling their labor for wages (if you could get them).

So capitalism produced, along with laborers, a mass of beggars and vagabonds—exiles and outlaws who were "vogelfrei." S.'s voice was thick with the German. *Bird-free, free as birds, but also free of any means of support in this life.*

So that's why we have to understand the urban-rural split historically, S. said, *rather than reifying it as ontological. And this is the significance of Trotsky's anecdote about the cows. Everything, for Trotsky, ultimately hinges on doing away with mythologies of rural exoticism and replacing them with "rational relationships"—"concrete relationships"—between the urban workers and the peasants.*

I was sitting against the wall, legs crossed, and definitely not going to ask what "ontological" meant. S. had her head resting on one of my crossed knees, enjoying her cigarette. She reached over her head and poked the window open with her pinky, ashing into the night with her throat arched.

You can just replace the word rational with mutual or collaborative. S. dragged thoughtfully. *It's not about doing away with beauty and ornament. He's not Stalin. He's about making relationships that support more beauty. But beauty appears only when we strip away the veil of the exotic.*

She said this last urgently, looking up at me, clearly in danger of exoticizing S., the brilliant country cousin. Starlight filtered through the window and cast S. in a weak nimbus, her red hair peacocked around her head.

* * *

I gazed down at S. with an overly meaningful expression. Sentimental things were trying to force their way out of my mouth. You look unearthly, I triumphed in not saying. You are a staggering beauty, I also managed to not say.

Of course, of course. We need to maintain this Trotskyian distinction, I cracked out instead, running my hand through my hair like a poorly oiled robot.

It was very late and the expropriated fraternity house had gone quiet. Fluorescence from the hallway pulsed in milky strands in the gap under the door. S. rolled out of my lap, then slid on her back up to her pillow. She folded the blanket back and wriggled in—*You can sleep over if you want.*

When I woke I was in motion already—on top of S., my hand up her cunt and my crotch pressed against her ass. The night had darkened, clouds fleeing across the sky and wind thumping the panes. The window was still cracked from when S. had ashed, and the air was freezing, but S. and I were sweltering against each other. S.'s sweatpants were off, and her naked ass, round and full with yoga muscle, pushed back against my crotch, then fell forward pulling me down with her. We moved like this with my hand inside her—we were a single entity, cresting and valleying, soft and precise. A shamelessly tonal lyric (Adorno would not approve, I had to admit, as our bodies syncopated), a guileless animal relieved of thought or theory.

We're making love, S. shockingly uttered into her pillow. I had assumed "making love" was a ruse, a carrot held in front of straight people to make sure they did everything by the book. I thought it was "ideological." I did not know Marxists could make love, especially not gay ones. But now this Marxist who earlier that night had been dismantling truisms like a stagehand striking a set, was drenching us in cliché. The descent into banality of this titan of thought had an allure that exceeded (or descended beneath) language.

I held S. down against the bed. The broken-straw and salt aroma of her inner thighs and genitals rose between us. I parted her hair at her neck, and when I touched S. like this her stern shell began to fall off her like feathers at a molt.

S. was sweet now, utterly nondidactic. Her voice had changed, the hard edge dissipating into a cotton candy pitch. She was whimpering and writhing and saying, her face in the pillow, *Fuck me.* Then she turned over and her warm and muscular legs locked around my ass. My hand was being crushed into a squiddy beak inside her, pushing until it curled into a fist on itself and our fuck downshifted to a trance-slow gear. Maybe this is just what it is to fuck in general. Though this didn't feel "in general" to me.

Over breakfast at a diner in an airstream trailer in downtown Middletown, S. proposed that I drive across the country with her. *We'll make our way through Marx's* Capital. *We'll read it aloud.*

S. had already arranged to transport her thesis advisor's battered Volvo (as well as the advisor's sulky daughter and sulkier cat) to San Francisco, where the daughter, cat, and car-lost-in-custody are to be deposited with the thesis advisor's ex-husband. *Put as many miles on the damn thing as you want,* the advisor had instructed when she handed the keys to S. *Go the long way around. Make loops for all I care.*

* * *

I would like to loop around the country with S. endlessly, listening to S.'s world of songs created specifically for the purpose of being the ineffable soundtrack to sex with communist lesbian yoga practitioners. She keeps a shoebox of cassette tapes under her bed—mixes that seem to consist solely of Dead Can Dance and Cocteau Twins that she contemplates seriously, biting her bottom lip and scowling before carefully selecting a cassette. I really do not like this music, but I like the idea of a woman liking it.

S. is more beautiful than any girl (or boy) in Kathryn Bigelow's *Near Dark*. I cannot believe she wants to drive with *me* across that unimaginable expanse that separates our coasts, reading Marx's *Capital* while tornadoes black out the sky.

By Rochester we'll be thrown into prairies, she said, as we walked to my bus. *You already feel cut off from the East Coast in Rochester, with the green and brown shrublands rolling to the horizon, the trucks revving around you in a groaning herd. In Chicago we'll eat huge slabs of pizza downtown while clouds scud across the skyscraper windows.*

We'll pitch a tent in Nevada behind this one 7-11 where they let you camp, S. said. *Backing up to an expanse of rocks and scrub and the pine forests rising into the hills. Just beyond the yellow puddles cast by the spotlights of the gas pumps, we'll watch the stars from our sleeping bag until they blur.*

I'll be back in a couple weeks, I said, experimenting with a surety and adultness that my entrée into a sex life and

Marxism had introduced. *After school gets out. We'll go to California.*

April 5, 1988

I am not taking the road trip. My mother has told me I will do no such thing. Instead I am being sent somewhere terrible and clarifying.

ADDENDUM #2:

ABE ROSENBERG

TO BARBARA ROSENBERG,

MAY-JUNE 1988

MAY 12, 1988

FM: Abe Rosenberg
TO: Barbara Rosenberg

SUBJECT: YOUR DAUGHTER—INSUBORDINATION

THE TANKS WENT OUT NICE AND CLEAN AS SCHEDULED TO PARTICIPATE IN [REDACTED]. A MESS WHEN THEY RETURNED! DUST ETC. YOUR DAUGHTER WAS ASSIGNED TO WASH THEM DOWN BUT WILL NOT TOUCH THE VEHICLES.

MAY 27, 1988

FM: ABE ROSENBERG
TO: BARBARA ROSENBERG

SUBJECT: MORE INSUBORDINATION—DAUGHTER

LOOK IT IS NOT HARD TO HOLD A GUN. CRADLE IT ON YOUR SHOULDER LIKE A BABY'S HEAD I ALWAYS SAY AND I SHOULD KNOW I TEACH GUNS NOW! HOLD IT SOFTLY AT FIRST—THE TRIGGER CURLED AROUND YOUR FINGER LIKE A LOCK OF HAIR. IT'S A FATHER-DAUGHTER DANCE EXCEPT THE GUN'S BODY LEADS. THE GUN IS A BABY ALWAYS ABOUT TO CRY. HOLD IT HARDER. FREEZE TO ITS SHAPE LIKE A VINE IN WINTER.
YOUR DAUGHTER WILL NOT. WILL NOT CLEAN THE GUNS OR THE TANKS AS I SAID BEFORE.

JUNE 1, 1988

FM: ABE ROSENBERG

TO: BARBARA ROSENBERG

SUBJECT: STRIKE

DO YOU THINK WE COULD FIT A BODY IN HERE LOIS JOKED, SLIPPING A TUBE OF TOOTHPASTE IN A DUFFEL BAG. I SAID MAYBE A CHILD'S BODY? AND SHE LAUGHED. ALTHOUGH LIKE ALL OF US I PREFER THE GUN ROOM, I GO WHERE I AM NEEDED. TODAY IT WAS PACKING DUFFEL BAGS.
I SAW A PILLAR OF SMOKE OVER THE HILL AND WENT OUTSIDE WITH PRIDE TO WATCH. I SAW YOUR DAUGHTER "ON STRIKE" CROUCHED AGAINST THE BARRACKS. A ROCK FELL FROM HER NOTEBOOK.

JUNE 4, 1988

FM: ABE ROSENBERG
TO: BARBARA ROSENBERG

SUBJECT: MISSING

YOUR DAUGHTER HAS NOT BEEN TO THE MESS HALL IN DAYS. I DEPLOYED TO THE BARRACKS DUE TO THE SMELL. HER BUNK WAS SOUR AS AN UNTENDED TERRARIUM. UNDERNEATH IN THE DARK I DISCOVERED PITA BROKEN OPEN WITH MOLD—OLIVES WET AS MULCH, CADAVEROUS IN PLASTIC BAGS. IF YOU WANT WE COULD [REDACTED]
[REDACTED]
PAGE 02
ARRANGE A SECURE PHONE CALL ON MONDAY DURING WHICH I CAN EXPLAIN FURTHER.

ADDENDUM # 3:

SAR-EL TO BARBARA ROSENBERG

JUNE 5, 1988

FM: SAR-EL
TO: BARBARA ROSENBERG

SUBJECT: DAUGHTER

LAST KNOWN LOCATION OF YOUR DAUGHTER:
BEN GURION DEPARTURES LOUNGE 6/4/88 0800 HOURS STOP

ADDENDUM # 4: DIARY FRAGMENTS, J. ROSENBERG, JUNE-JULY 1988

June 5, 1988

I ARRIVED TONIGHT AT SFO from Ben Gurion. I called S. right away from a pay phone at the airport.

S. sounded a little surprised but mostly cold. She suggested I meet her at an alleyway burrito joint in the Castro where she refused to look at me, fussing instead over the menu, concentrating with her cassette-tape intensity, like a surgeon choosing an instrument. When the nachos arrived, she launched into an inquiry on Lacan, specifically his formulation that there is no sexual relation. I was having a hard time focusing; my hands were cold and blotched with purple.

The reason there is no sexual relation, S. said, *is that being exposed to another's desire is so anxiety-producing as to make relation impossible. Heterosexual people overcome this nonrelation by means of the State and the Family, which floods this abyss with documents, dailiness, and children, so that, at least for a time, one can behave as if it isn't there.*

Okay. I nursed a chip. For lesbians no such abyss-flooding methods seem to exist. But I had decided when I left the base that the declaration of the impossibility of something was the first step in making that thing possible.

Perhaps, I thought as S. went on, leaping into this abyss with S. would be something like leaping from capitalism to socialism? An unknowable plunge toward the possibility of some better world, a *salto mortale*—as Marx called finance's fatal leap into the unknown—except in a good way?

But now S. was saying something about how things were "too good" between us and how in fact this had caused her to tip over into a point of non-relation. I was unclear if this was a legitimate deployment of Lacan and did briefly try to out-reason her—twisting (I guess?) her own redactions of Lacan to argue that we could soothe each other in the face of the abyss, providing structure and social meaning.

The true function of the Father is fundamentally to unite a desire and the Law, I probably misquoted.—

Did you capitalize "Father" in what you just said? S. crunched her nacho mournfully. *This is the problem with butches,* she said, scowling and grinding the same bite of nacho over and over again in her molars.

It took me a moment to decipher that she had broken up with me. She let me walk her home anyway, as it seems that is what adult butches do.

June 7, 1988

I've found an apartment share for $225 a month. It's in Noe Valley with straight government majors recently graduated from Bowdoin—a chilly first-floor room with a bay window that looks out onto the small dark alley between our row house and the next. I've gotten a job waiting tables on the overnight shift at Sparky's Diner on Church Street in the Castro. And I also have found "gay science fiction," which merely intensifies my mournful desire to share with S. the cosmic sublime.

Most evenings during the 4:30 a.m. lull, with the neon SPARKYS sign casting a pool of pink onto the sidewalk, I perch on a stepstool in the kitchen's warm, bacon-soaked air—reading Samuel Delany out loud to the green-mohawked leatherdyke line cook and having sad thoughts about the sky.

I want to share my sad thoughts about the sky with S., but I live at Sparky's now, wiping tweakers' pancake-syrup finger paintings off Formica tables while S. is in her apartment on Fulton Street where the fog pours down from Golden Gate Park in the evenings turning the windows blue, supposedly nursing the misery of how "too-good" things had been.

June 16, 1988

I have taken a second job doing data entry during the daytime downtown—falling asleep on the keyboard while processing workers' comp claims for Aetna—so I can save up to buy a motorcycle, which, I feel sure, will deliver S. back. I know nothing about bikes, but there are many for sale in the classifieds. California has just passed its helmet law, and diehard riders are selling their bikes off for cheap rather than wear a helmet.

June 25, 1988

I've bought a Kawasaki 440 LTD. I don't know anything about Kawasaki 440 LTDs (or motorcycles in general ahem) but it was nearby, within my modest means, and the seller—a gay guy who lives in the Hayes Valley in a shag-carpeted apartment looking out over Alamo Square studded with framed photographs of young men on every surface and inch of wall space—was home when I followed the address in the ad and knocked on the door.

Do you know how to ride? the guy asked. He was a willowy man of maybe 27 whose eyes were older than my four grandparents' eye-ages combined. He's lost everyone in his life, like everyone has, and the motorcycle is a loss he could decide to lose first.
  Do you have a license? He squinted.
  I need a license? I asked with the entitled stupidity of a college student.
  The guy shrugged with that characteristically gay male dispassion about the possibility of a female human doing something incredibly self-harming and stupid. He did not care about me, but this not-caring wasn't personal. His life is about boys and their unstoppable disappearance.

After fifteen minutes of doing circles around the parking lot of his apartment complex, and the exchange of my savings, I rode the much-too-heavy vehicle back to my apartment share, where I sleep on a mattress on the floor and subsist on a diet of PowerBars and dried apricots.

June 30, 1988

Nights I'm not at Sparky's, I ride the Kawasaki to every lesbian club or bar night in the city—Snatch, Uranus, Club Q—searching for S., hoping to be seen disembarking or embarking this thing, silently praying not to drop it. Sometimes I don't even go into the clubs, but just ride around, half getting on or off the motorcycle, hoping to be witnessed in my capable, motorcycle-christened dykey-ness.

July 8, 1988

Outside Cafe Flore on Market Street, I spotted S. She was hugging someone who looked like another yoga teacher in a tangle of very fit asses in tight leggings. I arranged myself back on the bike and theatrically checked something on the odometer.

S. turned. I turned, swinging my leg off the bike.

The lack of surprise on S.'s face suggested she'd seen me already. Perhaps she'd even seen me do the entire pantomime of odometer-checking.

I cocked my head toward the bike in what I hoped was bad-boy nonchalance. S. raised an eyebrow, slinking closer in her fog of Drum tobacco and mango body butter.

I would never, under any circumstances get on a bike with you, she said, in a not-entirely unkind voice. S. was just conveying that some things are not worth dying for, and I am one of those things.

ADDENDUM # 5:

COUNTY RECORDS,

JULY 10, 1988

PROPERTY OF THE COUNTY OF SAN FRANCISCO EFFECTS
OF THE DECEASED, JORDANA ROSENBERG 07/10/1988

MOTORCYCLE FATALITY

- One notebook (red)
- Motorcycle (totaled)
- Backpack
- Copy of Marx's *Capital*

Part V:

Fawn*

---

*c. 1374—One of a class of rural deities; at first represented like men with horns and the tail of a goat

(Arise and fly The reeling Faun, the sensual feast. Lord Tennyson, *In Memoria*, cxvi. 183)

c. 1481—*intransitive*. To bring forth young. Now only of deer.

Old English—variant of fall: "to move more or less freely from a high [to a low place] . . . of rain, snow, lightning, etc.: to come down . . . Of leaves, hair, feathers, teeth, etc. ["the old feathers fall . . .] . . . to give birth"

ON *BAREFOOT CONTESSA*, INA GARTEN is preparing a dinner for six, a holiday dinner. Her kitchen is large as a battleship, the center island one expansive butcher block. A lamb shank seeps thin pink blood into the grain. Ina's stuffing garlic cloves into glistening pockets sliced into the side of the lamb. She grabs a bushy sprig of rosemary in her fist like it's a fat cock and tugs her hand down the spine, shedding rosemary leaves over the shank. *I have LOTS of this in my garden*—she gestures with one rosemary-coated hand toward the windows behind her—*and I just LOVE to get out there and pick herbs every morning.*

Huh, Fawn mutters. She is staring at the television, wrapped in the pilly yellow blanket up to her nose, practically mummified. It's late afternoon. In Manhattan, gloaming briefly gets brighter just before sunset, as the windowpanes of all the skyscrapers flash red with falling light. Fawn's room is cherry-lit.

Shomshing's wrong, Fawn slurs, wriggling her head and stretching her neck to get her mouth above the rim of the blanket. *Shomshing's really wrong! Ina's shupposed to be in the Hamptons. She broadcastsh from the Hamptons.* Fawn looks around for Sugar or her daughter, but Sugar isn't coming back and her daughter, well—

How do you know she's not in the Hamptons, she imagines her daughter asking, snidely, not looking up from a book. *The windowsh,* Fawn says out loud to no one. *There are buildings outside Ina's windowsh!*

Ina's kitchen is the same kitchen she always cooks in—her expansive Hamptons country kitchen—but instead of trees, there are skyscrapers clustered outside her windows like paparazzi. How is this possible, Fawn wonders in a panic. And why is Ina acting like everything is normal? Fawn is fixated on the screen, trying to make it make sense. Reality is out of joint and it doesn't feel like an oxycodone shift.

The sun crosses the horizon and sets. Fawn's room loses its crimson hue and darkens. Fawn blinks rapidly to clear her eyes.

Ina is in the Hamptons after all. Fawn had been been seeing the reflection of the buildings outside her own window. She exhales. Green branches fill the panes behind Ina now.

Ina's hushband is a profeshor, Fawn—lonely enough to try to explain the life of Ina Garten to her dead daughter—says. *He comesh on the weekendsh.*

Her daughter would probably say something sarcastic and cruel, like: *Ina's husband is gay. Think about it. Why does he live in New Haven and Ina lives in the Hamptons? He's a beard.*

Must her daughter ruin Ina Garten for Fawn. Must she destroy every last thing.

Not everyone is gay! Fawn shouts into the silence of the room, finally getting her mouth above the rim of the blanket. *Some people just live separately!*

Some *people do,* her daughter would say.

Fawn returns her attention to the television. Fuck her daughter. Fuck her for not being here to help, and fuck her for her sick cockamamie ideas about life, and her made-up ideas about what is possible. Anyone can see Ina is a woman in a heterosexual marriage preparing a lamb.

* * *

Ina seasons the roast with big pinches of salt and pepper from decorative little ramekins, then starts pounding with a meat mallet. *You have to hit it hard,* Ina says, slamming the mallet down. Ina's capable forearm does look a little gay. Fawn banishes this thought. Thwack thwack. Fawn's stomach turns. Sometimes these cooking shows are a bit much, in her condition. She closes her eyes, waits for the splosh of mallet into the flesh to stop. But it doesn't stop. In fact, it is going on for longer than possible. This isn't right. Ina's cooking show has slipped genres. Splosh, splosh, splosh, thwack. *Lamb is a tender animal, a young animal, but because it's young its flesh can seize up in the oven,* Ina growls. Ina is destroying this meat like Anthony Perkins stabbing Janet Leigh in *Psycho*. Thwack. Thwack. *It has a lot of collagen,* Ina shouts over the thwacking. *You have to really get in there. Really break down the fibers.* Splosh.

How long can this go on? The lamb must be threads of flesh now—Fawn imagines with her eyes squeezed shut—a skein held together by gristle, splayed out on the butcher block like a spider's web. Fawn has never thought about the term "butcher block" before. How strange that the ordinary, graphic meaning of the term has become a distinction of high-end kitchening. Splosh splosh. Fawn feels like she's going to vomit. This segment of lamb-destroying will not end. Even with her eyes closed, Fawn's head starts spinning. Every second stretches interminably while the sound of mallet hitting meat continues. Time is lengthening, and Fawn is stuck inside one sploshing second that is bloating too long.

She wakes screaming.

Fawn flutters one eye open, expecting a scene of television carnage.

Ina is merrily pulling a round roast out of the oven. How much time has passed? Fawn's eyes scan down her own body. She half expects her legs to be gone, or minced to bits, bloodying the yellow blanket.

But no, everything is in place. Ina is bringing the roast to the table and demonstrating how to properly carve it. Perfect pink discs of meat stack like dominos on a serving platter ringed by a gleaming moat of lamb juices. Fawn has woken with her throat so dry it hurts to swallow. Watching the lamb spill its juice, and Ina filling crystal stem glasses with sparkling water, is torture. Fawn looks to her dresser top. Her water glass is empty. It's been over twenty-four hours since Sugar was there. Fawn cannot fathom how, in her condition, she will refill the glass herself.

Jeffrey walks into Ina's kitchen, clad in his professorial trench coat, briefcase in hand. Fawn gets a memory-gust of the smell of Stephen's trench when he, too, would come in the door, the addictive scent of A MAN. Dry cleaning, shoe polish, mint.

Fawn closes her eyes, reveling in reminiscence, the many masculine odors of her husband. Selsun Blue, musk, the raw tang of a recently shaved neck. The odors swirl in her imagination, becoming edible, like a soft-serve twist. Fawn is licking it up, the cold milk of her husband's smells coating her throat.

Fawn begins drifting off to this fantasy. The scent gets stronger as she descends into sleep. She is diving into all of Stephen's smells. The cracked corn of his arm hair, the powdery millet of his beard. So many scents! But then the millet and corn and raw-wound scents begin intensifying, drowning out the mint and shampoo. Soon they are a barnyard stench, a dense fog of unwashed bodies and oily grain going rancid.

Fawn gags. The scent is choking her from the inside. She rouses herself with a start, coughing, and looks around wildly.

She expects, in some still-hopeful corner of her mind, for the smell to have been a dream smell, and to dissipate. It doesn't. So it is real. But coming from—where? Fawn's heart pounds. Has she shit herself again, she despairs, shifting around to feel for the terrible warmth inside her diaper. She is dry.
 The room feels hotter, the air denser. Fawn may be developing a fever. But also the lightbulb in Fawn's bedside lamp is searing through its rime of permanent dust, scorching the side of Fawn's face. And there is a sound coming from somewhere, or everywhere—so ubiquitous Fawn hadn't noticed it. Like drumbeats peppering the walls. She sees that the Food Network is no longer running Ina's show. There's an emergency announcement playing, which Fawn realizes has something to do with the drumbeat sounds. A hurricane has descended on Manhattan, tossing marbles of rain against the windows. She changes the channel. NY1 News is looping footage of scuba divers swimming up the FDR Drive. The river has surged over the seawall, strewing whitecaps along the highway.
 No one will be coming anytime soon, Fawn realizes, not even the murderous Jewish Family Services. Fawn is relieved that not only she, but all of Manhattan, is suffering tonight. She turns the volume on the TV down but not off (never off) and twists to her side to give her aching tailbone a break.

A gust of cold wet air blows in from the window next to Fawn's bed, washing over her face and shoulder in a stream of wonderful, pool-cold respite. But—she realizes—the rain is going to soak the floor! Fawn grits her teeth in frustration with Sugar, who must have opened and forgotten to close it. Now who will help her with this.

Just then something rustles at the corner of Fawn's vision, and a shadow flicks across the wall. She cranes around, straining against the pull of the blanket.

The bird is perched hugely in the window frame like a ragged, tweedy Nosferatu, its eyes blazing. Its scabby claws are curled like thick iron horseshoes around the sill.

Fawn is tiny under the yellow blanket, her limbs limp as yarn. Her eyes lock with the desolate primeval eyes of the bird. Fawn's lips wrinkle and purse, trembling with speech that will not come. She raises one eyebrow and glares.

The bird steps from the frame down into the room, surprisingly dainty on its claws, moving with strange lightness like a marionette. It hops to the foot of the bed, its bulk blocking the television, backlit by blue shadow splashing off the wall behind.

The bird bobs up and down several times and then hops onto the bed, looming over minuscule, shrinking Fawn, the size disparity so wrong, like a train has jumped a track and come to rest on the lip of a goldfish bowl. The bird begins to extend its neck and lower its beak.

The bird's wings close around Fawn like a rank cave. She can see the bird's nostrils close-up, a huge horned ridge crawling with mites. Squalls of reptilian air pour from them, boiling and acrid. The bird opens its beak—its gray tongue a lewd stone phallus, disgusting and surprising, urgent and hard—and grasps Fawn's neck, pulling her against its feathered chest, its breastbone sharp against Fawn's face. Then it steps to the window and bobs again, testing their combined weight. Now she and the bird are dropping through the open air.

Fawn feels her neck released by the bird's beak and her head swings down in a nauseating arc as the bird begins to flap, straining against the sheets of rain and wind. Fawn flashes on an image of her body breaking like a mollusk onto the hard pavement below, but then she and the bird are lifting—her feet, swollen from lack of use and edema, gripped fast in the bird's claws. Fawn is tossed by the wind like a yo-yo at the end of the talons. Blood runs down her legs and is washed away in the hammering rain.

Fawn and the bird ascend higher, out of the range of the city lights, into real darkness. Outer-space black, black like the inside of a thick leather Bottega Veneta purse. They are sailing far over Yorkville, rocked by torrents of cold rain. Fawn wonders, in semi-lucidity, if she is dreaming, and if so why she can't dream of a big Passover dinner, or a vacation in Paris. But no, she has to dream the bird's dreams, science fiction dreams, on top of everything. More than her cancer ever has, this has made Fawn realize that she is dying. Because all the parts of her that have flown out into the world—specifically the bird, who is a part of Fawn however much they would both like to forget it—have returned and are taking Fawn apart, bit by bit, carrying her off like crumbs in a mouth. Soon Fawn will be only the part of her that is the bird.

Fawn wants to tell Sugar that she didn't mean it about eating the seafood tower at Googie's Diner. Honestly she would just like to sit around with a bunch of other mothers and sip a

Tab, ice snapping in a tall glass, smoking Camel Lights while little girls play at their feet.

This ungrateful fucking bird, Fawn thinks, slewing violently in the talons' grip, glints of Manhattan hurtling past. Yorkville is a slash of blurred yellow light below. A little forest of post-war brick high-rises, Irish burger joints, off-track betting saloons, and nut-and-yogurt shops stretching from Fifty-ninth Street in the south to Eighty-ninth in the north, and from Third Avenue to the river.

Here she, and Stephen, and the other boys of Nyack and the girls of Brooklyn had made bridges of their bodies so their children could cross to that slice of Manhattan ringed in the rubble of the Luftwaffe. The boys took Route 9 to the Palisades Parkway to the George Washington Bridge to the FDR Drive, and at some point it all just became tentacles of home to them. Nothing was alien. Everything could be remade in their own image. And it's true, as everyone knows, there is no aristocracy here, just extrusion engines melting the past into a usable goop. In the FDR Drive, that imported geological layer, the horror of old Europe softened like a malleable gum, a padded understory for Manhattan's artificial offshoot, ordered up at the behest of Detroit with its legion of cars waiting to be rolled off the assembly lines to advance on the cities of the East Coast, an army of screaming babies.

For Detroit, Manhattan had grown a new orbit, a coil of hardened gasses. A narrow, furious highway. And there, off the FDR Drive, the boys of Rockland County and the girls of Brooklyn thought they were laying down history, sedimenting a layer of their own.

But if all of bombed-out Bristol unrolls itself like a carpet for a swarm of on- and off-duty taxicabs, then surely an I Can't Believe It's Yogurt! on Seventy-fourth and Third holds no claim to permanence.

The bird has hauled Fawn up against its breast and is beating the air with a wing. They careen in the hail and cold. Fawn looks down at the lights of Yorkville shrinking to pinpoints as she and the bird bobble in the currents. The bird's breath is at her neck—hot blasts that Fawn grudgingly welcomes against the frigid night. Fawn is drenched, though her body lacks the strength to shiver.

She and the bird climb fitfully against the weather when all at once the air turns even colder, condensing into a single arctic note, and the rain stops. Silence falls over everything. Fawn's ass begins lifting, rising into the air of its own accord. Her feet waggle in front of her. When she cranks her neck against the beak-grip to look up, she sees the bird is going horizontal too. Its wing tips are gleaming, haloed with lavender. Fawn spins back around to see a neon purple aurora flush across the sky—a luminous topography swirling and gullying. Towers of violet rise around them. Canyons of violet spiral beneath, bright throats opening to the heavens.

Neon particles sparkle on the bird's wings as it bucks and tumbles like a glittered horse, Fawn waving in its beak like a flag. Columns of violet waves build and pour toward them, one after another. Fawn braces herself for the sound of crashing and then realizes that waves don't break in outer space; instead, they sail through the void. Towering, violet animals, rocking in the air. Or lack of air.

Fawn is not really breathing. She is dying now, she understands, or is dead. She is becoming elemental. Atoms sing off her skin and fizzle into the dark. Then the bird's beak opens in a wide yawn that is also maybe a grin, or an attempt to make sound in the voiceless cosmos. Night night, the bird mouths as Fawn coils into a tapestry of space light, whistling on her own through the violet sea.

Acknowledgments

THREE PEOPLE HAVE read multiple drafts of this work, and I am tremendously grateful to them for all their engagement with it. I am very lucky that this book found its way to Nicole Counts, a wise and capacious editor, able to move brilliantly from the microscopic to the gestalt. My sister Amanda Rosenberg has been an unfailingly supportive and wonderfully astute reader. My partner Jasbir Puar's extraordinary acumen and comradeship—and her inimitable sensibilities about the stakes and aims of satire—have sustained me throughout.

I thank MacDowell, the Banff Centre, and the Lannan Foundation for support. For reading venues and opportunities to workshop this writing, I thank Patty Gone, Jon Ruseski and PLATFORM talks, Calvin Gimpelevich and the T4T reading series, Amy De'Ath and Topos Too, the Beck Lecture Series at Denison University, Emma Heaney and the Experimental Humanities and Social Engagement program at NYU, Max Haiven, Leigh Claire La Berge and the Alexander von Humboldt Foundation, Oberlin College, Elizabeth Freeman, Rana Jaleel and HATCH at UC Davis, Annie McClanahan and the English Department at UC Irvine, and Karen Tongson, Maggie Nelson, and the English Department at USC. Sarah Mesle at the *Los Angeles Review of Books* was an excellent editor for some very early versions of this writing.

At Random House, in addition to Nicole, I would like to thank Chris Jackson for helming this inimitable imprint, and Oma Beharry for taking this project on with remarkable ease and thoughtfulness. I have been repeatedly moved by the art and expertise of Shannon Barr, Avideh Bashirrad, Rebecca Berlant, Sarah Feightner, Andy Lefkowitz, Fritz Metsch, Raaga Rajagopala, and Erin Richards. My wonderful agent, Rob McQuilkin, has been a steady guide and a critical first reader. Michael Taeckens, Sarah Jean Grimm, and Electra Colevas are simply the best.

Andrea Lawlor, Carmen Maria Machado, Torrey Peters, and Michelle Tea lent their collective genius to a manuscript workshop that was the basis for fundamental revisions to this work. The manuscript benefited immensely from George Abraham's dazzling poetic, political, and editorial eye. Allison Page and Craig Agule reviewed a draft with characteristic precision and care. Katie Brewer Ball, Cornelia Reiner, Britt Rusert, and Maya Wind provided excellent feedback on early portions. Charmaine Chua, Noura Erakat, Laleh Khalili, Zohran Mamdani, Wadie Said, and Diala Shamas generously spoke with me for a different investigative project that involves research into the history of North American tax-exempt organizations that support the Israeli military and state project. Those conversations, and that research, also informed some of the writing in this novel. That these scholars and lawyers took the time to speak with me during a genocide, when their work is so urgent elsewhere, is deeply humbling.

Finally, the process of writing this book was long. Its debts are many, and include a great number of other friends and colleagues not named here, who provided critical fellowship, debate, and conversation that shaped this work along the way. Hopefully the combined support of so many wonderful interlocutors has resulted in a worthwhile contribution to a satiric tradition that subjects far-right fantasies to a withering light.

About the Author

JORDY ROSENBERG is the author of the novel *Confessions of the Fox*, which was a *New York Times* Editors' Choice selection; shortlisted for the Center for Fiction First Novel Prize, a Lambda Literary Award, a Publishing Triangle Award, the UK Historical Writers Association Debut Crown Award; longlisted for the Dublin Literary Award; and named one of the best books of the year by *The New Yorker, HuffPost, BuzzFeed, Kirkus Reviews, Literary Hub, Electric Literature*, and others. Jordy's work has been supported by fellowships and residencies from MacDowell, the Lannan Foundation, the Banff Centre, the Ahmanson-Getty Core Program Fellowship, the Society for the Humanities at Cornell University, and the UCLA Center for 17th- and 18th-Century Studies. He is a professor in the Department of English and Associated MFA Faculty in the Program for Poets and Writers at the University of Massachusetts Amherst.

https://www.jordy-rosenberg.com/

About the Type

This book was set in Walbaum, a typeface designed in 1810 by German punch cutter J. E. (Justus Erich) Walbaum (1768–1839). Walbaum's type is more French than German in appearance. Like Bodoni, it is a classical typeface, yet its openness and slight irregularities give it a human, romantic quality.